Taste
of
Darkness

by

Victoria Noxon

The Síoraí Legacy, Book III

Taste of Darkness

Cover Art by *Rae Monet, Inc. Design*

The Wild Rose Press, Inc.
PO Box 708
Adams Basin, NY 14410-0708
Visit us at www.thewildrosepress.com

Publishing History
First Black Rose Edition, 2013
Print ISBN 978-1-62830-066-6
Digital ISBN 978-1-62830-067-3

The Síoraí Legacy, Book III
Published in the United States of America

Dedication

To my parents for a lifetime of love and support.
To my husband...my very own hero of 28 years.
And, as always, a special "Thank You" to the readers
who enjoy playing with me in my other worlds!

Cara melted beneath his sizzling touch, lost in his masculine scent. He tasted of peppermint spice. She smoldered with a passion that burned to her core. Never before had she experienced such craving.

His lips left hers and traveled across her cheek where his whisper brushed her ear. "Stay with me tonight?"

Oh how she wanted to say yes, but common sense warned her of the dangers that action would bring. She turned her lips into his neck.

"I canna." Even as she denied her need to him, and to herself, she couldn't stop the instinctive reaction his scent and his nearness created.

Her mouth burned and stretched. The tips of her incisors pierced through her gums, taking the shape of large, sharp fangs.

No! No! She cringed as the words echoed in her thoughts, a cruel reminder of what she was. She battled within herself, but knew she'd lost when her teeth pierced the flesh of his neck. An overwhelming power of electricity shot through her when the coppery taste of his blood filled her mouth.

Overcome by an erotic hunger, Cara was reluctant to step away.

When she did, remorse shot through her.

What had she done?

"From Murias, a huge and mighty treasure,
the caldron of the Dagda of lofty deeds."
The Yellow Book of Lecan

Prologue

Scotland, 1250 AD

Cahira O'Leary clenched her hands into anxious fists. Her knuckles whitened and her fingernails burrowed into the soft flesh of her palms. She cringed in discomfort, inhaled a deep breath then exhaled on a sigh.

Beside her, Braedan, her husband and the love of her life, grasped leather reigns between his long fingers. Oh, how she loved those hands, strong, yet gentle. She tilted her head to glance at his profile. An easy smile played at the corners of his mouth.

The gods help her. She wanted to slap him for it. How could he look so calm and unruffled at a time like this? Didn't he understand the uncertainty that twisted her insides?

Her parents' opinion meant the world to her. Would they be happy? Or was it too soon?

Her stomach twisted. With each rut in the road, the knot tightened further into a nauseous ball. She gulped hard in an attempt to swallow the lump in her throat.

Telling herself she acted foolish, Cahira steered her

attention to the countryside. She loved the short ride to her parents' farmstead, and today proved to be no exception despite her growing uneasiness.

The cart bounded across the old, rutted dirt road. The wooden wheels creaked in protest at the bumps in their path.

It was a glorious afternoon.

Cara closed her eyes and tilted her face. Her body swayed in tune to the rocking motion of the dray beneath her. Heat from the sun warmed her cheeks, and she drew a deep breath. The light aromas of floral and musk filled her nose with the fragrance of late blooming heather.

She opened her eyes, cleared her throat, and dug deep for the courage to ask the one question that nagged her all day.

"Do ye think they'll be happy?" she asked as casually as she could manage, and then held her breath while she waited his reply.

Cahira didn't have to look at him to know his eyes brushed over her. After six months of marriage, she knew the man who sat beside her...his mannerisms, his thoughts, even his bad habits...the latter of which he boasted many.

Braedan laughed and jerked his wrists to slap the reins on Molly, their black Highland pony. In response, the mare picked up the tempo in her pace. Instead of the unhurried saunter, Molly now traveled at a brisk trot.

Cahira's stomach pitched and rolled. She drew a deep breath and willed it to settle before she attempted to speak again.

The bubble of unease swelled and pressed against her lungs until it became hard to breath. She waited for the sensation to pass before she glanced up at him. And then, she did something she'd never done before. She backhanded his arm. Not hard, but enough to gain his attention.

Braedan yanked back on the reins drawing Molly to a stop. He pushed the wooden brake handle forward and locked the wheels. Then, he wrapped the leather reins around the lever before he turned and captured her eyes with his own.

"What was that for?" he asked, his brows creased. He cocked his head to one side and studied her. A half smile slanted his lips.

"Because ye deserved it," she exclaimed, a faint hint of frustration in her voice.

He weighed her with a critical squint. "Oh, aye, and why's that then?"

"I asked ye a serious question, and ye laughed." She nibbled on her lower lip, concerned she may have pushed his patience. A woman should never strike her husband.

His expression softened. "I'm sorry, lass. I thought ye were jesting with me."

"I wasna." She lowered her eyes, clutching the material of her skirt in both hand. "Do ye think my parents will be happy with our news?"

With an index finger, he slanted her chin up until her eyes met his. "Is that why ye've been quiet all day? Ye're worried how they'll react?" When she nodded, he gripped her hands in his and gave them a gentle squeeze. "Yer parents are going to be thrilled to hear ye're with child."

"Do ye really believe so?

He wrapped his arms around her. His chin rested

on the top of her head. "I know so." He laughed. "In fact, yer father has even gone so far as to question the fertility of my manhood."

She stiffened in shock and glanced up into his face. "He dinna," she wheezed, her eyes wide.

Braedan nodded. "Aye that he did."

She drew a quick lungful of air. "But we've only been married six months."

"A lifetime to some." He must have recognized the bewilderment on her face and smiled again. "Och, come on, love, doona look so surprised. Yer momma is aching to hold her grandbabies in her arms. 'Tis natural she blame me."

"That isna fair. 'Tis the will of the gods."

"Doona find fault with her. She's getting on with age and wants to see her only daughter's bairns before she passes."

"She isna that old, Braedan." Cahira blew out an annoyed breath.

Braedan chuckled. "Yer parents are no'..." he hesitated. Sympathy flared in his eyes, and he sighed. "They're aging, love. Ye may no' see it, or maybe ye do and refuse to admit it, but yer parents wilna live forever. None of us will."

"Braedan, please. I doona want to talk about this."

Braedan's arm tightened around her waist. He pressed a kiss to her forehead. "I love ye, lass, and ye're right. This is a time for happiness, no'—" His words faded.

She nodded and snuggled against him. Keeping his arm around her, he stretched a hand over to release the brakes and grab the reins. He gave the leather strap a gentle snap. Molly strolled forward.

Cahira closed her eyes and listened to the soft thump of his heartbeat. Oh, how she loved this man.

Braedan's parents moved from Ireland to her village of Berwick when he was a wee lad. Cahira and Braedan grew up together, spending most of their waking hours down by the old creek bed skipping rocks. When they matured, no one seemed surprised when romance blossomed between them. In fact, the entire village joined in celebration of their marriage.

And now, Cahira couldn't imagine a life without him.

Braedan's chest tensed beneath her cheek. With a quick jerk, he yanked back on the reigns, drawing Molly to a halt.

Cara lifted her head, opened her eyes, and tipped her face to look at him.

"What the hell?" His deep voice simmered with strained control. He stood and glanced across the valley.

She followed the direction of his stare.

Orange and yellow streaks of color flashed above the trees to the West. The brief bursts of color mingled with a black haze that swirled into the white, puffy clouds. Cara squinted, attempting to see between the branches of the pines, but the foliage proved too thick to see anything but greenery.

The forest hushed. Even the animals held their silence.

She lurched to her feet. "What is that, Braedan?"

Braedan shook his head. "I canna be certain, but if I were to guess, I'd say something's been set afire over there."

"Fire, but what…?" Her voice broke at the

5

realization of what lay in that direction. "Braedan, my parents."

Braedan dropped to the seat and gave her hand a sharp tug. The wagon bobbled when she landed with a thump on the hard wooden seat.

"Hold on, love," he yelled. He whipped the leather straps. Molly neighed at the unexpected contact and hurtled into action.

Cara's hands clutched the wagon seat in a death grip. The terror in her heart swelled.

When they rounded the final bend, an icy fear twisted her insides.

The farmhouse and barn were engulfed with fire. Flames shot from the rooftops and rose thirty feet high. She cringed. Her eyes prickled and nose burned from the acrid odor of burning wood that hung heavy on the breeze.

"No!" she screamed and jumped to her feet. The cart swayed, and she toppled to the left. Braedan caught her wrist and steadied her.

"Cahira, sit down before ye fall," he bellowed.

She ignored him and yanked her hand from his grip. Her nerves tensed, and she glanced around in panic. Braedan drew back on the reigns, stopping the cart on the outskirts of the yard.

Her gaze scanned the farmstead in a frantic search. "Where are they, Braedan? I doona see them."

A desperate need to find her parents filled her, and she leapt to the ground. The instep of her foot landed on a rock. Thrown off balance, her ankle twisted. Pain radiated up her calf. With a cry, she pitched forward and fell to her hands and knees on the small pebbles in the front yard. The gravel, marred by sharp edges, bruised her kneecaps and scraped her palms.

"Cahira!" Braedan's anxious voice echoed from a long way off, but in the next instant, his arms wrapped around her. "Ye need to take care, love. Doona forget the bairn," he pleaded.

"I have to find my parents." She shrugged off his embrace and bounced to her feet. "Ma! Da!" she yelled and ran across the yard toward the house.

She stopped twenty feet from the front door. Flames blazed from the windows. The pungent odor of burning wood seared her nose and throat. Her cheeks burned from the heat. She raised a hand in front of her face to shield her skin while she attempted to peek inside.

Braedan wrapped his arms around her and pulled her into his embrace. His ragged breath brushed her hair.

"Ma, where are ye?" Her voice cracked. The hiss and crackle of timber her only answer.

Tears streamed down her cheek, and she spun away. A hint of red beside the chicken pen caught her attention. Her heart stopped at the realization her father often wore a shirt that resembled the color.

A low, tortured sob passed her lip.

"Father!" she screamed. She gripped the front of her skirt in both hands, yanked it up, and raced toward the building. Chickens cawed and flapped their feathers, scurrying from her path.

As she drew nearer, the cloth took shape, and her steps slowed. Her hand covered her mouth to prevent another agonized howl from escaping.

Her father slumped motionless against a bale of hay. His neck skewed at an odd angle and rested on his right shoulder, eyes closed as if asleep. A dark maroon stain shadowed the area around the handle of a blade that protruded from his chest. Blood seeped to the ground and formed a red pool beneath him.

Cahira dropped to her knees beside him. "No, da, no!" Deep sobs racked her insides. She placed her hands on his shoulders and rocked back and forth, shaking him as though the fierce motion would bring back life.

"Cahira, love, he's gone. Come away," Braedan ordered in a stern voice. He wrapped a hand around her upper arm and tugged, attempting to pull her from her father's motionless body.

She refused to budge, and his grip tightened.

"We have to leave! Now!" Braedan urged.

Grief held her prisoner, and she yanked her arm away.

"Leave me be." She swiped at her tears and jumped to her feet.

"Ma!" she screamed.

Once again, she picked up her skirt and ran with no clear direction in mind. "Momma, where are ye?"

Braedan's footsteps crunched the gravel close behind.

She rounded the corner of the barn and came to an abrupt halt when she reached the thin wired fence that surrounded her mother's garden. On the ground, a pair of legs spilled from between the rows of corn. Cahira jumped the barrier and rushed forward. She pushed aside stalks, beating them down with her foot until she uncovered her mother's still body. Blood poured from a wound on her forehead.

Cahira dropped to her knees.

"Momma," Cahira whispered in a small panicked voice.

Her mother's eyelids fluttered and opened.

"Cahira," she croaked in a hoarse voice.

Braedan knelt and wrapped an arm around her waist. "What happened here, Mrs. McNair?" he asked in a gentle voice.

A weak smile curved her lips. "When are ye going to learn to call me momma, boy?" She stretched out a hand toward Cahira who clasped it and held on tight.

"Ma, what happened?"

"Reivers. Yer da tried to stop them." Her voice broke and she looked at Cahira. "He's gone, isna he?"

Cahira read the search for truth and couldn't lie. "Aye."

A lone tear slid from the corner of her ma's eye, and she nodded. She glanced at Braedan. "Ye take care of my daughter, ye hear?"

"Momma, stay with me," Cahira begged, although the death rattle in her mother's chest swelled louder with each breath, a sign of impending death.

"I love ye, Cara."

Cahira swallowed hard and bit back the tears at the nickname she hadn't heard since she was a wee, troublesome child of ten.

"Doona leave me, momma." She leaned forward and whispered in her ear. "I'm with child. I need ye. We need ye."

Her mother glanced toward Braedan and bobbed her head in approval. She coughed and squeezed Cahira's hand. Blood trickled from the corner of her mouth.

And then, her mother expelled her last breath.

Cahira laid her head on her chest and cried. Violent sobs racked her body.

Horses neighed, followed by loud, boisterous male voices that resonated from the trees.

Braedan grabbed her by the arm.

"They're coming back. Come on, Cahira. We've go' to go now," he whispered in a voice gruff with concern.

"What about my parents? I wilna leave them."

"We'll come back to bury them. Keep low and head toward the trees. With luck, they wilna see us." He grasped her upper arm, pulled her to her feet, and steered her toward the woods.

They'd only traveled half the distance to the forest when a coarse voice bellowed, "Whoa! Hold up there. Where do ye think the two of ye are going?"

"Doona turn around. Just keep walking," Braedan murmured.

"Are the two of yer deaf or something? I said *stop*." The voice boomed. The raspy tone rumbled through Cahira and sent chills racing up her spine.

Braedan's hand, on the small of her back, stiffened yet urged her to continue.

"Run," he shouted.

The pressure of his hand left her back. Cahira took off head first for the forest and the sanctuary of the trees.

Behind her, a loud hum ricocheted across the breeze. Braedan let out a snagged cry.

She dared to glance back at the noise, gasping at the spear that emerged from the center of her husband's chest. His face pale and eyes wide as he stared at her. His hands gripped the pointed tip, and then he fell onto his knees.

"No!" she screamed and rushed to his side.

"Go!"

She dropped to her knees, tucked her hands beneath each armpit and tugged.

"I wilna leave ye," she cried and yanked again. "Braedan, stand up."

He wobbled and fell forward. Her hands moved to his chest. With a mighty shove, she pushed his shoulders, but he was too heavy for her slight frame. He slammed against her, pinning her on the ground beneath him. The tip of the spear pierced her side. White hot pain filtered across her abdomen. His weight pressed down on her, and she struggled to breathe.

"Stay. Down. Cara." He pressed his lips to her cheek, each word a stilted syllable. "Close yer eyes. Let them believe ye're dead," he urged in a pleading tone.

"I need to get ye help, Braedan." Cahira rasped, ignoring the pain flaring through her middle. "Ye're bleeding."

"'Tis too late for me, love."

She shook her head and shoved at his shoulders. He didn't move. "Nay! Ye canna leave me, Braedan," she pleaded in a low, tormented voice.

"I love ye, Cahira," he rattled in a weak whisper. "Forever."

Braedan's body slumped against her, and he ceased to breath. Despair lanced through her and she closed her eyes.

"Two for one. Nice shot, Neimus."

Fear lanced through her at the voice. The anguish in her heart became a sick and fiery gnawing which shattered the last remaining threads of her control.

She would die this day.

The pain in her abdomen grew. A warm, sticky liquid pooled on her stomach, and spilled down her side. Blood. Her teeth chattered and her body trembled. And then, the pain eased, her body relaxed, and darkness settled behind her eyelids.

This day should have been blessed, but now, she hovered in a black void, left alone in the dark. She tried to breathe, to fill her lungs with air, but even that most natural action lay trapped in her throat.

She struggled to roll over, to shake herself free from the invisible bonds that held her paralyzed.

Panic overpowered her until terror engulfed her in a black, invisible cocoon. She teetered on the edge of an abyss, a part of her yanked down, and, the gods help her, she wanted to give in to that final plunge.

She searched for an image of what happened. And then, the memories flooded back in a flash. Her parents, Braedan, and then another painful realization hit.

She'd lost their child.

Just as that last thought swirled through her mind, a dim light filtered through her closed eyelids.

Cahira opened her eyes and gasped for breath. She'd escaped from the darkness, and now stood in her parents' front yard.

She glanced around. The house and barn had burned to the ground. Smoldering ash littered the ground, the only evidence that a homestead once existed in this small clearing.

She fell to her knees, and wrapped her arms around her chest. Tears streamed down her cheeks.

"All will be well again, child."

Cahira jumped, startled by the softly spoken words.

She raised her eyes and blinked. Swiping the tears from her cheek, she scrambled to her feet.

A silver-gray haired woman stood before her. Wrinkles lined her eyes and crinkled her cheeks. A gentle smile graced her aged features. Cahira gauged the women to be five and eighty years old.

"Who are ye?" she stammered.

"I am Semias, Druid of Murias. I am here to help you."

Overwhelmed by grief, Cahira turned away. "Leave me be."

"Your future waits. The world needs you."

"I have no future. It is gone, taken from me all in one day," Cara hissed through clenched teeth. Anger burned a lava river through her veins, and she made a dismissive gesture with her hand. "Why would I care what the world needs? Look at what it has done to me, taking everything I ever loved. I doona care what happens to it."

"Many innocent people will depend on you for their survival."

Cahira wavered, struggling to comprehend what she heard. "What are ye talking about?"

"Centuries ago, the gods of the Tuatha Dé Danann banished an evil Vampryss to a realm of unconsciousness. A great oracle of the past foresaw her escape and counseled us to prepare. She will wreak havoc upon the world. You've been selected to become a grand warrior, known as the Síoraí, and protect us all, but you will not be alone in this war."

Disbelief poured over her. "Warrior? Me?" she asked in a broken whisper.

Semias nodded and stretched out a wrinkled hand

to Cahira. "Take my hand. Let me help you through your pain."

Cahira shook her head and took two steps back. "Nay," she whispered. "Why would I protect innocent people? Who was here to protect my family? They never hurt anyone."

Semias' lips curved into a gentle smile. "This was predestined, child. Your parents, your husband, and your baby boy are safe, tucked away within the gods' loving embrace."

Cahira's breath caught. "Baby boy?"

Semias nodded. "Your husband holds him close."

"How do ye know this?"

"Take my hand, Cahira O'Leary, and let me show you."

Cahira's heart thudded in her chest, and her eyebrows shot up in surprise. "Ye know my name?"

Semias inclined her head and smiled. "I know all there is about you."

Cahira shrugged to hide her confusion. "Why? What is so important about me that ye would even care?"

"Because you are vital to the continued existence of the world," Semias declared again. She wiggled her fingers. "Come."

Cahira needed to know the fate of her family and slipped her hand into Semias'.

Semias smiled.

Peace engulfed Cahira and lifted her from the horror of her surroundings. Anyone coming into the meadow at that moment would see the cinders of a once loved homestead.

Nothing more.

Chapter One

Santa Monica, California
Present Day

Cara leaned over the rail, her gaze fixed on the rolling waves of the Pacific Ocean. Twenty-five feet below, the surf crashed against the moorings of the Santa Monica pier. The sea struck the supports and formed a shower mist that rose fifteen feet high. A sharp gust of wind captured the fugitive droplets and carried them upward where the cool beads splashed her face and mixed with the tears that slid down her cheeks.

The noise of late night partiers blared in the distance, but to her delight, this portion of the pier lay in shadows. The aquarium lights and three of the four pier lanterns lay dark. Only the haze from the remaining lamp cast a faint glow over the area.

The smell of sea salt permeated the air and rose from the waters. The odor was so strong, she remembered the taste of the bitter seasoning and the tingle as it touched her tongue. A cool chill raced up her spine, and she frowned. Her hands tightened around the rail.

The memory sent a sharp spasm through her chest. A raw and primitive grief overwhelmed her in a torrent of emotions she hadn't felt in more than seven hundred and fifty years.

A sharp pain tore through her palm. She gasped and jerked her hand into the pale light. A glint of metal caught her eye, and she grimaced. With her thumb and forefinger, she plucked the splinter from the soft tissue. A bubble of crimson blood trickled from the wound.

In spite of the ache in her hand, she laughed.

Two months ago, she came to California to do what she'd been trained to do. Kill vampires, werewolves, shifters, every evil creature that lurked in the shadows of this world.

Whoop dee friggin doo!

Before she arrived here, she took up temporary residence in Arlington, Virginia. By her standards, that city embodied perfection, comfy with its divine weather and phenomenal hunting.

But then, as usual, duty called, and the gods assigned her to this scorched, oven-baked place where the high temperatures generated a river of sweat that trailed a continuous path down her spine. The humidity hung so heavy in the air, even the simplest action of breathing proved difficult.

Centuries and centuries of killing, destroying, and fighting brought her to where she was today. An immortal protector for the Tuatha Dé Danann, honor bound her to their decree, even while she sought to live her own life.

No one lives forever. Words spoken by Braedan on the day he died. An ironic chuckle escaped her lips, and she shook her head. What she wouldn't give to see him now. How would he react to her life? To the danger she faced every day?

Evil inhabited the world, all corners scarred by the ravages of inhuman creatures. Their malevolence radiated in an insidious aura of death. They crept through the darkness and left a path of destruction in their wake.

Cara witnessed the carnage of their innocent victims.

She should be hunting, but, damn it, she just didn't feel like it.

Cara ran a hand across her neck and massaged the stiffness in her muscles. She wanted to blame her melancholy on the silence of the night, but, deep inside, she knew it was more than that.

Earlier in the day, her best friend and fellow guardian, Cameron MacLean called to share some good news about guardian, Fallon O'Callaghan. Early this morning, Fallon's wife, Lizzie, gave birth to a son. The boy, christened Nathaniel Mitchell, would be called Nate for short. Mom and son were doing great.

Although she maintained an enthusiastic demeanor over the phone and sent her good wishes, the grief and sadness she'd buried deep within her heart inundated her in a long overdue depression.

Unashamed tears slid down her cheeks.

"I miss ye, Braedan," she whispered.

For so long, bitterness and anger fueled her actions and fed her rage. But look at her now. She should be happy for her friend, not feeling sorry for herself.

The undeniable and dreadful fact remained. The survival of the world at stake meant no time for self-pity.

She glanced toward the sky and swallowed hard, certain Braedan and their child watched over her from the heavens.

"I will see ye again, my love. I trust in ye to care

for our son, and I know ye'll tell him about me."

Cara brushed the tears away and lifted her chin. Her inner spirit strengthened with resolve. She would never forget where she came from, what molded her, but she needed to look toward her future. No matter how long that may or may not be.

Being an immortal, demon-hunting, kick-ass woman, one never knew, she shrugged.

She smiled at the analogy and swiped the tears away.

"Hey, you shouldn't be out here."

Startled by the deep male voice, Cara jumped and spun around. A tall, dark figure stepped from the shadows into the light. Cara's eyes widened at the man's six-foot, athletic physique. Tight blue jeans accentuated muscular thighs, and a blue shirt, the top three buttons undone, revealed a chest covered with light-colored hair.

Her gaze moved over him, and she stepped back. She stopped when her butt bumped into the rail.

Sandy blonde hair framed his face and complemented a deep tan. Firm, sensual lips were defined by the shadow of facial hair along his cheekbones.

But his eyes were a sparkling shade of blue that reminded Cara of polished sapphire gemstones.

Cara's breath caught when he smiled. Hip lips parted in a dazzling display of straight white teeth.

He waved a hand in front of her face. "Woo hoo. Anyone home in there?"

Cara snapped out of her trance. "What?"

"Oh, there you are." Despite the slight edge of humor in his voice, his tone, deep and sensual, created a spiral of warm goose bumps that raced over her skin. Disconcerted, she crossed her arms and avoided his gaze, annoyed when heat stole into her cheeks.

"What the bloody hell are ye talking about?" she retorted. She dared to glance over at him. "I'm right in front of ye. Are ye blind?"

His eyes widened as if surprised by her sharp tone. He stared at her for a brief moment then shook his head. "No, I'm not blind, but you look a bit out of sorts there. Are you all right?"

She smiled, sure to betray nothing of her irritation at having her peace interrupted. "I'm fine. What do ye want?" she blurted, scarcely aware of her own voice.

His expression hardened at her harsh question. "You shouldn't be here."

"Last I heard this is a free country. Something change I didn't know about?"

The man chortled with a dry, cynical sound. "You're a regular smartass, aren't ya? This may be a free country, but it's not safe here."

She glanced around. "I doona see any problems."

A shadow of irritation hovered in his eyes. "You need to leave now."

She threw her head back and placed her hands on her hips. "And who are ye to tell me what to do?"

"Lady, this is my beat, and I'm sick and tired of people dying on my beat. Why don't you go home and save me the hassle of peeling your body off the pier?"

She dropped her hands at her sides. "Are ye a cop?"

"I'm a detective."

"Detective, eh? And do ye have a name, detective?"

"Doesn't everyone?" She raised her eyebrows. "The name's Jake Bradshaw."

Cara released a deep sigh at the hint of censure in his tone. "Detective Bradshaw, I'm going to admire the view for a little while, and then I'll go home." She made a cross over her chest with her fingers. "I promise."

"I know you will, but could you please admire the view from somewhere else? It's been a long day and I'd like to go home and get some sleep."

She sighed then gave a resigned shrug. "No one asked ye to stay."

"I can't leave you out here by yourself." His lips thinned and sudden anger lit up his eyes. "You really don't get it, do you?"

"Look, detective. I doona need a gallant knight to save my virtue. I am capable of taking care of myself."

"Lady—" He paused. "What is your name, anyway?"

She forced her lips to part in a curved, stiff smile. "Why? Is it yer goal to arrest me?"

He leaned his forearms on the rail. He tilted his chin, glanced at her and smirked. "Have you done something that might warrant your arrest?"

"If no' that, then why do ye want to know my name?"

He chuckled. "'Cause it's a bit rude to keep calling you *lady*, don't you think?"

She bit down hard on her lower lip. He did have a point. "I suppose so. The name's Cahira O'Leary."

He stood up and pushed his hands deep into his pocket. "Cahira? Nice name."

She bent her head and studied the knotted pine

timbers of the deck before she looked at him. "Thanks, but most people call me Cara."

"Well, Cara O'Leary, I must insist you leave this area."

Her hands clenched at her waist and she laughed to cover her annoyance. "Wow, ye wilna let it go, will ye? I'm no' hurting anyone."

"Because you're trespassing," he replied with a heavy dose of sarcasm.

She stiffened and cocked her head. "Excuse me?"

His eyebrows rose. "Didn't you see the tape over there?"

"What tape? Over where?"

"The yellow police tape that says 'Do not cross. Crime Scene.'" With a slight incline of his head and a wave of his hand, he pointed to an area over his left shoulder. "That tape was put there to keep people off this part of the pier."

Cara peered in the direction he indicated. A bright six-inch wide fluorescent yellow tape lined the area from the aquarium to the rail.

Oops!

She looked at him and smiled. Grateful for the semidarkness that hid the flush in her cheeks, she shrugged. "Sorry, I must have missed it."

"You missed that?"

She flinched at the confusion in his tone. "I just said I did. Dinna ye hear me?"

"But you had to have stepped right over the top of it."

She lifted her hands in a sign of defeat and clamped her lips closed. Instead of responding to his observation, she spun around and walked away.

"Hey, where are you going?"

Cara didn't turn, but she did start to laugh. "Ye tell me to go and when I leave—" She broke off her sentence and twisted around. "What's it to be?"

"You're going home then?"

"I guess so. Why? Do ye want to come?"

His eyebrows shot up. "Are you propositioning me? You know, I might have to arrest you as a—"

Her mouth dropped open. "Ye have got to be jesting?"

"Jesting?"

She pressed her lips together in anger. "I am *no'* a harlot."

"Damn, woman, what century are you from?"

She stared at him. Her heart pounded a rapid beat. *It was time to go.* Aloud, she said, "Well, Detective Bradshaw, it was a pleasure, but I'm going home—" She paused. "*Alone.*" She stressed the final word.

He grimaced and offered her an apologetic smile. "I'm sorry about that. Why don't you let me make it up to you and walk you home?"

Cara lifted her hands, palms outward. "Thanks, but no. I'm a big girl and can find my own way."

Chin held high, she turned and strolled fifty feet until the beach appeared in the corner of her eye. She stopped and glanced down at the sand. Did she dare? She peered over her shoulder. Mr. High-Strung Detective stood rigid, his arms crossed over his broad chest, his bright eyes fixed on her.

She made a split-second decision to give Mr. Smarty Pants a topic to discuss at his next psych exam. With a mischievous grin, she stepped up on a nearby bench and pulled her body upward.

"Hey, get down from—"

She gripped the rail with both hands and heaved her body up. Swinging her legs to the other side, her butt rested on the metal bar. She took a moment to glance at the detective.

Intense panic filled his expression, and he rushed forward, his hands outstretched.

She giggled. Before he wrapped his hand around her arm, she pushed herself over.

His shout faded against the maelstrom of crashing waves on the beach below.

Her feet landed in the sand, her knees buckled just for a moment. She stood, spun around, and glanced up. Jake Bradshaw, his mouth open in stunned surprise, stared wide-eyed at her from the top of the pier.

Cara smiled and waved. "Good night, Detective," she shouted.

He snapped his mouth shut and frowned. "How the hell did you do that?" he hollered in a loud voice that carried across the breeze.

"'Tis a secret," she yelled back. With a final wave, she turned and walked into the white mist that floated across the shoreline.

****

Jake stared at the auburn-haired woman until she disappeared from sight. His stomach knotted, and he drew a couple of deep breaths. She nearly gave him a heart attack with her unanticipated leap from the pier.

That woman jumped the equivalent of a three-story building, rose to her feet, and walked away as calm as she pleased. She should be dead or at least sporting a few broken bones.

"A woman with secrets can't be a good thing," he

whispered, although he hated to admit it, she intrigued him.

His thoughts returned to the first moment he saw her. Before he approached, he took a minute to study her. He read sadness in her expression and fought the temptation to offer her comfort. It'd been a strange reaction to someone he didn't know.

But when he confronted her, she changed. No longer the demure, sad woman, she became argumentative, yet tantalizing. Unusual iridescent emerald green eyes highlighted a perfect oval face with exotic cheekbones. Even in the shadows, her beautiful, bright auburn hair gleamed of deep gold and red tones. Black jeans emphasized her curved hips, and a black tank top revealed the soft cleavage between her uplifted breasts.

It took every ounce of his willpower to look at her face.

He blew out the breath he held.

"Wow!" he muttered under his breath.

Cahira O'Leary was a woman he wasn't likely to forget, and one he certainly hoped to see again.

Chapter Two

Deidra Sidhe strolled along the crowded pier, manipulating her hips in a soft sway.

Since her arrival on this plane, she'd learned one thing about the species that shared her new home. The power of persuasion could be found in the crotch of the male's pants. She caught a glint of interest in several men's eyes, but when she made her move, the women at their sides intruded.

A hard object jabbed into her ribs. She spun around to face the culprit, but he had already vanished into the crowd. Her hands fisted at her sides. She wrinkled her nose and shook her head. These creatures reeked with a putrid smell of weakness that burned her nose and throat with every breath, but for the moment, her survival depended on them.

She straightened her robe and pulled the hood over her face. The coppery scent of human blood no longer appealed to her taste buds. She would have to search for food, but later, when she found someone in a solitary setting where the overwhelming stench of tainted blood didn't make her want to vomit.

Her jaw tightened, and her incisors scraped her bottom teeth. A grinding noise flooded her ears. She cringed in annoyance and eased up. She flashed furious eyes to the skies, certain the objects of her anger received the message.

The gods of the Tuatha Dé Danann destroyed her world. They took her beloved Ághmach and imprisoned him in the Underworld, far from her reach.

She would have her revenge.

Bright lights filtered through the veil of her cowl. She glanced around and searched for the source.

Madame Elena.

Painted with a white substance, the words stained the center of a discolored, grimy window. Splintered wood surrounded the glass, the flaws hidden by multi-colored lights that flashed around its edges. Deidra squinted against the glare and took a step forward. The pain behind her eyes intensified.

She stretched out a hand and touched a blue bulb with her fingertip. Electrical sparks shot outward and sprayed her hand before the bulb dimmed and grew black. The other lights in the string followed and darkened in a chain reaction that eased the sting in her eyes.

Ah, that's better. Her gaze traveled over the face of the dilapidated, beige shack. Paint chips blemished the wooden siding and littered the sidewalk. The brown and tan awning over the door was ripped and shredded. The tattered strips fluttered like a flag in the soft breeze.

She took a step to the side, scuffing her feet on the pavement until she stood in front of the words that labeled the building's contents. *Medium. Fortune Teller. See the Future. Speak to a lost one. Madame Elena can do it all.*

Her heartbeat sped up with excitement and created a rapid succession of thuds against her breast. She hurried to the shabby entrance where she gripped the doorknob. With a quick twist of her wrist, she whipped the door wide. It slammed against the outer wall with a loud *crash*.

Inside, two warped mud-stained steps led up to a ten-by-ten room. At the top, she gazed around. She grinned at the annoyed expressions on the faces of the occupants. Their opinions mattered little to her.

She ignored them and glanced around the room.

A tattered olive shag carpet blanketed the floor. A pathway of dirt and mud on the floor's surface led from the door to the sitting area. Mismatched chairs, upholstered in various shades of grayish-colored vinyl, lined the grunge-smudged walls. Two oak end tables, their surfaces scratched, sat on each side of an uninhabited puke-green couch, the fabric shredded, cigarette-burned and coated with grime.

An object on the stand beside the sofa caught her eye, and she wandered toward it. A woman slid from a nearby chair, walked across the room and took the only other empty chair. Paying no attention to the obvious slight, she touched the globe. Her pointed fingernails rested against the dusty translucent glass. A thrill of surprise rushed over her at the red and blue electrical current that followed her touch.

"Simon."

At the low-toned female voice, Deidra turned. A woman dressed in old English Gypsy garb held back a curtain of black acrylic beads. A strip of braided black hair tinged with gray streaks hung over one shoulder.

The man sitting in the corner stood and walked over to the old woman. He smiled and nodded in greeting. "Madame Elena. Thank you for seeing me on such short notice."

Madame Elena stepped aside and motioned the

man inside. "Come. The moon is bright, and the spirits have been very vocal this eve. Shall we see what Natalia has to say?"

They disappeared behind the sequined curtain. The beads clinked and rattled for a few moments before they stilled.

She trembled with excitement and swiveled to the others in the room.

"Get out," she ordered, in a low, ominous tone.

When no one moved, she lowered her hood, and narrowed her eyes. Her mouth stretched and gums burned as pointed incisors broke through the tissue and filled her mouth.

And then she smiled.

Their eyes widened. They almost tripped over each other in their stampede for the door. Deidra bit her lip to suppress a giggle at their comical scramble.

When the room emptied, Deidra raised her hand. She used her mind and propelled a burst of energy through her fingertips to slam the door shut. With a sharp twist of her wrist, she flipped the lock.

She retracted her incisors and sauntered to the curtains where she peered through the slits of the stringed beads. Elena and the man called Simon clasped hands in the center of a table covered by a dingy white cloth.

The apparition of a young woman, with wavy blonde hair and a slender body, gyrated in the air above them.

Anticipation sent tingles of delight across Deidra's flesh, and she licked her lips.

"Simon, you must leave this place." The woman's voice rose in a shrill note of panic. Deep lines of

concern creased her translucent face.

"Natalia, I'll never leave you." A soft smile curved his lips. "I love you."

"No, Simon, leave now," she cried. *"Get out of this building. You are in grave danger."*

"There is no danger here," the medium assured.

The woman spun to Elena. *"Please, you both must leave."*

Deidra pushed the curtains apart and stepped into the room. The beads jangled which drew the attention of the room's occupants.

"Wouldn't that be rude since you came so far to see him?" Deidra asked. She arched her brows in interest.

Natalia shook her head. Her mouth opened then closed as if she wanted to speak, but couldn't. Her shoulders dropped in defeat, and she looked at Simon, an apology in her eyes.

"Forgive me, my love," she murmured, then faded and disappeared.

The gypsy rose from the table, her expression tight with strain. "You need to wait in the other room. This is a private session."

"I'll wait right here," Deidra replied then ambled across the room. She stopped behind Simon's chair.

Simon twisted in his seat and glared up at her. Stunned anger lit up his eyes.

"Who the hell do you think you are? You're interfering with my time. Get out," he roared. He set his hands on the table and pushed himself to his feet.

Deidra slammed her hand down on his shoulder and shoved him onto the seat with a heavy *thud*.

"Release him this instant," Elena insisted.

"Oh, I will. It is time for him to join Natalia," Deidra commented. Her gums burned as her incisors once again emerged from between her lips.

Simon struggled, but Deidra held on tight.

Deidra lowered her head and clamped her open mouth onto his neck. His skin popped when her points penetrated his flesh. The coppery tang of his blood, the rich flavor filled her mouth and enflamed her senses.

When Simon's body grew limp, Deidra released him. Motionless, he slid from the chair and landed in a heap on the floor. Wide, lifeless eyes stared up at her, his mouth open in a silent scream.

Deidra straightened, brushed her hands together, and licked the residual blood from her lips. She gazed at Elena who stood on the opposite side of the table. The corner of her lip twisted at the medium's ashen face. Elena's eyes were fixed on Simon's motionless body.

"What are you?" Elena whispered. She gazed at Deidra.

Deidra's brows rose. "Elena, isn't it?" At the woman's nod, she tilted her head. "I am your Queen," she replied in a sharp tone, daring the woman to defy her.

Deidra kicked Simon's feet from her path and grabbed his vacated chair. She lowered into it and inclined her head toward the other chair.

"Sit, Elena. We need to talk," she insisted in a soft voice.

Elena took a deep breath and stared at her with wide eyes. Her eyes narrowed. After a brief moment, she shook her head in defiance.

"I have nothing to say to you. Now, please leave,"

Elena ordered in a sharp, yet unsteady voice. She took a step away from the table and pointed an index finger at the door.

Deidra grinned. The woman's attempts at bravery pleased her.

Before Elena retreated to the corner of the room, Deidra leaned across the table, grabbed the Gypsy's hands, and gave a slight squeeze. Elena grimaced.

"You will suit me well." A muscle clenched in Deidra's jaw. "Now, stop this nonsense and sit!" she demanded.

When the medium refused to move, Deidra applied more pressure on Elena's hands and forced the elder to sit.

"What do you want from me?"

Elena's hands trembled, but she managed to pull them free.

"You cannot fight me." With a brief nod of her head and a mental call, Elena's hands returned to hers. Once clasped, she squeezed hard, then smiled when Elena cried out in pain. "Now, I wish to speak to my beloved Àghmach, and you shall be my link."

"Is he dead?" Elena asked in a shaky voice.

"He is in the underworld."

Elena's lower lip trembled, "Underworld? Then that makes him dead," she replied in a low, composed voice.

"No, it doesn't. He is very much alive and I wish to speak to him."

"If he's not dead, I can't help you." Elena attempted to pull her hands away again, but Deidra gripped them tighter. Elena whimpered.

"Do you wish to end up like Simon?" Deidra asked

in a tone as soft as velvet yet edge with steel.

Elena took a quick glance at Simon's body before her attention returned to Deidra. She whipped her head back and forth. "No," she murmured.

"Then you will connect me with my Ághmach." Deidra demanded in a loud voice that ricocheted off the walls in such a small room. "Now!" Deidra shouted. Her lips twisted into a grin when Elena flinched.

"I don't know who you are, nor do I care, but what you ask is not something easily accomplished under duress."

Deidra smiled. "Duress makes people do things they would not do otherwise."

"If you insist on doing this, then—"

"I do."

"You must close your eyes and concentrate on Ághmach's face."

Deidra hesitated. She waited until Elena closed her eyes before she did. After a few minutes, a dark shadow appeared behind her closed lids. An icy chill seeped through the air and caressed her skin.

Deidra felt it, recognized it, and opened her eyes. "Ághmach, my love."

A black figure of a man emerged from the center of the table and materialized piece by piece. First the distinct shape of a face, followed by the contours of broad shoulders and then muscular arms appeared until his inky shape became visible as a whole.

His eyes blazed fiery red.

"It is about time, Dee. What has taken you so long to come for me?" Chills of excitement flared up Deidra's back at Ághmach's arrogance. An erotic hunger settled between her thighs. Her breath quickened, and her cheeks warmed.

She choked back a laugh before she explained. "Until a year ago, I was confined in a realm of unconsciousness, oblivious to my surroundings and to the rest of the world."

"What of the Camarilla? Our people?"

Deidra's shoulders drooped. "Gone. The gods have destroyed the cabinet and all of our followers."

Anger flared in Ághmach's eyes.

"They shall pay for their actions," he vowed, his tone full of promise.

"Since my escape, I have searched for a way to release you from your prison so together we may seek our revenge."

His brows drew together in an angry frown. "You have not been successful, dearest. I am but a spirit of my former self."

Deidra bowed her head, chastised. "I am ashamed of my failure, my liege."

"As well you should be." Ághmach's eyes moved around the room, his brows wrinkled. "This is not our time."

Deidra shook her head. "It is not. The sustenance is not the same as our Camarilla, but it suffices to keep us alive. I have already begun to create our followers, our minions on this plane, but we need our leader returned to us."

His left eyebrow raised a fraction. "How is it that you have contacted me now? In this way?"

"I have found a woman with the mental ability to speak to others not of this world."

Ághmach nodded as if satisfied. "It is a first step."

Suddenly, he shuddered, groaned and closed his

eyes. Silence permeated the room.

Deidra shot forward in her chair. "My love?"

When he reopened his eyes, his mouth curved in a smile.

"Are you well?" she asked in an anxious voice.

Ághmach nodded and waved a hand through the air as if brushing her concern to the side. "Fine, fine." His eyes met hers. "Dee, a child resides nearby, a very powerful girl who holds the power of a psyche. Find her. On the eve of the celestial solstice, draw upon the child's power and those of the medium to perform the 'Ligint Saor' connotation."

Deidra's face brightened. "Of course, the ancient Gaelic spell meant to release into freedom." She nodded. "It is a good plan. I will make the necessary arrangements."

"Good."

Her gaze met his and his eyes softened.

"I miss ye, beloved," she whispered.

"Bring me back and I'll show ye just how much I miss ye." His voice held the promises of a lifetime lost. "Bring me back, Dee. Bring me back."

And then he disappeared. His essence lingered heavy in the air. She closed her eyes, drew a deep breath, and savored his scent. Oh, how she missed his arms around her.

She cleared her throat, faced Madame Elena and chuckled at the medium's ashen face. She patted the woman's cold hand in reassurance. "It appears you will become my personal guest for a while. Do not fear. I will free you when I have my beloved, Ághmach, at my side." She glanced at Simon's body. "Just as I have released him."

A visible shudder attacked Elena's body.

"God help us all," she muttered.

Deidra narrowed her gaze as bitterness rose in her throat. "No one can help you or anyone else in this pathetic world," she growled, then smirked when Elena flinched.

Chapter Three

Jake gripped the steering wheel with both hands as he maneuvered his '93 coupé along Ocean Park Boulevard in downtown Santa Monica. The traffic moved at breakneck speeds, bumper to bumper, and he struggled to maintain the harsh pace.

Headed home after another thirteen-hour stretch at the precinct, Jake focused on the rash of unsolved homicides that plagued the city over the past six weeks. He reflected on the similarities of each murder and counted them off on his fingers.

All of the murders occurred during the twilight hours. No survivors, no witnesses, and, although the crime scenes were blood-splattered, they were also evidence-free. Not one fingerprint, other than those of the victims, was found that might lead police to the identity of the killer or killers. Lastly, the coroner had to rely on dental records to identify the mangled remains.

Even the city's criminal profilers remained stumped, having never seen a case similar to what the city experienced now.

So far, the investigation ruled out drug-related or gang attacks. With the exception of two prostitutes, eighteen of the victims were model citizens with no history of priors.

This morning they found the bodies of college

students, Janice Hopkins and Timothy Stoles, near Venice Beach. Parents reported the teens missing three days ago.

Jake ran a hand over his tired eyes and drew in a deep tortured breath. Damn, his temples throbbed, and a large knot formed in his throat. He swallowed hard and blinked, vowing to find the culprit or culprits responsible for these horrific crimes and send them to prison for the rest of their days.

All too quickly, the direction of his thoughts switched gears.

Visions of a red-haired beauty assaulted him. As hard as he tried to forget Cahira O'Leary, he couldn't. Not only did that woman haunt his dreams at night, she tormented his thoughts during the day.

What was so special about her that he couldn't forget?

No woman, except his late wife Lisa, ever had this effect on him. A stab of pain speared through him, and he drew another deep agonized breath as he thought of how much he missed her. She was gone, her death his fault.

A car materialized from a side street. Stunned by its sudden appearance and the anxious blowing horn, he whipped the steering wheel to the left, and jerked the car back into his own lane.

"Damn," he muttered then clenched his jaw.

He shook his head. That woman was going to be the death of him, and he didn't even know who the hell she was.

Static crackled from the radio under the dashboard followed by the dispatcher's voice. "Any car in the district of Woodlawn Cemetery, respond to a report of trespassing on cemetery property. Possible vandalism involved."

Jake looked at the nearest street sign. The next lane up would take him to the front entrance of the graveyard.

Reaching for the handset beside the radio, he picked it up and pushed the button. "This is Detective Bradshaw. I'm in the vicinity of Woodlawn and will investigate possible trespass."

"10-4, Detective," came the reply over the speaker.

"10-4, my ass," he mumbled under his breath then dropped the microphone into the cradle, wondering why he'd been so eager to volunteer.

After a few moments of berating himself, he arrived at his destination. He flicked on the directional, slowed the car and made the right hand turn onto the grounds.

Woodlawn was one of the largest cemeteries in Santa Monica and most of the teenagers in the area came here to party. Jake figured he had at least an hour and a half drive, along twisted roads, just to make it to the other side of the site. And there was a nine out of ten chance the trespassers had already left.

He shook his head, braked and shifted the car into park.

Stretching a hand across the car seat, he picked up the LED spotlight from the floor, and plugged the adapter into the lighter socket. He rolled down the window, aimed the device out the opening and flicked on the switch.

Light splayed across the headstones. With his right hand, he slid the car into gear and inched his foot on the gas.

An hour later, Jake was about to call dispatch and report the area clear when a small group of dark figures launched from the shadows and ran within six feet of the car's front fender.

He slammed his foot on the brake. The tires squealed. The car juddered to a standstill a split second before he hit the petite young girl with brown hair who trailed the pack.

Shrieking laughter, both male and female, ricocheted through his open window. The five teens hit the edge of the trees on the opposite side of the road. Before they disappeared, one of the boys turned to stare at Jake. He grinned, stuck up his middle finger, and spun around to vanish behind a cluster of headstones. Within seconds, the teens' laughter faded into the distance.

"Shit," he cursed.

He tossed the light onto the passenger seat and slammed the car into reverse. With a glance over his shoulder, he backed up to the edge of the pavement. He faced forward, shifted into drive, and navigated the car the automobile down the road beside the area where the group vanished.

He glanced sideways and stretched out a hand to grab the light. When his eyes returned to the road, his heart thudded against his ribcage. A lone figure appeared from the gloom of the trees into the path of his car.

"What the fu—," he started. Shock wedged the words in the throat. Every muscle in his body tensed, and he slammed his foot on the accelerator instead of the brake.

The car shot forward.

Realizing his blunder, he jerked his foot off the gas and thumped on the brake. The car shuddered to a stop. The seatbelt jammed into his shoulder and upper chest. Pain raced down his arm, and he gasped for breath.

He glanced out the windshield. An icy panic gripped him. As if in slow motion, the figure hit the front bumper, rolled across the hood, up the windshield and disappeared over the top of his car.

Jake whipped the car into park. Frozen in disbelief, he gripped the steering wheel with both hands. His gut twisted, and he swallowed the bile that rose in his throat. He shuddered and forced air through his lungs.

What the hell just happened?

His hand trembled as he reached for the microphone and brought it to his mouth. He pressed the button.

"Dispatch, I need an ambulance at Woodlawn Cemetery. I have a pedestrian who has been hit by an automobile."

"10-4 detective." The box squawked a reply.

Jake leaned his head back against the headrest and closed his eyes. His hand dropped into his lap. The microphone plummeted to the floor with a clunk.

Oh God! He'd hit someone. The sickening thud and the sight of the body as it flew across the hood and over the roof replayed in his mind. What had he done?

His eyes shot open when the microphone crackled and the dispatcher's voice echoed in the car. "Jake, rescue squads for most of the San Diego area have responded to a thirty car pileup on Interstate 5 near Claremont. I've put out a call to Lemon Grove. Their EMT rescue is en-route to your location, ETA twenty-five minutes."

Jake shook his head in disgust. Lemon Grove was more than thirty miles away. He picked the microphone off the floor. "10-4." He grumbled into the receiver and then dropped it into the center console as if it burned his fingers. "Probably get there quicker if I took them to the hospital myself," he muttered under his breath.

Raising his hand, he adjusted the rear view mirror. The shadow of a prone body lying on the ground ten feet behind his car came into view.

He shook his head in denial, and continued to stare. His heart pounded so hard in his chest, he was afraid it might burst through his skin. Regret weighed him down. Remorse ate at him. He'd injured, possibly killed another human being.

"This cannot be happening," he murmured aloud, trying to force his brain to work.

And then, the figure moved.

He blinked, afraid to believe, but there it was again…a slight movement.

Jake seized the inside car handle, whipped the door open and leapt from the vehicle. He crossed the distance between his automobile and the body in two seconds flat.

"Hey, are you all right?" he asked as he dropped beside the figure.

A soft feminine moan answered his question.

With care, he eased the woman's body over. When her face came into view, he gasped and stumbled backward.

"Cara?" he whispered. His heart pounded with an uneasy mix of panic and pleasure. To find her again only to lose her was not a thought he could fathom…not now.

At the sound of his voice, the heavy lashes that shadowed her cheeks flew up and her lower lip trembled.

"Hi," she whispered.

"Hi yourself," Jake replied, his voice soft.

Her eyes flickered over his face as if she were glad to see him. She must have recognized his concern for her smile died, and she averted her eyes.

After a few seconds of thick silence, he couldn't stop his next words. "What in the hell are you doing out here, Cara?"

Chapter Four

Cara struggled to sit up.

"Ouch," she murmured. Her side throbbed in pain, and she winched. She wrapped an arm around her midsection, flopped to the pavement, and closed her eyes.

A brilliant mixture of rainbow colors swirled behind her eyelids. Her stomach lurched. Bitter acid rose in her throat.

She swallowed.

What if the vampires came back while she lay incapacitated? Jake would be unprotected and open to attack.

She pushed past the pain and opened her eyes. With her nerves on edge, she scanned the area for the presence of enemies. Finding none, she forced herself to relax.

"Don't move." Jake ordered in a tense voice.

She waved his concern away with the brush of her hand. "I'm fine."

"Cara, you've been hit by a car. You may have internal injuries. Stay put. The rescue squad will be here in a few minutes to take you to the hospital."

She ignored the stabbing agony in her ribs and pushed herself upward. "Really, I'm fine, and I'm no' going to the hospital."

He frowned in exasperation, wrapped an arm

across her lower back and helped her sit. "You don't look so good."

She grimaced. "Thanks. Ye're such a sweet-talker."

A smile ruffled the corners of his mouth. "You've got blood all over you. Not exactly flattering," he remarked in a soft, chiding voice.

"I can assure ye that nothing's broken." She bit her lip to stifle a grin at the doubt that colored his eyes bright neon indigo. With her bloodied hand, she patted his arm in reassurance. "I just need to sit here for a few minutes. Doona worry. I'm a quick healer."

His brows shot upward, and he snorted in disbelief. "Yeah right."

"Jake, please. I'm fine." She looked at his parked car then back at him, an eyebrow rose in question.

"What?" he asked. His eyes narrowed, and he frowned.

"Are ye the one who hit me?"

A pink flush flared into his cheeks, and he glanced away, avoiding her gaze. "I never saw you until it was too late to stop, so yes," he hesitated, spread his arms wide then met her gaze. "I am your one and only runner-downer."

She giggled at his self-proclaimed name. "Nice!"

In the next instant, his expression turned grim. "Cara?"

"Aye?"

He measured her with a cool appraising look. "You didn't answer my questions."

She rubbed her aching middle. "Sorry, what question was that?"

"What are you doing out here?"

Her mind whirled and she shrugged to hide her concern. She couldn't exactly tell him she was chasing a group of vamps. Instead, she shrugged. "Why? It is a free country, isna it?"

Jake shook his head. His lips twisted into a cynical grin. "Stop with the free country, already. Yes, it is, as you well know, but think about it. You're in a cemetery, for Pete's sake."

She looked around. "Who's Pete? Is he here?"

"You're kidding, right?" He must have recognized the confusion on her face for he shook his head. "Never mind, let's just say you show up in the strangest places."

"Thank ye," she said with an innocent smile.

A shadow of annoyance crossed his face. "Do you always have to be a smartass?"

A warning voice whispered in her head telling her that she'd successfully pissed the man off. "I doona understand," she muttered.

His expression was tight with strain. "All I wanted was a straight answer, but you couldn't even do that. I should arrest you, you know?"

She flinched at the harsh tone of his voice. "For what?" she choked out.

"It may be a free country, but the cemetery has a curfew. It closes at seven in the evenings."

An unwelcome blush crept into her cheeks and she was glad of the semidarkness that hid the flush in her cheeks.

"So, that means you're trespassing. Are you going to tell me what you were doing running around with a group of wild teenagers? Aren't you a little old for that?"

Her embarrassment turned to raw fury. She bit her bottom lip stopping her bitter retort.

She swallowed hard, lifted her chin, and boldly met his gaze. "If ye must know, I happen to know one of those kids. I was hoping to get her home before she got into trouble." The lie passed her lips as easily as the sun rose in the morning, and she did it without batting an eyelid.

His expression softened. "I didn't mean to get in your way." He glanced out into the darkness. "It would appear they're gone."

"Yeah, I can see that," she muttered under her breath. She struggled to stand, grimacing at the pain her ribcage.

He rushed to her side.

"You really should wait for the ambulance and go to the hospital." Despite his assertion, he offered her his hand. She looked into his face, and placed her hand in his. He wrapped his fingers around hers and helped her to her feet. Still a little wobbly from the accident, she stumbled and would have fallen except Jake's arms caught her, drawing her against him.

Cara looked up into his face, surprised to see desire in his eyes. Her pulses leapt with excitement and a delightful shiver of wanting ran through her. She wanted him to kiss her, and would have encouraged it except for the nagging voice of common sense that whispered in her ear. There was no room for romance in her life, not now, probably never.

"I'm okay. Thank ye," she whispered, a little breathless.

"Hey, why don't you come to my place and get cleaned up a bit? I'll tend to your injuries."

Cara smiled. "Are ye hitting on me?"

Jake laughed. "Would it be a problem if I were?" His gaze traveled over her before somber eyes met hers. "Seriously, I wouldn't feel right sending you home by yourself especially since you're hurt."

"Ye really doona need to—"

"I know. I don't need to worry about you." Jake finished for her. "Please, Cara. Ease my guilt over plowing you over and let me take care of you."

Before she could comment, he raised his hands. "I know that, too."

"What?"

"You can take care of yourself. Please, for tonight, let me." He wrapped his arm across her shoulder. "Come on."

Cara didn't argue. Instead, she let him lead her to the passenger side of his car. He opened the door and eased her inside.

He walked around the front of the car. Her eyes followed him, admiring his confident steps. She didn't understand how she let him talk her into this.

She lifted her shoulders and flexed. Her body had already begun to heal itself. One of the perks of being immortal, she supposed.

She would heal, but not before she felt every bone-shattering and nerve-pinching ounce of pain. Depending on the severity of her wound, the injury could be gone in seconds or hours, leaving her ready to fight again.

Such was her life.

The slamming of the car door brought her back to the present. Jake slid behind the wheel. He glanced at her and smiled. Then, he picked up the radio microphone, and pushed the button. Cara cringed at the loud squawk that echoed in her ears.

"Dispatch." He released the button and waited for a response.

"Go ahead, Detective."

Again he pushed the button. "Cancel Lemon Grove EMT. Pedestrian refuses medical treatment. As for the trespassers, they slipped away. I didn't notice any vandalism, but its damn dark out here. For now, the cemetery is all clear."

"I'll file the report, and send a black and white over in the morning to check it out," the soft female voice said. "Have a good night, Jake."

Cara's eyebrows rose at the familiarity of the woman on the other end of the radio. Were she and Jake involved? She bit her bottom lip and refrained from making a comment.

"You, too, Julie. Tell Randall I said hello, and give the munchkins a hug for me," he said. "Out."

Ah, so the dispatch lady had a family of her own. For some reason Cara couldn't quite fathom, an intense sense of relief rushed over her.

He gave her a sideward glance. "Ready?"

She nodded and passed him a timid smile.

He winked and turned the key. The engine purred to life.

They drove through the streets of Santa Monica. As usual, the streets were bustling with activities. Inside the car, the silence was almost unbearable.

"The Night Lifers."

"Huh?" Cara turned her head at his words.

"Night Lifers. That's what we call them. They're the people who stay out all night partying."

48

Cara didn't tell him that half of those night lifers were vampires, shape shifters or werewolves. Santa Monica ran rampant with them.

"Doona they have a home or someplace to go?"

"Why? Why go home when you can be out with friends having a good time?"

"And what about ye? Doona ye have friends to go out with?"

He shook his head and chuckled. "I have friends, but I'm a homebody. I'd rather go home after work than spend my time getting drunk. It's not worth the memory loss."

"Do ye have someone for ye at home?" Cara held her breath waiting for his answer.

He smiled. His teeth shone white against the dimness of the car. When his answer came, an unexplainable deep stab of regret filled her heart. "Yeah, I do. She's the love of my life."

Cara bit her lip, stifling any response. Her hands clenched in her lap and she stole a glance at his profile. A nice proportioned nose, a strong chin overshadowed by a faint hint of whiskers. Manly. Her breath caught in her throat and she suppressed the urge to reach out and caress his jaw.

He's unavailable. Let it go. Her inner voice argued.

After ten minutes of more silence, Jake turned on the directional and slowed to a near stop. Turning left, he pulled into the front of a one-story house.

"This is where ye live?" Cara asked in a surprised high squeak. She swallowed.

Jake gave her a soft smile, his mouth softened as his lips curved upward. "You sound surprised?"

She cleared her throat of the disturbing peep. "It's

beautiful."

"Thank you," Jake replied. Pride filled his voice. He pulled the vehicle in front of a double door garage.

Cara glanced around. The grounds were stunning with its rolling lawns and towering palm trees. A winding white stone path led up to a front porch made of marble stone. Globe topped lampposts lined the walk, casting light and shadows around the building.

The one-story building reminded Cara of a Victorian mansion with its face smothered in ivy and creeper rose bushes. The plants looked in need of some tender loving care. However that slight detail didn't take away from the charming appearance of the home.

She envisioned a high cliff overlooking the Pacific Ocean behind the house.

He stopped in front of the garage and turned the key off. With his hand on the door knob, he faced her. "Come on. Let's have a look at your injuries."

"That wilna be necessary."

"Don't argue." He said as he opened the door. When she didn't move, he leaned down and peered inside. "Are you coming?"

She shrugged, and stepped from the car. "All this fuss and ye're going to find out 'tis all for naught."

"I'll be the judge of that, thank you very much," he responded in a soft and gentle voice.

His tone held such warmth and concern that shivers of excitement raced up her spine.

Instead of reacting, she followed him across the drive and up the steps. She stood to the side while he stuck the key in the key hole, turned the lock, and pushed the door open. He crossed the threshold and stretched out a hand.

A moment later, the room brightened.

"Come on in," he invited.

Inside, Cara's breath caught in her throat. The small foyer opened up to a larger, more spacious, living quarter. In awe, her gaze swept the area.

A glass chandelier hung from the ceiling, a round sphere in the center surrounded by hundreds of crystal diamonds. When the light passed through the shards, a prism of reds, yellows and oranges cascaded over the room.

The walls were made of the same oak toned panels as the floor. Photographs lined one wall on the opposite of the room, and Cara made a mental note to check them out later. To the right of the pictures, French doors led outside. To the left, a set of three steps led up from the living room into a kitchenette. A short railing, adorned by outdated spindles separated the two rooms.

A long black leather sofa sat opposite two leather bound recliners. In the middle, a large square table made of a light colored wood separated the two pieces of furniture. A small lamp adorned an end table between the two chairs. A forty-two inch flat screen television was pinned to the wall above the fireplace.

Fireplace?

She swiveled to face him, her brows high. "A fireplace? What do ye need a fireplace for? 'Tis hot as blazes in California."

A chuckle rumbled in Jake's chest. He walked forward, stepped around her, and grabbed a remote from the table. Aiming it at the fireplace, Cara heard a low beep a moment before the fireplace roared to life.

Cara walked to the blaze and stuck her hand out. "There's no heat," she said in wonder.

"Decorative purposes only." Jake walked to the couch and sat. He patted the seat beside him. "Now come over here, and let me see your injuries."

"There's no need." Cara held up her hands to show clear, unmarred flesh. The bruises were gone from her arms. "See, all gone."

Jake jumped from the seat, his eyes wide with amazement. In three steps, he stood at her side. He grabbed her arms, and raised them into the light. "How is that possible?" he muttered, his eyes wide.

"I told ye I'm a fast healer." She turned away so he wouldn't see the unease on her face.

"No one heals that fast."

Jake's breath brushed against her ear. She hadn't realized he stood so close.

She swallowed hard. "Oh."

"Daddy! Daddy!"

Chapter Five

Cara spun around at the high-pitched childish voice. A wee girl of seven, maybe eight, in a long strawberry colored nightgown ran across the wooden floor. Her bare feet slapped the linoleum. She clutched a ragtag six-inch brown teddy bear with green eyes under one arm.

Her eyes widened, and she glanced at Jake.

A smile curved his lips, and he knelt on one knee. The child flew into his arms.

"Munchkin," he said in a voice smothered with adoration.

He pressed a kiss to her forehead then leaned back to look into her face. "What are you still doing up? Where's Mrs. Denton?"

"I'm sorry, Mr. Bradshaw. She heard you come in and had to see you."

Cara glanced toward the hallway where a woman, about sixty, entered the room. Wisps of gray hair escaped from the bun pinned to the top of her head. Soft wrinkles lined her eyes. A laundry basket full of clothes rested on one hip.

The woman's gaze moved over Cara. Her lips curved into a gentle smile that brightened her face.

"Come on, Aimee. Your daddy has company, and its way past your bedtime."

"Aw, daddy, I don't want to go to bed." Her arms

tightened around Jake's neck, and she looked over his shoulder at Cara. Animosity lined the child's expression. "I want to stay with you."

"Aimee, go with Mrs. Denton," Jake said in a tone that implied there would be no argument.

Tears filled Aimee's eyes and her arms tightened around Jake's neck. Cara's heart broke for the little girl. The pain in the depths of her baby blues shook Cara to the core.

She took a step forward. "Hey, I've got an idea," she said in a casual tone. When all eyes turned on her, her stomach knotted, but she refused to give into the awkwardness, and continued, "Jake, why doona ye take Aimee and tuck her in." She bobbed her head and waved her hands for a semi-comical effect. "Maybe read her a bedtime story. I'm sure Aimee will fall fast asleep in no time."

Aimee's eyes brightened. "Will you daddy? Oh, please."

"Mrs. Denton can keep me company until ye get back." Cara turned pleading eyes to the woman who, the gods bless her, took the cue.

Mrs. Denton stepped forward and nodded. "I will be happy to, Mr. Bradshaw. You've been working so much overtime lately. It's hard not to see how much Aimee misses you."

Jake looked into Aimee's eyes and smiled. "All righty, then. I can see that I'm outnumbered." Bouncing her in his arms, Aimee giggled. "Let's go read that story."

At the door, he stopped, and looked over his shoulder at Cara. "I'll be back in a bit. Don't go anywhere."

"I'll be here," she promised.

Satisfied, he nodded and disappeared around the corner.

Left alone with Mrs. Denton, an uncomfortable silence permeated the room.

"I'm sorry. I dinna mean to throw ye under the bus, so to speak?"

Mrs. Denton smiled. "Not such a bad place to be at the moment." She tilted her head and looked at Cara curiously. "How did you know?"

Surprised at the woman's intuition, Cara shrugged. "Know what? That Aimee doesna see her father as much as a child at that age should? That she needs his attention? She has his love, I can see that, but there's something that draws him back, pulling him away from giving her his all." She spoke the words in a soft voice. "I wilna be one of those reasons," she murmured under her breath, and then turned to watch Mrs. Denton's reaction to her assessment of the situation she'd inadvertently found herself in.

Mrs. Denton nodded. Sadness flared in the woman's eyes. "For one so young, you see much."

Cara strolled across the room to peek at the pictures that lined the wall, but the only photos were those of Aimee.

Aimee as a baby, a toddler, and then the beautiful child Cara met tonight. Not only did the pictures portray the child's outer shell, but Aimee's inner light shimmered from within the frames.

Cara's senses heightened, and she stiffened with surprise.

Supernatural power existed in the soul of this child, strength more magical and breathtaking than Cara had ever felt in anyone, especially one so young. If Aimee's power could radiate from a simple photograph, what would it feel like to touch her?

She swallowed in spastic convulsions, two, three, four times, and then gulped for air. Her breath caught in her diaphragm and worked its way up—a hiccup, then another in a nervous habit she loathed. She stared at the little girl in the picture. Her heart pounded against her chest.

She inhaled a deep breath. "Where's Aimee's mother?" she asked, struggling to keep her tone casual.

"Mrs. Bradshaw passed almost five years ago. It was a very difficult time for Mr. Bradshaw. He hasn't been the same since." Cara turned away from the photographs and faced Mrs. Denton whose tortured eyes met hers. "Aimee has been forced to grow up too quick. She's only seven, but she's already lost much of her innocence."

Cara nodded, glanced to the pictures on the wall. "Mrs. Bradshaw's death was brutal, wasna it?"

Mrs. Denton gasped. "How do you know these things?"

"I have a sense for things that are different," she replied. She kept her expression deceptively calm even though her insides twisted like a whirlwind.

Mrs. Denton's eyes pierced into Cara's soul. "Very much like Aimee, but, tell me, how different are you from her?"

Cara giggled in a tone that sounded a bit shaky even to her own ears. "Ye've no idea, Mrs. Denton. I'm as different as they come."

Mrs. Denton's eyes widened. "Are you here to hurt the Mr. Bradshaw? I won't let you—"

Cara held up her hands halting the woman's words. She shook her head. "Oh, no, I would never hurt them."

As if she'd spoken the magical words, Mrs. Denton's tense frame relaxed. "You seem like a lovely young woman."

"Thank ye." Cara's eyes turned toward the French doors located near the fireplace. Over her shoulder, she glanced at the elder. "May I?"

Mrs. Denton nodded. "I don't see why not, but please be careful. The decking gets slippery at times."

Cara strolled to the doors and pushed them open. She stepped onto a large angled porch.

Just as she envisioned, the house, built on a cliff, overlooked a beach that bordered a small bay.

To the left of the doors, a set of stairs led to a stone pathway. Bordered on either side by red bricks, the marbled rocks created a trail that traveled across the lawn to another round of steps that trekked down the mountain face to the beach below.

Lovely!

Leaning over the railing, she glanced out across the ocean. The moonlight sparkled on the rushing waves, the only distinction between sky and sea. A gentle wind filtered across the air, bringing with it the scent of fresh sea air.

Suddenly, a shiver that had nothing to do with the breeze ran down her back. She was no longer alone and turned her back on the sea to face the man responsible for the goose bumps that dimpled her flesh.

"You're not planning on jumping, are you?" His brows dipped to a frown. His gaze shot to the rail, then to her, and back to rail as if he assessed his timing. "That's a little bit farther than the jump from the pier."

His analytical looks made Cara giggle.

She shook her head. "Nay, I wilna take that leap."

He weighed her with a critical squint for a moment before he burst out laughing. A full-hearted sound, his laughter wrapped around her like a warm blanket.

"No' right now anyways." She giggled, hesitated then raised an eyebrow. "Unless, of course, ye'd like me to leave?"

Jake took a step forward than another until he stood in front of her.

"I would very much like you to stay," he whispered. He grasped her wrists, drawing her hands toward his face where he pressed his lips to the palm of her right hand. His eyes never left her face.

She gasped and drew in a quick breath.

Jake pulled her into his arms. Heat shimmered and spread through her. The warm, male scent of pine swirled through her and enflamed her senses. Heat formed between her legs.

And then, his lashes lowered and his gaze rested on her lips. Warmth crept into her cheeks.

The corners of his mouth tightened. Fire danced in the depths of his eyes. "May I kiss you?"

"Jake," she breathed his name, lifting her lips to his.

The feel of his lips on hers was exquisite...soft, warm, and heated. When their tongues touched, fire licked through her, scorching her, melting her insides.

He pulled away. A soft breeze brushed Cara's heated skin and she trembled. She opened her eyes.

"What is it about you?" The vulnerability in his voice made her heart ache.

She didn't have time to reply before his mouth

moved over hers again. His lips barely touched her, and yet he teased and tantalized her with delicate nips. Her breath quickened when his tongue snaked out and touched her lips.

Cara melted beneath his sizzling touch, lost in his masculine scent. He tasted of peppermint spice. She smoldered with a passion that burned to her core. Never before had she experienced such craving.

His lips left hers and traveled across her cheek where his whisper brushed her ear. "Stay with me tonight?"

Oh how she wanted to say yes, but common sense warned her of the dangers that action would bring. She turned her lips into his neck.

"I canna." Even as she denied her need to him, and to herself, she couldn't stop the instinctive reaction his scent and his nearness created.

Her mouth burned and stretched. The tips of her incisors pierced through her gums, taking the shape of large, sharp fangs.

No! No! She cringed as the words echoed in her thoughts, a cruel reminder of what she was. She battled within herself, but knew she'd lost when her teeth pierced the flesh of his neck. An overwhelming power of electricity shot through her when the coppery taste of his blood filled her mouth.

Overcome by an erotic hunger, Cara was reluctant to step away.

When she did, remorse shot through her.

What had she done?

She covered her mouth, her eyes wide, and stepped away.

"Cara?" Jake asked in a tone filled with confusion,

his eyes glazed with desire. He took a step toward her, hands outstretched.

She shook her head and backed away. She couldn't stay here with him. She'd just changed everything.

"I'm sorry…so sorry," she mumbled.

Tears formed behind her eyelids, but she refused to cry in front of him. When he reached for her, she sidestepped his hands and skirted around him. Once she was safely out of reach, she spun around and sprinted through the living room to the front door.

"Cara?" At the sound of his voice, she hesitated. Her hand rested on the knob. She glanced over her shoulder. He stood in the doorway, his brows drawn together in bewilderment. His eyes pleaded with her not to leave.

"I'm sorry. I canna stay." Too late, the tears slid down her cheeks. With a furious swipe of her hand, she brushed them away. "Forgive me."

She swung the door wide and flew into the night.

"Wai—" The slamming door cut off his words.

Chapter Six

Like a beacon, the blue lights from emergency vehicles flashed over the beach.

Nerves tense and eyes alert, Jake edged through the crowded arena until he found a vacancy among the vehicles already on scene. Once parked, he sat for a moment. His hands gripped the steering wheel. He sucked in a breath while his gaze scanned the sight.

He counted six police officers in a circle. They stood at attention, their faces ashen, expressions haunted. Silent and immobile, they looked at each other, not at the object of their investigation. Emergency personnel loaded equipment into the ambulance, an obvious sign their services were no longer needed. His gut twisted and a sigh rose from deep in his throat.

Even the police photographer's expression held disgust as he rounded the scene, the flash of his camera a continuous stream of bright light.

A man in a dark suit bent over a blood-splattered mass in the sand. With a gloved hand, he knelt to retrieve an object with a pair of tweezers which he placed into an airtight cylinder. He held it into the lights of the vehicles, shook his head, and set the evidence into the steel briefcase at his side.

Jake recognized many of the uniformed and plain clothed officers. Why shouldn't he? He asked himself with a cynical smile. The number of murders in Santa Monica brought them together often.

What the hell was happening in this city? With more than twenty murders on the board with the same M.O., the department still had no leads.

Less than a half an hour ago, the shrill ring of the telephone startled him awake. His heart beat a rapid thud against his breastbone when he picked up the phone. He shot a quick glance at the alarm clock on his bedside table, and his heart dropped. It flashed 1:18 which could only mean one thing…another murder. After his mumbled "hello", Captain Dawson ordered Jake to the beach.

He returned to the present, drew another deep agonized breath and mentally prepared himself to do his job.

"Let's get to it," he mumbled to himself before he exited the car.

"Hey, Jake." A deep male voice hailed him from across the lot.

He turned. Matt Russell, his partner for the past three years, walked toward him, hand outstretched.

"Matt," he greeted, gripping Matt's hand in a firm shake. "So what have we got?" he asked, nodding toward the cluster of officers.

Matt shook his head. "We've got nothing. This one's the same as all the others. This bastard's smart."

"Cap said there was only one body. That's different than the others."

"Jake—"

At Matt's hesitation, Jake quirked an eyebrow as intuition took over. "More than one?"

Matt nodded. "Yeah, it looks like there are two,

maybe three bodies. They were ripped apart, so it's hard to tell."

"Shit!"

"That's what everyone is saying, in between puking their guts out."

"Well, let's go take a look-see, shall we?"

"Hope you've got a tough stomach tonight."

Jake laughed, although it lacked his usual humor. "Gotta in this line of work."

Jake primed himself for the sight of the victims. During his time on the force, he'd seen some messy cases. Each time, as the vomit rose in his throat, he dug deep and regained control of his errant stomach, although some moments proved easier than others. Steel stomach or not, he'd been forced to accept what each crime scene brought.

"Damn!" Jake exclaimed. He stepped past a female police officer and spotted what remained of the bodies on the sand. Nausea swirled in his stomach, and he suppressed the impulse to hack.

The beams from the car lights cast shadows and played over the remains as if performing some kind of ritual dance. Blood splattered the sands in all directions. A pool formed under the visible body parts that littered the ground.

"So, what do you think, Jake?" Matt asked. "It looks like we have ourselves an ax murderer here."

Jake shrugged. "At first glance, it would seem so, but look—" He pointed to the jagged edges of flesh that once belonged to part of an arm. "If it were an ax, the cut would be smoother, not shredded like that. What did the coroner say?"

"He's not saying. He found a tooth ingrained in the

sand and wants to analyze it before he finalizes his report."

"A tooth?"

"It looked like an old shark's tooth to me. Who knows?"

A soft breeze filtered across the air and drew Jake's attention from the conversation. His neck prickled. Goose bumps spilled down his back. A second sense warned him that they were being watched. He spun around. His gaze strayed across the crime scene, but the mass of officers were preoccupied in doing their jobs. They had no interest in him.

"Jake?" Matt waved a hand in front of his eyes.

"Huh? What?" He lifted his brow just enough to display a flicker of annoyance at the interruption.

"If you don't believe it was an ax, what do you think could have done this?"

Jake still couldn't shake the unsettling feeling, but tried to focus on the conversation.

He shook his head. "I don't know, Matt. To me, this looks more like an animal attack," he murmured.

"A shark?" Matt asked in an incredulous voice.

He glanced at Matt for a quick second. "One tooth doesn't make a herd. Not to mention, a shark doesn't swim on land."

Again his attention diverted, and he continued to scan his surroundings until they landed on a dark ominous figure on a sand dune high above the beach.

A flash of recognition rippled through him.

Cara.

Immediate questions formed in his mind. What was she doing here? Did she see who murdered these people? Was she looking for him? Would she skedaddle if he went to talk to her?

He turned back to Matt and slapped him on the shoulder. "We'll have to wait and see what the coroner comes up with. Do you think you can handle the rest of this by yourself?"

"Sure, but where are you going?"

"I'm going to check something out." Jake's gaze remained fixed on Cara, afraid she might bolt, and he'd lose her again. "I'll catch up with you tomorrow to get the full report."

With slow steps, Jake strolled across the sand toward Cara. His fear subsided when each step brought him closer to her, and she still hadn't run away.

****

More than a week had passed since she ran from Jake's house in stunned disbelief, and Cara still hadn't come to grips with what she'd done.

She'd bit him, her incisors breaking through the layers of his skin. His blood became an aphrodisiac that intoxicated her with an addiction she'd fought since leaving him. The taste still lingered on her tongue. To most people, this might be considered a minor offense, if one measured the heated moment, but to a guardian, it meant a lifelong commitment.

In that instant, their destinies altered, and a new course forged, one with no possible hope of escape. Their worlds were joined, and the core of their beings, their essences, would merge to become one.

Even now, the bond ran unrestrained in his blood and built a fire that would burn hot until it filled him with an inextinguishable inferno. Consummation of the bond, their acceptance would grant them both release from the flames and bestow upon him power and strength equal to hers.

She grimaced. A stab of regret tore through her. Jake Bradshaw didn't know the price tag associated with their chance encounter.

He desired her body, of that she was certain, but could he accept her for what she truly was? More than a mere woman, an immortal guardian created by the gods of the Tuatha De Danann assigned to protect the human race from demons, vampires, shifters, even werewolves.

Since Deidra Sidhe, evil Vampryss of the extinct Camarilla coven, escaped her prison, havoc ran rampant in the world. She sought a way to resurrect her evil counterpart, Ághmach. To date, the guardians put a kibosh on two of her campaigns, but they'd remained on their toes, on the defensive, waiting for her next move.

Cara lived in a dangerous world, a world she deemed a nightmare. It was her cross to bear, but now, she'd drawn Jake and his daughter into the midst of her battle.

Would he believe her if she tried to explain?

Jake Bradshaw was special. An inner astuteness glittered from his sapphire blues and emphasized the true depth of his character. He savored sun-drenched days, but didn't fear to glimpse beneath the cloud cover for concealed hazards.

She hoped her intuition proved accurate, because now she knew why she'd been sent to California.

Deidra Sidhe was here.

It had taken her the past week of solitude to realize that fact.

Sheer stupidity on her part!

How had she missed it? Especially given the

number of murders in Santa Monica? And if that weren't enough, the brutality of the murders themselves should have given her a sign. Deidra had her own destructive method of killing, unique only to her.

She couldn't tell Jake the murders he investigated were committed by a blood thirsty Vampryss hell-bent on revenge. If she did, she committed cerebral suicide. He would call her crazy and insist she see a psychiatrist.

He needed to know Deidra was dangerous, not someone to be taken lightly, but she couldn't just blurt that out.

Not yet, anyways.

And with those thoughts in mind, she arrived at an important decision. No matter how much it affected her, she needed to stay as close as possible to Jake and Aimee and protect them while she continued her search for the Vampryss.

High above the beach on the top of a sand dune, Cara glanced out over the ocean. With the tip of one shoe, she kicked the grains of sand.

The moonlight shimmered over the calm water. Stars twinkled against the darkened backdrop of the cloudless sky.

Below, a squadron of uniformed policemen scoured the area, searching for more victims of Deidra's latest attack. They would find them, but only in bits and pieces scattered across the sand.

When Jake emerged from his car, her heart skipped a beat. A delicious shudder heated her body. She knew he would be here. After all, this was his beat and this was his case.

His powerful well-muscled body moved with easy

grace through the crowd. He towered over the other men in the group. Flashing lights glimmered over his handsome face like beams of icy radiance.

And then, he turned in her direction. His eyes widened and his lips parted in a dazzling display of straight, white teeth. He said something to the man beside him and slapped him on the shoulder.

Would he come to her?

Moments later, he answered her question when he left the circle of lights and headed in her direction.

Torn between the need to see him and the overwhelming sense of self-preservation that assaulted her, she fought the urge to run to his arms. He radiated a vitality that drew her like a magnet and sent electric currents racing through her. Each time she saw him, the pull was stronger, more powerful than the last.

Blood coursed through her veins like an awakened river. It had to be the bond…the only explanation for the eruptions of long-buried emotions.

Long, purposeful strides carried him to her. When he stood before her, his gaze traveled over her face and searched her eyes.

"Are you okay?" he asked.

Her heart took a perilous leap at his deep-timbered voice.

Cara nodded. "I'm fine, and ye?"

He nodded and released a long audible breath, running a hand through his already tousled hair. Cara fought the urge to cover his hand with her own.

When he answered, his voice was tender, almost a murmur. "I'm doing. I'm glad to see you. You left in such a rush the last time I saw you, I was afraid I'd scared you away."

He stood close without touching, and yet, heat shimmered through her body.

If he experienced the same sensations, he didn't show it. And, at this point in their relationship, she couldn't tell him that her immortal blood raged through his blood, transferred into his bloodstream by her bite. The numbing venom and quick healing erased all signs of injury, but not the lasting effect. Soon he would want her with a fiery passion he wouldn't be able to ignore.

No way, nu-uh!

Instead, she grinned, opened her arms wide and twirled around once in a circle. "Well, here I am."

His gaze dropped from her eyes to her shoulders to her breasts. He grinned. His eyes twinkled when he looked into her face. "You certainly are." And then, his eyes filled with question. "What are you doing here?" With a sharp wave of his hand, he indicated the activity on the beach. "It's too dangerous out here. You could have been hurt."

She cringed at the concern in his voice then inhaled a deep breath.

"I knew ye would be here. I was out for a walk, thinking about things, heard the sirens—" she paused and lifted her shoulders in a brief shrug. "Hey look, Jake, I'm sorry about that night. I shouldna have run out like that."

"It's okay. I came on a little strong. I don't understand what happened. I've never...," he paused. "I usually have a little more charm."

Cara laughed. "It's okay. Really, it is."

Jake glanced around. "Are you telling me that you came out here to see me?"

She lowered her eyes.

He slipped a finger under her chin and urged her face up so she couldn't ignore the question in his eyes.

"Cara?"

She nodded. "Aye, I needed to see ye."

His eyes narrowed. "Are you sure you're okay?"

She nodded. "I'm fine, but—" she mumbled before she spun on her heels and turned away. It was time to put on the helpless female act, and she couldn't do that while looking him in the eyes.

"What's wrong, Cara?"

Guilt swelled inside her. She almost changed her mind until she remembered that this was the only way she could protect Jake and Aimee from Deidra's wrath.

Cara shrugged. "I'm fine, Jake."

"No, you're not. Something's wrong. Tell me what it is, Cara," he demanded.

She glanced over her shoulder. "'Tis silly really," she replied in a feeble voice.

He walked up beside her, grabbed her hand in his, and gave her a reassuring squeeze. "It can't be that silly if it brought you here."

"I got into a fight with my roommate—" She glanced at his face, pausing to catch her breath.

Eyes full of understanding met hers. "And you have no place to stay."

She shook her head. "I hate to ask, but I doona know anybody else. I havena been in Santa Monica long enough to make many friends. I was wondering if I could borrow yer couch. I promise it will be just a couple of days."

He smiled, wrapped an arm across her shoulder, and pulled her into his embrace. The warmth of his arms was so male, so revitalizing, that a warm glow spread over her. She relaxed against him, and buried her face into the corded muscles of his chest.

"You can stay as long as you'd like."

His breath, warm and moist, brushed her cheeks and her heart thumped. She stepped out of his grasp and flashed him a grateful, relieved smile.

"Thank ye. I promise I wilna get in yer way."

He gave her a smile that sent her pulses into a snit and winked. "You can get in my way anytime you'd like." He picked up the small black leather bag, grabbed her hand, and drew her down the bank at his side. "Come on, let's go home."

Pain squeezed her heart at the bittersweet memory of her home with Braedan.

In Cara's world, there was no such place called home.

Chapter Seven

When they rounded the corner block and pulled into the driveway, Jake switched the headlights off. The solar lights lining the pavement provided enough illumination for him to reach the front of the garage.

He slipped the car into park, switched the ignition off and turned to face her. He touched her cheek, a gentle slide of long fingers that traced heat upon her skin.

She shivered.

A shaft of moonlight slanted through the windows and captured his face in a halo of light. Tenderness glowed in the incredible blue depths of his eyes, a gentleness that slipped past her defenses. Beneath the warmth, passion unfurled inside her like the petals of a morning glory opening for the sunshine.

"I meant what I said. You're welcome to stay as long as you need."

Beneath the soft-spoken words, he issued her a passionate challenge that would be hard to resist.

"Thank ye, Jake," she responded over the choked beat of her heart.

His gaze moved over her face. He hesitated when his eyes landed on her lips. She thought he might kiss her, even hoped he would, but, instead, he cleared his throat and swung away.

Heat rushed into her cheeks, and she swallowed

hard.

The first test in his challenge and she would have failed. Damn, this might be harder than she thought.

"It's late," he muttered then turned and jerked the door open. The dome light flashed on and she averted her face so he wouldn't see her uneasiness. She turned the handle and slipped from the car. He grabbed her bag from the backseat and strolled up the walk. She followed close on his heels.

Inside the house, Jake dropped the car keys on the table, set her case on the floor and slipped off his jacket. He hung it on the coat rack beside the door.

When he faced her again, his lips twisted into a crooked grin. "You can have my room. It's the last door on the left at the end of the hall."

Cara shook her head. "Thanks, but I wilna take yer bed. I'll bunk on the couch."

"Cara." Annoyance brought a slight lift to his timbre voice. His disapproving gaze met hers, his mouth set.

She ignored him, moved to the couch and dropped, spreading her arms across the leather back. Swallowing hard, she lifted her chin and met his gaze. Her lips curved into a stiff smile.

"This is a comfy couch. Do ye have a pillow and blanket? I doona need much," she said with easy defiance.

His blue eyes pierced the distance between them, and he studied her for a moment. And then, his lips arched into a sour grin before he spun around and disappeared down the hall. She jumped when a cabinet door slammed shut.

Wow, she hadn't meant to piss him off.

73

He reappeared a moment later. In his arms, he carried a pillow, blanket, and a set of sheets. He plopped them on the seat beside her, and then dropped down himself. "I really don't mind giving up the bed," he said in a low, composed voice.

In spite of herself, she chuckled. "I know, but I really doona mind sleeping here."

He released a long, audible breath. "Cara."

"Let it go, Jake, but I do thank ye just the same."

Jake looked as if he were about to say something else but changed his mind. "Well, good night then." He slapped his legs, stood and walked toward the hallway.

"Jake," she called.

"Thank ye," she said in a soft voice when he glanced at her.

He nodded. "You're welcome."

****

A noise, more like soft thud, crept into Cara's sleep drugged mind and stirred her awake. She squint her eyes open and glanced toward the direction of the sound. Jake moved around in the kitchen. He wore a pair of black patched pajama bottoms, and a black tank top. Good heavens! What a powerful set of shoulders, and the way his muscles rippled with every movement made her mouth water. Just the sight of his body sent molten lava racing through her blood.

Was it any wonder she didn't sleep much last night?

Of course, she couldn't blame her entire lack of sleep on Jake.

Nocturnal by nature, she'd been granted the same characteristics as a vampire. Her normal routine found her asleep during the day while she hunted for vamps at night.

A necessary sacrifice to protect a family, she needed to adjust her lifestyle if only for a little while.

She sat up and brushed the wayward locks of hair from her face.

"Good morning, Jake," she called.

He glanced in her direction and walked to the top of the steps where he leaned against the wall. His muscular arms crossed his chest. Blood surged from her fingertips to her toes, and warmed the areas in between at the glimpse of his strong golden body.

His gaze traveled over her body. When his eyes met hers, they contained a sensuous flame. "I'm sorry. Did I wake you?" he asked.

She stretched her arms above her head, groaned, and shook her head. A draft hit her stomach. Her tank top rose above her navel.

His gaze followed her action. He cleared his throat. "Did you sleep well?"

"I did." She pulled the shirt down and covered her naked skin. "Thank ye."

The warmth of his laugh sent shivers over her spine. "I didn't do anything." He grinned. "Can I get you some coffee?"

"No thanks."

"Really? You don't do coffee?"

She crinkled her nose and shook her head. "I never acquired the taste."

He winked. "I, myself, can't live without it," he commented before he stepped back into the kitchen. He poured himself a cup and sat at the table. He picked up his mug with one hand and a newspaper with the other. With a quick flick of his wrist, he whipped the paper open.

Cara reached for her jeans on the floor and, from beneath the sheet, tugged them over her waist. Fastening them, she stood, walked across the room, and stepped up the three stairs that led from the living room into the kitchen.

"Mind if I join ye?"

With a nod of his head, he indicated the chair opposite him in an invitation to sit. He glanced at her over the top of the newspaper. "There's juice in fridge if you'd like. Help yourself to anything you want."

"I'm fine," she reached across the table and nabbed a section of the paper.

He stared at her, complete surprise on his face.

Her eyes widened, and her brows shot upward. "What? Ye told me to help myself."

He shook his head and chuckled. "So I did."

She glanced down, and giggled, pleased with her selection. "I go' the funnies. This is my favorite part of the paper."

Jake laughed at her enthusiasm. "Yeah, mine too, so don't mess it up. I get it next." And with that he turned back to his section. A grin twisted his lips while his eyes scanned the news.

Cara flipped open the paper. Within minutes, her eyes drifted over the top. She marveled at the sandy blonde color of his hair that matched the perfect arch of his broad eyebrows. Long, thick eyelashes drew down, startling against the firm surface of his face. She could only imagine his eyes, a very light, crystal blue with tiny shards of light that sparkled from the center, surrounded by a thin rim of black.

Featherlike stubble shadowed his cheeks. Her gaze

moved to his mouth where the memory of his kiss sent a shiver of pleasure across her skin. The gentle massage of his lips firm, yet soft at the same time with a teasing resilience she wanted to experience again.

As if he sensed her scrutiny, Jake dropped the paper to the table, his firm mouth curled as if on the edge of laughter.

His eyes twinkled beneath his brows. "What? Is my nose crooked or something?" Jake drawled. His silky voice held a dare.

Her breath quickened, her cheeks warmed under his gaze, and she lowered the funnies.

"Actually, no," she said in a quick rally. "But ye may have the beginnings of a wart." She reached across the table and touched her finger to the tip of his nose. "Right there."

His brow shot up in surprise and a crooked grin twisted his lips. "And does it have that crinkling hair poking from the center?"

"Well, I'm no' certain. Let me look," she said, barely able to keep the laughter from her voice. She leaned forward, rested her elbows on the table and peered at his nose. She squinted, and wrinkled her nose. "Hmm, I doona see any, yet, but I suggest ye see yer medical doctor afore it grows more than a few hairs. That thing doona look healthy."

He stared at her and then burst out laughing. "You are a smart ass," he commented in a voice choked by his laughter.

In the next instant, his expression grew serious, and his laughter stilled. His hands cupped her cheeks with a tender touch that made her toes curl and heart race.

His gaze locked with hers in an intensity that made

her both nervous and stimulated.

"Would ye consider it rude if I ask what ye're thinking?" she whispered. Her voice shook.

"Nah, it wouldn't be rude," he said, his voice husky and deep. "But I hope you don't take it personal if I decline to answer."

She swallowed. Without looking away, she backed out of his grasp. "I suppose no'. It is a free country, isna it?"

He chuckled. The deep, rich sound caressed her, and her nerve endings tingled. His eyes smoldered. "It certainly is, and if I were to ask what you were thinking, would you answer?"

"I believe it best to keep my secrets to myself. At least, until I get to know ye better," she said, fluttering her eyelashes.

His face split into a wide grin. "More secrets? I wonder just how many secrets you might have."

Her heart skipped and her smile faded. "Everything in life isna as it appears, Jake. A person's destiny, chosen for them a long time ago, steers them over winding roads that twists and turns. Sometimes, 'tis best they keep a few secrets to maintain the balance between the forces."

Jake's eyes widened, and he blew out a sharp breath. "Wow, heavy stuff. What do you mean? What forces?"

She inhaled then exhaled before she raised her eyes to his. "The forces of good and evil."

"So you're a philosopher?"

"Huh?"

"You're one of those people who try to find the truth in everything. There will always be a battle between good and evil. People are inherently evil. That will never change."

Once again, Cara leaned across the table, her face inches from his. "Sometimes good things can overshadow the bad if one has the strength to fight for it."

"And have you ever seen the good?" he asked in a soft, serious voice.

"Only once," she whispered. "And ye?"

"Once," he murmured. The words left his lips in a rush of soft air that stroked her cheek.

"What are we doing, Jake?"

His fingertip stroked her cheek. "Perhaps we're both trying to find the good again."

Cara held her breath, afraid to move and end the moment.

"Perhaps." His mouth captured hers in one heart-stopping moment.

He tasted of peppermint, mixed with the nutty tang of coffee. Coffee wasn't so bad.

Leaning over the table, she moved closer to him. Her tongue slid along the seam of his lips, teasing and enticing. She tempted him until his lips took charge. His tongue swept inside her mouth and melted her insides in a fiery blaze.

"Daddy?" a small childish voice called from the hallway.

Cara flopped back into the chair with a loud *thump*. She sucked in air in quick, shallow gasps. Dazed by desire, she peered across the table at him.

He leaned away, his breathing just as ragged as hers. A deep groan slid past his lips. He glanced at her, and then blinked as if trying to bring her face into focus.

When his eyes dilated, his lower lip curved into a crooked smile. "It would see that my daughter doesn't always have the best timing."

Chapter Eight

"Daddy, where are you?"

Jake shuddered, glanced toward the hallway, then back at her. He cleared his throat.

"I'm in the kitchen, honey," he called out in a rough voice.

Cara bit back a grin at the huskiness in his tone, even as she struggled to control the blaze that boiled her insides. Her heart hammered and pulse pounded as she remembered the flaming power of his kiss.

Damn, test number two...disastrous. She came to a sudden realization that no matter how hard she tried, she was doomed for failure, especially where this man was concerned.

The soft patter of footsteps came closer. Cara spun around in her chair and stared toward the doorway just as the beautiful little girl with strawberry blonde curls and rosy cheeks entered the kitchen, a brown bear clutched in one hand.

Barefoot, Aimee wore a bright yellow nightshirt with a big green butterfly pasted in the center of her chest. Yellow happened to be Cara's favorite color. The shade reminded her of sunshine on a glorious Highland day.

Rubbing her eyes, the child stepped across the threshold and shuffled over to Jake where she climbed on his lap and snuggled into his neck.

Envy stabbed through her like a sharp tack at the picture of father and child. Once, a long time ago, a child rested in her womb, beneath her heart, but fate ripped that dream from her grasp.

"Good morning, sweetheart," Jake said. He pressed a kiss to the top of Aimee's head then inclined his head toward Cara. "You remember Ms. O'Leary, don't you?"

Aimee kept her head tilted, but lifted her eyes just far enough to get Cara in her sights.

"Hi," she mumbled then pushed her face back into Jake's shoulder.

Remembering the girl's previous reaction to her presence, Cara gave her a small, tentative smile.

"Hi, Aimee. It's a pleasure to see ye again. If ye wish, ye can call me Cara."

Aimee's head shot up. Her blonde brows furrowed. "You talk funny."

"Aimee Alysse," Jake admonished. "That's not polite."

Cara burst out laughing. "'Tis okay, Jake," she said. She leaned toward Aimee, her expression secretive. "I talk differently because I come from a different country. Do ye know what that means?" she asked in a soft voice.

Aimee's head shot up. A spark of interest lit up her eyes, and she leaned forward. "Yes, ma'am, we learned all about countries in Social Studies at school. What country do you come from?"

"I was born and raised on an isle called Scotland on the other side of the world." She smiled.

"Really?" At Cara's nod, Aimee's voice rose in excitement. "Wow! You mean you came all the way across the ocean? Here?"

"I sure did."

"Wow!" Aimee said again. "What's it like there?"

"I havena been home in many years, but, as I remember it, Scotland is a beautiful country, wild and untamed with acres upon acres of rolling green meadows and streams as blue as the skies. I used to frolic with my best friend amongst the heather and skip pebbles across the creek. We traipsed through fields, looking for lucky four leaf clovers, but, alas, the leprechauns werena as giving as they are in the Unites States. I never found a one."

"They hid them from you?" Aimee's eyes widened in awe.

Joy bubbled in her laughter. Cara's heart sang with delight, and she gloried in this shared moment. Aimee was a charming child, a bit mature for her age, but delightful never-the-less. "I believe they did."

"How rude!" Aimee declared. Her eyes widened with curiosity. "What else did you do?"

"I chased butterflies and bunny rabbits."

"Did you ever catch them?"

"What? The butterflies or the bunnies?"

"The bunnies, of course."

"Of course." Cara laughed before she shook her head. "Nay, they were much too fast for me."

Over the top of Aimee's head, Cara's eyes met Jake's baby blues. He studied her face with an enigmatic stare. For a long moment, she held his gaze until heat flared into her cheeks, and she cast her eyes downward.

Without warning, Jake stood, hiking Aimee high into his arms. "Hey, darling, I've got to get ready for work. Can I get you some juice before I jump into the shower?" he asked as he settled her on the chair he'd just vacated.

"Apple juice, please," Aimee said.

"You got it." Jake walked to the cabinet for a glass, to the fridge for the juice, then back to the table. Cara's eyes followed his every movement. When he tipped the carton over the glass, his eyes caught Cara's and held.

"Daddy! That's too much," Aimee's squeal broke the silence of the room.

Jake jerked, spilling juice on the table.

"Oops," Jake grumbled over Cara's laughter. He grabbed the dish towel from the countertop and slopped up the spill.

"You made a mess, daddy," Aimee giggled.

Jake shot her a smile, and ran his hand across the top of her head, ruffling her hair. "Quite observant, aren't ya, little miss?"

"Uh huh," Aimee commented. She reached for the glass, and sipped at the juice.

"Where's Mrs. Denton? She's usually awake by now."

Aimee shrugged, indifferent. Excited eyes returned to Cara waiting for her to continue her story-telling.

"I'm here, Mr. Bradshaw." Cara glanced up. The woman stood in the doorway. A twinkle lit up her eyes when she spied Cara. "Good Morning, Ms. O'Leary. It's good to see you again." She walked into the room and came to a stop beside Aimee. "And a good morning to you, little lady. Why didn't you wake me up?"

"I heard daddy's voice."

Jake pressed a quick kiss on Aimee's forehead. "And now, I have to shower and get ready for work. I'll be back in a bit." He stood, winked at Cara then left the room.

Mrs. Denton walked to the draperies in the kitchen, prepared to whip them open.

Cara's stomach knotted, and her nerves tensed. If Mrs. Denton let the sun in, Cara's secret would be out. She couldn't risk that.

"Mrs. Denton," she called in a shaky voice.

The woman turned. Her brows rose in question. "Yes?"

"Could you leave them closed, please? My eyes are sensitive in the morning and take a while to adjust to the light."

Whether she recognized the panic in Cara's voice or the sheer terror in her expression, Mrs. Denton smiled. Bless the woman, she left the curtains closed.

"Okay. We can wait a little bit," she said, walking back to the table. "What would everyone like for breakfast?"

"Corn flakes," Aimee piped up.

Mrs. Denton laughed. "Corn flakes it is." She turned to Cara and raised an eyebrow in question. "And what can I get for you, Ms. O'Leary?"

"I'm fine, Mrs. Denton, and please call me Cara."

"Cara." Mrs. Denton nodded. "A pretty name for a pretty lady." And with that, she turned and shuffled around the kitchen. She poured Aimee's bowl of cereal and placed it in front of the child. "Don't forget to drink the milk. It's good for you," she said with a stern expression before she spun away.

Aimee rolled her eyes, opened her mouth and mimicked Mrs. Denton. Cara bit her bottom lip to stifle the giggle that threatened to escape.

Mrs. Denton continued to toil around the kitchen, placing dirty dishes in the sink. She wiped her hands on her apron and turned back to the table. "While you eat, I'm going to get the laundry started. Today's bed day." Mrs. Denton must have recognized the confusion in Cara's expression for she smiled. "It's time to change the sheets," she explained.

"Ah ha," Cara laughed. "I wondered what ye meant. Ye doona seem the type of person to spend their day in bed."

"I must admit, there are days when my body would love to lie around all day. Age creeps up on a person too fast." She glanced at Aimee, then back at Cara. "Do you mind keeping her company?"

"It will be my pleasure."

"Thank you. I'll be back in a bit." She glanced at Aimee who picked at her cereal. "And you, little miss, eat. Don't play with your food," she said.

For the next twenty minutes, between mouthfuls of corn flakes, Cara and Aimee talked, laughed, and even giggled, something Cara hadn't enjoyed in a long time.

"Hi, daddy." Aimee's eyes twinkled.

"Hey, munchkin."

Cara's heart skipped at the deep baritone voice behind her. Chills skittered up her spine at the confident footsteps that echoed on the hardwood floors.

And then he came into view.

Jake's hair glistened of small droplets of water, and oh he smelled delicious, of leather and sandalwood. He wore a pair of tight black jeans, which outlined his butt very nicely, and a blue short-sleeve button up shirt. The top two buttons undone. Cara's breath wedged in her throat at the sight of golden-haired locks.

He glanced around the room. "Where's Mrs. Denton?"

"She went to strip the bedding," Cara volunteered.

"Ah, bed day." He ruffled Aimee's curls, his lips curved. "It looks like you're in for a busy day, munchkin."

"Oh, daddy," Aimee groaned.

"What?" His eyes locked with Aimee's and he frowned. "Aimee, on bed days you're expected to clean your room so Mrs. Denton doesn't have to scoot around your toys."

"I picked it up last night," Aimee protested. "It's clean." At Jake's raised eyebrows, Aimee persisted. "I'm telling the truth, daddy. It is."

Jake laughed in a rich buoyant sound that boomed in the room. "Okay, then you will have to find things to occupy your time without getting in her way."

"I've got an idea," Cara said. When both sets of eyes turned in her direction, a flush crept into her cheeks. She shrugged. "I doona want to step on anyone's toes, but I've got nothing planned today. If Aimee and Mrs. Denton doona mind, I'd be willing to stick around and sit with Aimee—." She winked at Aimee. "—and keep her from getting underfoot."

"Oh, please, daddy. Please," Aimee begged.

"I don't know," Jake said. His eyes narrowed, and he rubbed his chin with one hand as if deep in thought. He sure was making the little girl squirm. "Let me think on this one for a moment."

"Please." Aimee begged again. She lowered her voice to a near whisper. "Mrs. Denton is boring, daddy."

"Is that right?" he asked in a choked voice. His

eyes held a twinkle, and Cara knew he struggled to hold his laughter in check.

At Aimee's anxious nod, he caved. "Ok. I'm sure Mrs. Denton won't mind having a little peace and quiet from you today." He looked at Cara. "Are you sure you don't mind taking care of the rug rat?"

Cara smiled. "Absolutely no'. Aimee and I are going to have a grand time today, wilna we?"

"Oh yeah!" Aimee piped up.

Jake's eyes passed between the two girls at the table. "Well, then, I'll let the two of you get on with it." He leaned down, gave Aimee a kiss on the cheek and a quick hug before he stood again.

He glanced at Cara. "Thank you," he mouthed in appreciation.

"Have a good day," she said.

"Imagine that," he muttered under his breath, his expression doubtful.

"Ye can always stay home with us," she suggested in a tentative voice.

Aimee's eyes glowed and she bounced up and down in her chair. "Yeah!"

Jake laughed at his daughter's enthusiasm, but shook his head. "Oh munchkin, I would love to, but unfortunately, I can't. Not today."

With one last kiss on Aimee's forehead, he headed out the door.

****

It turned out to be one of the best days Cara had experienced in a very long time.

They played hide-n-go-seek, baby dolls, watched television, and even had a pillow fight.

Around five o'clock that evening, they sat on the

couch in front of the television watching one of Aimee's favorite shows. Only the gods knew what was so entertaining about a couple of boys creating mischief on a cruise ship, but Aimee found it amusing.

The child snuggled against Cara's side. Cara's arm rested across her shoulder, and she leaned over to press a soft kiss to Aimee's forehead. Aimee held up the well-loved teddy bear that she'd seen on the day of their first meeting.

"You need to kiss Tillie Bear too," Aimee giggled.

Cara smiled. "I do, eh?" She leaned over and planted an exaggerated kiss on the bear's forehead. "Uhmmm Wah." She turned her gaze back to Aimee and tickled her on the nose.

The girl giggled and pulled Tillie against her chest. "My momma gave me Tillie a long time ago. I was a baby when my mom went away, and don't remember her much. Tillie's my best friend." Her eyes clouded. "Will you be my friend, Cara?" she asked.

Cara nodded. "I already am, Aimee."

Aimee was an adorable child, full of spirit, life and laughter, the power that lay within her strong, innocent, and dormant for the moment. The lass had no idea of the magic she carried, or, if she did, she didn't acknowledge it.

Such power was inherited, and Cara concluded she must have inherited it from her mother because Jake's aura didn't emit the same stir to her senses.

Did Jake even know his wife was a powerful witch? That his daughter possessed the same magical energy? Perhaps his wife kept it secret and never used her powers within his presence. Or maybe, Jake refused to believe such things were possible. She'd seen it before.

Tough questions to answer and Cara shoved them aside, best to overlook the subject for the moment.

The truth always emerged when one wasn't looking.

Chapter Nine

Cara strolled through the dimly lit living area. The two etched glass wall scones positioned on each side of the television illuminated the room in a soft glow. She ran her hand along the back of the couch, the smooth leather surface cool to her touch.

She glanced at the clock situated on the wall above the couch.

Quarter after ten.

She'd tucked Aimee into bed two hours ago. While the girl snuggled beneath the covers with Tillie Bear, Cara read her a story from the Grimm's Fairy Tale. She'd no sooner finished the last page when the girl's eyes fluttered shut.

Cara enjoyed the day spent with Aimee. So young, the innocent girl trusted so easily. Cara's heart softened for the wee lass who'd suffered the loss of her mum at such an early age and had to grow up too fast.

Mrs. Denton also retired for the evening, claiming that bed day always took a toll. She needed a good night's sleep to recuperate from the day's chores.

Jake called around seven to say he had to write up another report, but once he finished, he would be on his way home. His voice, weary and strained, sounded through the earpiece and pulled at her heartstrings.

She walked to the pictures on the wall. The soft light shimmered across the glass. With her fingertip, she traced the smile on Aimee's face. Wrapped in her father's arms, the picture portrayed a child who adored the man who held her.

The front door opened and closed behind her. Startled, she jumped and whirled around.

Jake dropped his keys on the table beside the door and leaned against the table. He ran a tired hand over his face.

Cara's heart ached at the weariness in his features.

Anger pounded through her veins. Deidra's rampage did this to him. Cara clasped her hands at her waist in an attempt to still the violent tremble that shook her to her core.

"Ye look exhausted," she murmured, stomping down the intense rage boiling inside her. He didn't need to hear resentment in her voice, especially since it wasn't meant for him.

His head jerked up and he faced her. His eyebrows rose as if shocked to see her standing there. "Yeah, well, all in a day's work." He slipped off his jacket and hung it up before he turned back to her. "I didn't expect anyone to be awake."

Cara shrugged. "I'm sorry. I dinna mean to alarm ye."

He walked across the room and stopped in front of her.

"Don't be sorry. It's a nice surprise." His eyes searched her face, and he raised his hand to caress her cheek. A tired smile creased the ashen shadow around his lips.

Cara covered his hand, and turned her face to press her lips to the calloused layer of his palm. Her eyes remained locked with where she glimpsed the true Jake

Bradshaw. Gorgeous blue eyes full of warmth and life, but in the depths, hidden from all, she recognized self-inflicted pain.

"Jake," she murmured against the palm of his hand.

He slipped his hand from hers and placed an index finger across her mouth to silence her.

"Sh!" He traced a path across her lips, down her chin to the tender flesh of her neck.

He tugged her into his arms. His chin rested on the top of her head. "Don't talk," he whispered into her hair. "Please." He drew away.

She stared into the infinite depths of his eyes. Tortured incredulity filled his expression. "I don't want the memories of the day anymore. Help me forget," he whispered in a voice thick and unsteady. His eyes implored her to understand his need.

Speechless, Cara stared at him. Her heart pulsated at the unexpected warmth that swelled within her. She tried to ignore the knot in her stomach, the tingle between her thighs, but the sensations persisted. She couldn't deny him, and raised her arms, wrapping them across his broad shoulders.

Passion burned in Cara, and a shiver of desire ran through her. It grew until her insides burned with fever.

One of his hands settled on the small of her back, and he eased his other toward her face, across her cheek to rest in the tender area behind her ear. His fingers slipped through her hair, and he drew the strands to his face. He buried his nose into the auburn locks as if inhaling her fragrance.

When he pulled away, he swallowed hard and lifted a hand to touch the side of her throat.

Cara licked her lips in anticipation of the feel of his

mouth on hers.

"Jake," she breathed his name. His lips lowered. The flames in his eyes burned hotter.

And then their lips met.

His mouth intoxicated her. When their tongues touched and danced, fire licked through her, deep and low. Spirals of ecstasy burned her up in a tantalizing blaze. She groaned at the hot ache that began in her belly and raced through her bloodstream.

Cara leaned back. With the tip of her index finger, she traced the full curve of Jake's lower lip along his jaw. He recoiled from her innocent, provocative touch.

Shaken, she dropped her hand and glanced away.

Instead of releasing her, he pulled her close.

"No, please," he whispered into her hair. "I didn't mean to…it's just that I haven't been this close to anyone in a long time."

Cara nodded and leaned away. "I do understand." She smiled. "I havena…" She hesitated a brief moment then continued, "'tis been a long time for me as well. 'Tis a bit scary, isna it?"

His lips curved into a crooked grin. "They say that once you learn how to ride a bike you never forget."

Cara giggled at the analogy, and opted not to tell him she'd never learned to ride those two-wheeled contraptions.

"Ride, eh?" she asked. Her voice simmered with barely controlled passion.

Jake chuckled. His lips recaptured hers, more demanding this time. His mouth moved a leisure pace against hers until a small whimper escaped. The tip of his tongues slid out from between his lips. Her lips parted for the tender penetration of his tongue.

A sharp stab of conscience speared through her. She couldn't let this continue. She needed to stop this before it passed the point of redemption. Jake needed to know, to understand what she was before he made that final commitment. It would change everything. Perhaps he wouldn't want her then, but it was a risk she had to take.

His teeth captured her lower lip and he nibbled. She made a tiny, throaty sound of pleasure, but the caress only lasted an instant.

It took everything within her to draw away from his embrace. "Jake, we have to talk."

Jake's gaze locked with hers. After a moment, he cleared his throat and took a step back.

"I'm sorry. I shouldn't have—" He clamped his lips together, turned and started to walk away.

"No, Jake." She grabbed his arm and drew him to a stop.

He glanced at her hand on his arm, then into her face. "I don't understand," he whispered.

Cara led him to the couch.

In a nervous habit she couldn't control, she bit her bottom lip until it hurt. Then, she moistened the stinging lip with the tip of her tongue and tilted her head. "Please. Why doona ye sit so we can talk?"

Jake sat and Cara claimed the seat beside him.

"What do you want to talk about?" Jake murmured. He dropped onto the couch. With a soft tug, he pulled her against his chest and wrapped an arm around her. Her head fit snug into the hollow at his shoulder.

She glanced into this face. Her brows drew together in a frown. "Ye doona know anything about me."

"Should I be afraid of you?"

"Nay, I would never hurt ye, or anyone in yer family, but ye know nothing of my past."

"And you know nothing of mine."

"Doona ye think we should get to know each other better before we—?" She smiled. Warmth flared into her cheeks and she lowered her chin, hiding her face into the curve of his shoulder. "I wilna deny I want ye. I want ye with a passion I havena felt in years." She glimpsed up at him from beneath half-closed eyelids.

He grinned. "Well, that's good to hear."

"What you doona know about me is that I was married once a long time ago," she blurted the words out, and then waited for his reaction.

Jake tensed beneath her cheek, but relaxed a second later. "It couldn't have been that long ago. You're not that old."

She tilted her head and looked into his face, surprised to discover his lips curved into a smile.

"Jake—"

He leaned down. His lips touched the base of her throat where her pulse pounded a mad rhythm. He retreated and stared at her a moment before he shook his head. He sucked in his breath, as if the movement pained him.

"Perhaps you're right, Cara. We should get to know each other better." He slid away from her and moved to the edge of the couch.

She opened her mouth to speak, but he held up a hand to still her words. He shook his head and slid a hand through his hair down to massage the back of his neck. "Let me start. Once you hear my story, maybe you'll realize you're better off not knowing me. I'll even give you the chance to run away."

"I know about yer wife, Jake. Mrs. Denton told me she died, and how ye shut yerself off from the world after her death."

"Did she also tell you I was responsible for her death?" His voice lowered to a harsh whisper that sandpapered across her already sensitive nerve endings.

Her eyes widened and her body stiffened with shock and disbelief.

A grim smile crossed his lips as he ran a finger down the middle of her nose. Then, he leaned forward to kiss the end of it.

"Don't look so surprised. Lisa's death *was* my fault."

She shook her head. "I doona believe that."

He laughed. A harsh, raspy sound that sent a whirlwind of mixed emotions churning through her stomach.

"Aimee was two, almost three. I worked in the covert ops unit of the police department. We were investigating the operations of one of Santa Monica's biggest crime lords, Senor Lucas Levithus. We'd been on his trail for years, but could never pin anything on him. I got too close, and my cover was blown, although I didn't know it."

Cara put her hand on his. "Jake, ye doona need to tell me any of this."

Jake released his breath and nodded. "Yeah, I do. I don't know why, and it may sound strange, but I feel a connection to you. I want you to know." He paused. "I need you to know."

Cara eased her fingers into his thick, warm hair and pulled his mouth to hers. With sensual deliberation, she traced the outline of his lips with the tip of her tongue before she closed her teeth with exquisite care on his lower lip. A shudder rippled through his powerful body.

"You make me forget," he whispered huskily against her lips.

"Perhaps 'tis best if ye did."

"No." He cleared his throat and leaned forward. His gaze focused on the lights near the fireplace. In his mind, he relived the day his wife died. "It was Saturday. Lisa decided to run some errands since I was home and could watch Aimee. Her car was in the shop getting some minor repairs done so she decided to use mine." Tears filled his eyes. "I held Aimee in my arms and we waved good-bye to her mother. The last thing I remember is Lisa's smile as she looked at us—" He hesitated, swallowing hard. "—and then the car exploded. The demolition's team found the remnants of the bomb that was meant for me."

"That doesna make it yer fault."

"If it wasn't for me and my stubbornness to nail that bastard, he would never have gotten that close."

"Ye dinna cause the explosion. He did it, no' ye."

"Maybe I didn't set the bomb, but that doesn't make me any less responsible. After that, I vowed to protect Aimee at all cost. She was all I had left. I swore to Lisa on her grave that I wouldn't let anything happen to our daughter. I took a leave of absence from the force for about a year. When I went back, I returned to the department as a detective. No more undercover work. The price tag was too great."

"What happened to Senior Lucas Levithus?"

"Word on the streets was he pissed off the syndicate. They found his body washed up on the beach."

"Ye dinna—?"

His lips twisted into a cynical smile. "Didn't what? Didn't feed him to the sharks in the bay?" At her look of astonishment, he shook his head. "It wasn't me, although I'd be lying if I said the thought hadn't crossed my mind."

"Ye're a good man, Jake Bradshaw. Ye werena the cause of Lisa's death."

"Yeah, well, I will always carry that burden inside me. Every time I look at Aimee, I feel the guilt over what happened to her mother."

"Is that why ye avoid her?"

His gaze shot to her face. "I don't avoid her," he denied, a bitter edge of cynicism in his voice.

Cara leaned toward him. She gripped his hand in hers and squeezed. "Jake, I've seen how much ye love yer daughter. Ye're very protective of her, yet I've also seen ye shy away from her when she wants yer attention."

Jake ran his fingers through his tousled hair. "I didn't realize I did that."

"Self-preservation is not uncommon after everything ye've endured."

"Are ye a psychologist?"

"No' really, but I tend to see things that others doona." And then Cara took a gamble. "Like how special yer wife truly was, and the gifts she possessed and passed to Aimee."

Astonishment lit Jake's face and he jumped from the couch. "Cara, I don't know what you're talking about."

"I think ye do," she said in a low voice.

"Cara, let it go. You don't know anything." A silken thread of warning spilled into his words.

She released a long, audible sigh. "Jake?"

An inexplicable look of withdrawal came over his face. She recognized that as a sign she wasn't going to get any answers about Aimee's magical powers. He didn't even want to acknowledge its existence. If that was what Jake wanted, she'd let him have it…for now.

"Thank ye," she said in a soft voice.

"For what? Telling you what a bastard I am?"

"For telling me that ye're human." She laughed. "Hmmm, now I guess it's my turn now." She patted the seat beside her that he'd recently vacated. "Come sit back down, and then ye can tell me if ye think I'm human or no'."

Chapter Ten

Jake strolled across the room and sat beside her. He seized her hands in a soft grip and captured her eyes with his. A faint light twinkled in the depths of his baby blues.

"Cara, I have a good sense for people. In my profession, it's how I stay alive. There is nothing you can tell me that I don't already know about you. You have compassion. There's gentleness in your voice when you talk to Aimee, and to me. You have a big heart. That's who you are, so there's nothing you can say that will change my opinion of you," he said, in a calm, sincere tone.

"That's where ye're wrong, Jake. There is so much ye doona know about me, about my past," she said in a shaky whisper.

He brushed a loose tendril of hair from her cheek with a touch so light and delicate that shivers raced down her spine.

And then he leaned forward. His lips skimmed over hers in a kiss as tender and light as a summer breeze. He raised his mouth from hers and gazed into her eyes.

"You are so beautiful." He murmured in a voice that shimmered with barely checked passion.

He feathered kisses over her lips. His tongue drew a warm, moist line around her mouth. She whimpered and parted her lips for his kiss. He took the offering.

His tongue plunged inside her mouth to mingle with hers. Desire blazed through her, spiraling through her like a raging river.

Her emotions whirled and skidded. She should stop this before they went any further, but his power to baffle her senses overran common sense. The heat of his kiss stopped all thought except the need to be with him.

Cara closed her eyes and counted her heartbeat in its violent race for blood. The thought of making love to this man made her lose control, and yet, deep inside, her conscious warned her that this union would be more than sex.

It would be a lifetime commitment.

The moist invasion of his tongue between her lips created a spasm of heat that rippled over her skin. He stroked her mouth in slow, sensual rhythms. Her limbs weakened, and she melted against him, indecision shattered by the hunger of his kisses.

What began as a simple kiss became a sensual obsession.

Her senses short-circuited, and she clung to him. When he made a move to pull away, she made an incoherent sound of protest and tightened her arms around his neck, wanting more.

"Sh," Jake said, nipping at Cara's lip. "I'm not going anywhere without you. You're going to be with me every inch of the way even if it kills me." He chuckled, a husky vibration against her lips. "It most likely will, but I have a feeling it'll be worth it."

He shifted and positioned his arms behind her shoulders and beneath her knees. With little effort, he swept her, as if she were weightless, into his arms. Cara wrapped her arms around his shoulders. She buried her face against the strong tendons in his neck and breathed in his masculine scent, pressing a kiss to his collarbone.

Filled with a burning desire, an aching need, for another kiss, she lifted her chin. As if he read her mind, he lowered his head. Their lips fused in a passionate kiss that lasted only for a moment.

He carried her from the room. Cara marveled at the strength in his arms. At the end of the hall, he hesitated at the last door on the right.

"Open the door, darling," he murmured in a low, seductive voice.

Cara shivered in delight at the endearment and stretched a hand down to twist the knob. The latch clicked and she pushed it open with a slight nudge.

Jake crossed the threshold. Inside the room, he stopped and released her legs. Her already heated body slid the hard length of his. His manhood, thick and hard, brushed her abdomen.

With his free hand, he reached over her shoulder and pushed the door closed with a soft *click*.

He wrapped his arm around her waist and guided her. As they neared the king-sized bed, he pulled her into his arms and spun around.

She touched her lips to his.

He drew away and pressed soft kisses to the tip of her nose and across her cheek. His breath brushed her earlobe. The minuscule action tickled her toes.

He sat on the edge of the bed, grabbed her hips, and pulled her forward until she stood between his legs. His hands inched upward and pushed her T-shirt up to bare her stomach to his gaze. His eyes met hers before he pressed his lips to the exposed skin. Cara gasped at the heat of his mouth on her flesh and ran her fingers through his hair.

In the next instant, Jake released her shirt, lowered himself to the bed, and tugged her on top of him. Her hair fanned across his face. He stretched out his hand and traced the line of her cheek with his fingertip. Her pulse quickened, and her heart fluttered violent thumps against her breast.

Cara rose above him and straddled him between her knees. He lowered his hands to her hips. She caught one of them and raised it to her lips. With a slow, secret smile, she ran her tongue across the length of the thumb before she closed her lips around the small appendage and suckled.

A low, very male growl radiated from deep in Jake's chest. His eyes swirled the color of smoked sapphires and he licked his lips at the sensual gesture.

He pulled his thumb from her lips, and smoothed his fingertips over her jaw, across her chin and down her throat where he paused at the pulse that beat just beneath her skin. And then, his hands continued their journey downward, skimming each side of her body across her hips, then back up to cover her breasts. The stroking of his fingers sent pleasant jolts cascading across her skin, and she gasped in sweet agony.

Nothing but the thin material of her tank top stood between his hands and her breasts. Blood surged from her fingertips to her toes. Her heart thundered with the beat of music when he cupped her breast, rolling her hardened nipple between his fingertips.

Cara cried out in surprise. His touch sent her to higher levels of ecstasy. She moaned and arched against his touch, the pleasure pure and explosive.

"That's it, baby," he murmured in a hoarse, choked voice. He rolled the sensitive nubs between his fingertips then gave them a light pinch.

Cara gave up trying to speak, her breath a heavy gasp at the molten fire that spread through the soft core of her body. She held Jake's hand against her breast and pressed herself into his palm.

And then his hands moved lower. He gripped the bottom of her shirt and, inch by slow inch, pushed it upwards. Cara leaned toward him, raised her arms, and allowed him to draw the thin material over her head.

His gaze dropped from her face to her shoulders to her bare breasts before his eyes returned to her face.

"You're exquisite," he whispered.

Passion pounded the blood through her heart, chest and head. She tried to throttle the dizzying currents that raced over her. Her limbs weakened and she leaned forward, her breast brushing his chest. Streaks of fire sizzled through her veins at his nearness, every nerve ending sensitized.

"You're burning me alive," he muttered in a hoarse voice. "My insides are being ripped out. I want to touch, kiss, and taste every inch of your body."

Cara tried to speak, but couldn't. His words, like a caress, stole her breath away.

With a swift motion, Jake turned, and rolled Cara onto her back in the center of the bed. He followed, turned his face into her neck and drew a deep breath.

He planted a kiss in the hollow of her neck. His lips continued their intoxicating exploration that seared a path along her neck and shoulders. As his lips traveled, he traced a warm, wet trail with his tongue.

His right arm slid behind her and held her while his

mouth closed over her breast. He devoured a sensitive nipple. His tongue tantalized the buds which had swollen to their fullest, his teeth scraped in a gentle, yet sensual vise.

She squirmed with pleasure. Her nails dug into his powerful shoulders.

"Jake," she cried, each inhale strangled gasp.

His hot, wet caresses on her naked breast created a fever that heated her thighs and groin. Passion rose in her like the hottest fire and clouded her brain.

After a few more moments of pleasurable torture, he rose above her, lacing his fingers through hers. With a soft wrench, he stretched her arms above her head and held her hands in his. Her body arched toward his mouth, her back a taut curve, her breasts full and flushed, begging for the heat of his kisses.

"Doona stop," Cara moaned. She squirmed beneath him. Her nipples throbbed against his hard chest. "Please, Jake, doona stop."

"I don't plan on stopping, sweetheart, but I want to see all of you."

His fingers drifted over her stomach and circled her breast. A trail of molten lava followed in their wake. She reached for him and pulled him back to her.

The hard thrust of his tongue between her teeth cut off her pleas. His lips pressed into hers, and controlled her wild moans of passion while his hand reached for the buttons of her jean. With a quick flick of his wrist, he unsnapped the button and unzipped them.

With another teasing kiss, he moved away. He slid down her body, pressing kisses on her bare breasts, down her stomach until he sat on his knees near the foot of the bed. He grabbed a hold of her jeans at her thighs, and gave a soft tug.

She lifted her hips, and she shivered as the material slid away from her heated flesh. He tossed them to the floor and returned to remove her underwear. She shivered at the look of absolute admiration on his face.

Desire sparkled in his eyes. "Oh my God, you are gorgeous," he breathed.

He nipped the inside of her thigh before he pressed a tiny kiss to the area. She whimpered and stretched out her arms to him.

He rolled off the bed, stood at the side, and gazed at her. With deliberate slowness, he stripped off his shirt, unbuttoned his jeans and unfastened the fly.

Humor glittered through the passion in his blazing eyes.

And then, as though he were an erotic male dancer, he peeled his jeans off his body, taking his underwear in the same sweep. He kicked the clothes aside and stood before her as though waiting her approval.

Cara's eyes widened. Her lips parted over a silent rush of air.

By the Gods, this man's body was superb.

She held out her arms to him. He knelt on the side of the bed, lowered his head, and latched onto the sensitive tip of her nipple. Cara arched toward his mouth, her back a taut arch, her breasts full and flushed with the heat of his kisses.

He drew away. His hands shook, and his body trembled as he parted her legs and settled between her thighs. His manhood rested against her, touching the very core of her center.

Her body arched against him. "Jake!" she moaned on a plea.

"Easy, sweetheart, easy," he said.

He turned onto his side, drawing Cara with him.

Her arms clutched at his shoulders.

"That's it, sweetheart. Hold onto me. There's no hurry. It's just the two of us and all the time in the world."

Cara felt a quick stab of disappointment at his words. Once he learned what she was…

She brushed the thoughts aside and vowed that nothing would spoil this moment.

"You're more beautiful every time I look at you," Jake said in a deep voice. His warm breath brushed her ear. His strong hand stroked her back.

Cara savored the fire that flared in her nipples and traveled to the pit of her stomach before the flames radiated outward like a heated kaleidoscope.

"By the gods—" Cara's voice broke as Jake moved between her legs. The warm, hard weight of his body pushed upward until he pressed against her softness. A slow, sweet lightning exuded through her body.

****

Cara gazed at him with dazed lilac eyes.

Jake's body tightened at the moist heat of her core, but he didn't enter.

"Jake?"

At the uncertainty in the way she said his name, he rolled to her side and looked into her eyes. "Um huh?"

"D-do you like being touched?" she asked. Her voice trembled.

He smiled. "Yes," he whispered against her lips. "Do you want to touch me?"

"Aye, but—"

"But what?"

"I doona know what ye like," Cara admitted then bit her lip. "I want it to be good for ye. As good as ye make me feel."

Jake closed his eyes for an instant. He fought the urge to pull Cara's hands down his body until they wrapped around the hard, burning flesh between his legs.

"If it gets any better for me, it could be all over." He smiled. "Feel free to put your hands on me, anywhere or everywhere. Your pleasure."

Cara's hand shook when she lifted it to his face. She traced the fullness of his lips. Her fingers traveled across his strong jaw then moved to the rim of his ear.

Her breath caught. She returned to the sensitive rim, but this time it was her mouth that caressed him. In a leisure pace that tormented him, she outlined the curve of his ear using only the tip of her tongue.

A shudder rippled through Jake at her soft touch.

"Do ye like that?" she murmured.

"Hmmm…I'm not sure," he said huskily. "Maybe you should try it again."

She looked startled, and then smiled. "Ye're teasing me."

"No, sweetheart, you're the tease."

He gave a low growl when her teeth closed on his ear in another caress, this time a little bit harsher than before.

"Ouch," he groaned in a gruff tone.

She pulled back a bit to look into his face.

"What? Dinna ye like it?" she asked, with wide, innocent eyes.

He growled low in her ear. "I loved it."

Jake caught Cara's mouth and kissed her until his

self-control reached its breaking limit.

He released her.

Her eyes snapped open. She watched him with an intensity that nearly made his breath stop. His gaze followed her actions while her tongue licked a path down the center line of his chest, delving through his thick hair to the hot skin beneath.

She smiled and continued past his ribs. When she reached his belly button, she stopped. His breath came out as a puff of air when she kissed the skin just above his navel, nibbling softly along his flat stomach.

Her lips stroked a random pattern across his ribs and over his abdomen. He laced his fingers together above his head to keep from reaching for her and interrupting her sweet exploration.

She wrapped her hand around him. She hesitated at his hoarse groan. He covered her hand with his own and guided her. In slow, soft strokes, he moved their hands up and down his shaft. He removed his hand and let her take the lead.

After a few moments, he couldn't take any more. His hands closed around her narrow waist and tugged her up beside him.

He shaped the rich curve of her buttocks, sinking his fingers into her flesh. His long fingers rubbed down her thighs, then swept back up in a rocking motion that made her tremble.

His hand moved between her legs where he cupped her in an intimate clasp. His fingertips parted her tight curls until he found her inner core. He slid his finger inside her, moving in and out, preparing her for him while his palm continued to stroke her sensitive bud.

She squirmed against his hand.

"Please, Jake," she begged.

Jake closed his eyes and groaned deep in his throat. A shudder ran through his body. He moved his mouth over hers and devoured her softness. His tongue explored the recesses of her mouth.

And then, he eased himself into her body.

He slid his hand between their joined bodies, rocked his hips while his hand caressed the hard bud of her passion.

As their mouths merged in the ancient ritual, his hips drove forward and he buried himself inside her. She gasped aloud. He withdrew only to plunge deeply again and again, each strong plunge sparking a flame that burned hotter.

He moved in an agony of restraint holding back with all his strength, never wanting it to end.

Her sweet cries of ecstasy filled the air.

Fire pulsed through him. His body constricted until he could barely breathe, and he picked up the tempo of his hips. She met him, thrust for thrust.

Cara's cries glittered through the fevered darkness until the muscles surrounding him clenched, released and tightened in a pinnacle of release. Her fingernails dug into his shoulders which added to his pleasure. Her body called to his to join her in release. He wanted to, yet he wanted to stay where he was and stroke the fervor in both of them.

Suddenly, he could no longer hold back. The colors swirled around him, a thousand tiny pulses of ecstasy prickled his nerves to life.

With a hoarse broken cry, his hips pushed forward and he entered her body until he could go no further, and then he surrendered to the sweet violence that ripped through his control.

Jake's last coherent thought was that Cara had taken him to a place he had never known before, and he never wanted it to end.

Chapter Eleven

Madame Elena sprung upright, her mind clouded with sleep. Her eyes widened, and she searched the room for the source of the loud scratching sound. Her breath lodged in her throat, and she inhaled shallow quick gasps while her hand pressed against her breast in an attempt to silent the rapid thud of her heart.

An icy fear twisted her insides.

Similar to the sound of a shovel or other metal implement scraping against stone, the grating racket reverberated from the other side of the twelve-by-twelve prison near the ten-inch square window. The clamor chafed her nerves and sent an eerie shiver up her spine.

She glanced at the window, but saw nothing except the trees outside. Branches swayed in the wind and tapped against the dirty glass with an occasional rap.

Was that the cause of the noise?

She drew a deep breath and released it in a *puff*.

Her gaze wandered around her surroundings. She'd been thrown in this room two days ago or had it been three? Staring at four concrete walls and empty space would make anyone lose track of time. Wouldn't it?

Only a twin-sized bed adorned the dreary dust covered, cob-webbed ridden space. Her nose burned from the rancid musty odor that lay stagnant in the air.

The sound came again followed by a childish

giggle.

The hair on the nape of her neck rose and she glanced at the window, frosted by a half inch of dust. Her blood turned to ice. A pair of reddish beacons, like eyes, glared through the glass. When they met her gaze, the color sparked a brighter shade of cherry.

Elena screamed and jumped to her feet.

And then another sound joined the melody of scuffing metal.

Rap. Rap. Rap.

Long, bony-like finger appendages tapped on the window's glass. Elena's pulse quickened and she jumped onto the cot behind her. Her back pressed against the wall.

Her heart pounded in her chest.

"Leave me alone," she yelled.

Rap. Rap. Rap.

A single footstep pounded on the tile floor outside the door, and then another, and another until the door thrust open, hitting the wall with a solid *thud*. Startled, Elena glanced toward the entry where Deidra stood.

The witches red eyes blazed.

"Maire! Go away!" Deidra said in a sharp tone. She stared at the window, her brows curved into a dissatisfied frown. A high pitched squeal sounded through the glass. Elena covered her ears at the shrill cry that threatened to pierce her eardrums.

"Stop!" The sharp reprimand quieted the creature. "It's okay, doll," she consoled in a softer voice. Then Deidra smiled and nodded. "Go find your fun elsewhere. I wish to have a little talk with our guest."

Turning back to Elena, Deidra smiled. Yellowed fangs peeked from beneath her upper lip. "Children!

She is newly formed and still learning our ways. Maire was just trying to play with you."

Elena recoiled in terror. She bit the corner of her lip to quiet her panicked cry. Her insides swiveled with horror. She extended her arms, palms outward as if that small action would keep Deidra at bay.

"Let me go, please," she begged.

Deidra advanced another step into the room. She stopped then smiled, displaying sharp incisors that made Elena cringe. "Do you not understand? I cannot release you until I have freed Ághmach."

"Please!" Elena pleaded. "Why won't you listen to me? I cannot do what you ask."

Raising fine, arched eyebrows, Deidra paused, tilted her head and look at Elena in curiosity. "Why do ye lie to me? I saw you. You connected me to him."

Deidra's expression clouded with anger.

Elena recoiled from the growing embers that burned in the other woman's eyes as she advanced.

In an attempt to avoid Deidra's wrath, Elena spun around. She stumbled over the cot and fell forward. Her hand slammed into the concrete wall. She whimpered, but ignored the stabbing pain that raced through her fingers, and pushed herself onto her knees. Her insides trembled as she turned to face Deidra.

There was no way out. Deidra stood between her and the door, blocking the only avenue of escape.

Deidra wrapped a hand around Elena's throat.

Elena's gasped, then gagged in reflex. With both hands, she clawed at the hand choking her. Deidra's grip tightened, and with a swift jerk, the Vampryss wrenched Elena off her knees, and lifted until the ground disappeared beneath Elena's feet. Deidra held her aloft with little exertion, despite her hysterical efforts to kick free.

Elena tried to speak, to assure Deidra she'd do whatever she asked, but the crushing grip of Deidra's hand on her voice box prevented speech. Only a strangled gurgled escaped.

Grief and despair tore at her heart with the realization she was going to die.

Deidra raised her other hand, her fingers hooked and rigid. God help her. What was she going to do?

Elena sputtered and continued to claw at the hand wrapped around her neck.

And then, Deidra lowered her other hand to trace Elena's arm with a sharp talon of her fingernail. A choked scream escaped Elena when pain flared across her skin. Blood spilled from the wound and trickled down her forearm.

"Do not lie to me again, Elena. I do not like it. Do you understand?" Deidra asked in a voice that held a silken thread of warning.

Although weak from lack of oxygen, Elena managed to nod in agreement.

"Good." Deidra nodded and released her grip. Elena dropped to the cot in a heap. She rubbed the ache in her neck and gasped for breath, dizzy and weak.

"Now that I have yer agreement, I wish to speak to my Ághmach. We have plans to make."

"You must give me a moment to catch my breath," Elena wheezed.

Deidra bent over and grabbed Elena's hands in her firm grip. With a quick yank, Deidra yanked her off the bed. Elena gulped at the pain in her wrist.

"We do not have a moment for you to catch yer

breath. Connect me with him now." Deidra's hands tightened.

Elena cried out. "Okay…okay…stop, please stop," Elena cried. Deidra released her hold. Elena dropped to the cool concrete floor. She drew in a couple of deep breaths and closed her eyes. "You must concentrate," she muttered.

After a few moments, an icy cold wind whipped into the room. Elena's eyes shot open to discover a flat, undistinguished black figure looming above her. The black mist floated four feet above the ground and moved toward them.

And then the figure took shape.

One instant the shadow's face was an indistinct void before two red oval spheres appeared. They glittered and flickered with the vividness of a lit wick on a candlestick. Those fiery red pinpoints demanded Elena's attention, hypnotic, and controlled her will and drained her energy.

She forced her gaze from the monster's face, flinching at the sight of his massive physique. His chest, a mass of dark, swirling snakes, radiated of heat and cold. Both sensations touched Elena's cheek and reminded her of fire and ice.

"Dee!" Ághmach loud thundering voice ricocheted through the room. "Where the hell have you been?"

Deidra bowed her head and knelt on one knee. "I have been preparing for your return, milord."

"Is all ready?"

Deidra stood and walked toward the apparition. "Not yet, my love, but we will be ready. In less than three weeks, the three celestial bodies of the Camarilla will merge. When they do, I shall draw upon their

117

powers to unite the souls of the medium and the magical child to tear down the barrier that disconnects this world to the underworld."

"What of the child?" he asked, spacing the words evenly.

"I have located her essence and will begin drawing her away from the protection of her father."

"Do not let anything get in the way of this, Deidra? I need to be back in the physical world. I need to feed." And then his voice softened as he looked at her. "I need to feel your arms around me."

Deidra licked her lips as if in premature anticipation. "And I need to have you at my side."

"Then get it done, Dee, so we can be together again, create our children, and rule the world side by side."

Deidra bowed her head. "Your will be done."

When Ághmach disappeared, Deidra looked at Elena who watched the exchanged in stunned surprise.

"What child do ye seek?" Elena choked.

"The child is of no concern to you, but in time, she will complete my world."

"A child is innocence. I beg of you, do not corrupt her. Use me instead."

Deidra's lips twisted into an evil smile. "Oh, I plan to."

Just as Elena would have begged again, Deidra held up a hand to stop her words. "Now, I will take my leave. I have a child to speak with."

And then Deidra was gone. The door slammed shut behind her followed by the click of the bolts, locking Elena inside.

****

A flash of pain shot through Aimee's head. She woke with a moan. Sitting up, she squinted her eyes shut and held her head between two hands. She winced, but as quick as the pain came, it faded away.

She'd been dreaming of the puppy dog daddy promised to get her when she grew up a little bit more. Just like the scruffy terrier she'd seen in the pet shop at the mall. She loved its big brown eyes.

The pain returned. Just a little, but it hurt. She needed daddy to get her some medicine.

She opened her eyes, about to jump to the floor when she realized she wasn't in her room. Her heart pounded. Scared, she lay back on the bed and whipped the covers over her head. Her ears met silence, and she lowered the blanket and peeked out.

Where was she?

A red glow lit up a room full of people. Her head hurt, and she whimpered, but continued to look around. They were all strangers to her. Some of them were so white they looked like the zombies she saw in that movie last week.

And then they smiled. A scream welled up in her throat at the big teeth that stuck out from their mouths. She clamped her hand over her mouth, muffling the sound.

Her eyes watered at the smelly odor in the air. It burned her nose when she breathed. A loud buzz rang in her ears. Goose bumps raced down her back and across her legs.

The pain in her head grew into a sharp stab that started on one side and went to the other. The hum in her ears grew to a scream and the redness in the room flashed with bolts of black and white.

A hand with long, sharp black-painted nails grabbed at her.

Aimee's gaze followed the hand up the arm into the face of a woman with straight black hair and bright red lips. The centers of her eyes burned red in her white face.

The woman smiled. Huge eye teeth spilled from the corner of her mouth.

Just like the others.

And then the hand touched her.

A bitter chill crawled across Aimee's skin, and she screamed.

Chapter Twelve

Cara snuggled against Jake's warmth.

Sandalwood filled her nose, and she drew a deep breath, drugged by the clean scent of the man in her arms. Her head rested in the crook his shoulder. With her fingertips, she traced a figure eight in the hairs of his chest, down around his belly button then back up.

"If you keep doing that, I'm afraid you'll have to live with the consequences," he murmured.

Cara giggled. "Afraid? Ye doona frighten me at all." She glanced into his face.

He chuckled, gave her a squeeze before his expression grew serious. He sighed, rolled her onto her back, and leaned above her. His eyes searched hers. "What is it about you? I've never experienced lovemaking so powerful before," he whispered.

Blood coursed through her veins like an awakened river at the heart-rending tenderness in his gaze. His nearness wrapped around her like a warm cozy blanket and comforted her.

The feeling only lasted a moment when it was ripped away by a sharp dose of reality.

By the gods, what had they done?

They'd consummated the Síoraí blood union. Although Jake didn't know, nor could he possibly understand the repercussions of their love-making, she did. The bond they created would only grow stronger each day and draw him into her dark and dangerous world.

The harder she tried to ignore the truth the more it persisted, and with it came a pointed surge of the same uneasy apprehension that claimed Cara's dreams since the first time she met him. What would happen to them now? By the very act of their love-making, their relationship now forged for an eternity.

Jake swept into her life like a summer storm cascading down from the high peaks of her beloved Scotland, leaving everything it its path wind tossed, shivering and glistening with new possibilities.

Aye, she could build a new life with Jake and Aimee? But how did he feel about her?

Jake lay back and pulled her against him. His hand caressed her hair, across her shoulder, and pulled her close. Cara closed her eyes when his lips touched her forehead.

She needed to tell him about herself and what made their relationship so special, so powerful. He deserved to know, didn't he?

Cara pressed a soft kiss to his chest, slipped from his arms, and out of bed.

"Where are you going?"

She pulled on her jeans and shirt then turned to look at him. Her breath caught in her throat at the sight of his endless blue eyes. She found warmth in their sapphire depths; a tenderness that slipped past her defenses.

"Ye're so handsome," she murmured, then flushed at the realization she spoke the words aloud.

He sat up, leaned against the headboard of the bed, his lips curved into a devilish grin. "Why thank you.

You're quite the looker yourself." He patted the mattress beside him. "Now, come back to bed, beautiful."

A wave of apprehension swept through her, and she released her breath in a long drawn-out sigh. "Jake, we need to talk."

"We will, Cara." He smiled, but she read the uncertainty in his eyes. "Later. I promise. I can think of better things to do at the moment."

Cara laughed. "Ye're insatiable."

He winked then chuckled at the stunned expression on her face.

Just then a high-pitched scream rent the air. A shiver of panic speared through her, and she shot to the door. There was no hesitation in Jake as he whipped off the comforter and jumped from bed. He grabbed his jeans from the floor, yanked them on and buttoned them before he reached the door.

Jake followed Cara down the hall into Aimee's room where the child thrashed on the bed in the middle of a nightmare.

Cara rushed to Aimee's side. Jake followed close on her heels. He dropped on the bed and grabbed the child up in his arms. His hand caressed her hair with soft comforting strokes. "Shh, baby, it's okay. I'm here. It's just a bad dream," he crooned.

Aimee didn't wake up, but continued to moan and cry. "Daddy, make her go away."

Cara moved to the other side of the bed and sat on the floor. She reached up and placed her hand in the center of Aimee's back, hoping to help her break away from the night terror. She closed her eyes and eased into the dream realm and into Aimee's dream.

A black mist surrounded her and clouded her vision. Her gaze searched the fog, but she saw only darkness. Concerned, she used her mind and called out. *"Aimee, I'm here. Where are ye?"*

"Cara, I'm over here." And then Cara saw her. Less than sixty yards away, the child stood above her on the edge of a cliff. With her mental powers, Cara shifted her body until she stood beside Aimee, a trick only done in a dream. She knelt down and pulled the child in her arms.

"It's ok, Aimee. I'm here now," Cara reassured and squeezed her tighter.

"What about her? Make her go away." Aimee raised her hand. Her index finger pointed at something over Cara's shoulder. Without releasing Aimee, Cara swiveled and followed the direction of Aimee's finger.

A flicker of apprehension coursed through her which quickly turned to fear. Anger knotted inside her, and she tensed under Deidra Sidhe's withering glare.

Deidra's body stiffened and her eyes widened as if she were just as surprised by her appearance as Cara was to see her.

Deidra recovered and took a step forward. *"Get away from her. She's mine,"* she yelled.

Cara jumped to her feet and pushed Aimee behind her. *"Like hell. Ye stay away from her."*

"She's mine, guardian," Deidra sneered. Her lips curled and displayed her yellow incisors. *"Remove your hands from her. That child belongs to me."*

"Go to hell. I will never let ye take her. This child has my protection and that of the other Síoraí. Doona doubt my words. We'll stand against ye and ye will lose, Deidra. That I promise." Cara pledged in a voice

edged with steel.

"We shall see." She waved her hand as if in nonchalance. *"Take her, but trust me when I say, your possession will only be temporary."* No sooner had the words left her mouth then Deidra disappeared.

Cara pulled Aimee into her arms. *"She's gone, Aimee."* She stood, and picked Aimee up in her arms. With a reassuring smile, she plucked Aimee's nose.

"Come on, let's go home. Yer daddy is plenty worried about ye."

Within seconds, their minds returned to their bodies. Cara jerked and opened her eyes. Jake held his daughter in his arms, and murmured soothing words into her hair.

The tears had almost dried on Aimee's cheeks when she opened her eyes and looked up at her father.

Aimee squirmed in his arms. "I'm okay, daddy. Cara saved me."

Cara stiffened, and stared at him speechless. Her heart pounded while she waited for his reaction. What would he think if he discovered she'd traveled into the dream world to rescue his daughter?

When his gaze met hers, she shrugged and masked her inner turmoil with a deceptive calmness.

Jake pressed a kiss to Aimee's forehead. "You must have been having a scary dream, darlin' and Cara came to your rescue."

"No daddy. She was really there." Aimee looked at Cara. "Tell him, Cara. Tell him how you saved me from that mean lady."

Cara looked at Jake who glanced at her. A strange glint flared in his eyes. She noted his set face, clamped mouth and fixed eyes. She begged for his understanding as she nodded. She reached up and stroked Aimee's hair. "Of course I was, dear," she replied in a soft, tender voice.

Cara watched the play of emotions on Jake's face. When Aimee relaxed in his arms, he smiled with relief. Although Jake appeared placated, a panic unlike any she'd ever experienced before welled in her throat.

What could Deidra possibly want with Aimee?

"Get away from her. She's mine."

Deidra's threat tore through Cara and reached deep into her gut. Cara had to find her before she succeeded in whatever devious plan she'd concocted. Truth be told, if Deidra got her hands on this child, Aimee was dead.

****

"How is this possible?" Deidra shrieked. She paced the small confines of her chambers in the mausoleum. When she arrived in California, she'd been drawn here by the essences of the dead. She thrived on the fear and panic that radiated from souls that lay beneath the surface.

It had taken very little persuasion for the groundkeeper to let her stay. He'd made quite a tasty meal. It soon turned out that this place was big enough to support her growing army, as well as provide enough protection from the sun. The thick concrete walls of the mausoleum even kept her cool during the hottest parts of the day.

And now, anger flashed blood red behind her eyelids. She was furious.

She glanced at her minions and growled through gritted teeth, "Find the female guardian and destroy her."

Chapter Thirteen

Cara nibbled on the corner of her bottom lip.

She leaned over the railing of the pier, in the exact place where she met Jake more than a month ago. The yellow tape had been removed, and a young woman and man sat on a bench at the far end of the wharf. His arm wrapped around her shoulders in a protective embrace as they gazed into each other's faces. The love she witnessed in their eyes tore at her insides.

She swallowed hard.

Thin, bleak clouds rippled in sheer veils across the face of the moon.

The night air swirled a tempestuous circle, as if trapped in a limbo of uncertainty. Just like her emotions. She dropped her gaze. Below her, the ocean stirred. White caps swirled across the water's surface.

She thought of Jake. Their relationship had seen drastic changes in the short time they'd known each other. They were mated for life, an immortal lifetime, and he didn't even know it.

Fear churned her stomach. How would he react when he learned the truth?

After the incident in Aimee's dream, Cara reinforced the protection spell around Jake's home. As an added precaution, she included an extra special charm to Aimee's bedroom. So far, the girl's dreams remained uninterrupted.

But it wouldn't last forever. Deidra would find a way around her defenses, which is why she had to find her first. And so, for the past four nights, she left Jake's arms for a couple hours of hunting.

She pushed away from the railing. It was time to get home. Cara smiled as she thought of the time she spent with Aimee and Jake. They were her family, and she'd do everything in her power to keep them safe.

Cara swiveled around, turned her back on the sea, and headed home.

****

"Hey, why don't we go to the park today?" Jake said. He glanced at Aimee over the rim of his coffee cup.

The girl jumped up. Her eyes widened with excitement. "Can we really? Do you promise?"

Jake laughed. "I don't see why not." He looked across the table at Cara. "What do ye say? I haven't seen you out of the house in—" Rubbing his chin, he looked thoughtful. "Forever sounds about right."

As much as she wanted to, Cara knew she couldn't, and a sharp stab of disappointment speared through her. To be out in the light of day would be her death. "Well—"

"Oh, please, Cara. Please," Aimee begged.

One look into Aimee's beautiful face, and Cara knew she couldn't say no. Not right now.

"Okay, okay, ye win. We'll go this afternoon," she conceded and held up her hands in a sign of defeat. Inside, she shuddered with the knowledge she would have to break the wee lass' heart. Not right now, but later.

"Yay!" Aimee ran around the table and threw

herself into Jake's arms. "I can't wait."

Jake caught her before she flew over his lap and wrapped his arms around her. He chuckled and pressed a kiss to the top of her head. His eyes smiled at Cara over the top of Aimee's head.

In the next instant, Aimee squirmed out of his arms, jumped to the floor, and ran for the hall.

"Hey, where are you going?" Jake called.

Aimee stopped in the doorway, spun around, and put a hand on her waist. "I'm going to pack, daddy," she said in a voice that implied he should have known that. She glanced at Cara. "Do you want to help?"

Jake glanced at Cara. His eyes widened, and he laughed.

Cara frowned at him, yet turned to Aimee and smiled. "I'm going sit with daddy for a wee while, honey. Can I help ye later?"

Aimee nodded. "Yep!" she said in a chipper voice, whirled and disappeared down the hallway.

"Well, I think ye made her day," Cara commented, with a fixed smile on her face. A cold knot chilled the lining of her stomach.

"And what about yours? Did I make your day?"

Cara reached across the table and covered his hand with hers.

"Ye make my days and nights," she said with a wink.

"Cool," he replied with a twinkle in his eyes and a trace of laughter in his voice.

After a few moments, the pleasure of their good-humored bantering left her. She sighed, clasped her hands together in front of her, and stared at them.

"Jake," she said in a hesitant tone, glancing into his

face. "Maybe it might be best if I doona go with ye and Aimee this afternoon."

Jake frowned. "Why not?"

"I think ye need to spend some quality time with yer daughter alone, without a third wheel tagging along and getting in the way."

He sighed with exasperation. "Cara, you are part of this family. To Aimee, you are."

"And what about ye?"

"I can't imagine my life without you." His voice remained calm and his gaze steady as he held her eyes.

"Jake," she began in a weak and tremulous whisper. Tears built behind her lashes.

The shrill ring of the telephone interrupted her, and she pulled her hand away. He stared at her for a moment. An inquisitive gleam brightened his baby blues.

With an irritated sigh, he stood and walked to phone.

He grabbed the phone from the base and brought it to his ear.

"Yeah," he growled into the mouthpiece.

Cara heard bits and pieces of the conversation. From what she gathered, there had been another murder last night at the north end of the pier. After that, Cara didn't listen. She knew Jake would go.

Jake hung up the receiver and turned to her, his expression grim.

Cara nodded. She understood his torment. After all, he did make a promise. "Ye go. I'll tell Aimee. We'll be ok."

Just then, Aimee ran through the door carrying an overstuffed backpack on her shoulder. She dropped it on the floor and ran to her father.

"I'm all packed. Can we go now?"

Jake dropped to one knee, his face clouded. "I'm sorry, honey. I have to go to work for a little bit."

Aimee's face fell, and Cara's heart broke at her forlorn expression.

"We'll go another day."

"But you promised we'd go today," she cried. Tears welled in her eyes.

"Aimee, I'm so sorry, but I have to go."

Defeated, Aimee lowered her chin. "It's okay, daddy."

Cara couldn't take any more of Aimee's dejected expression and stood. "Hey, Aimee, why doona ye and I do something together while dad goes to work?"

"Like what?"

"Oh, I doona know. Maybe we can make a cake or, maybe, some cookies. What's yer pleasure?"

"Really?" Her eyes lit up, and she smiled. "Mrs. Denton never lets me near the stove." The joy in her expression faded and she glanced up at Jake.

"Is it okay, daddy?" she asked in a small voice.

Jake looked at Cara and smiled in relief. "It'll be fine, as long as you let Cara do the oven stuff."

"Okay." Aimee smiled.

Jake kissed Aimee on the forehead and stood. "You have a good day, sweetheart."

"You too, daddy."

Jake stood and walked over the Cara. He wrapped an arm around her waist and pulled her close.

"Thank ye," he whispered in her ear.

Cara smiled. "Ye're welcome."

He kissed her on the cheek, stepped away, and

winked. "And for the record, you're my pleasure, and, if you'll let me, I'll prove it tonight."

An unwelcome blush crept into her cheeks and a warm glow flowed through her in anticipation. "Ye're on."

Jake chuckled and pressed a quick kiss to her lips. "See you later."

And then he walked out the door. "Bye Ladies. Happy cooking," he called over his shoulder just before the door closed behind him.

****

Cara and Aimee spent the afternoon making chocolate chip cookies. By two o'clock, the cookies were done and the kitchen cleaned up.

Cara wiped her hands on the dishcloth, and hung the towel on the oven door. She turned to face Aimee who sat at the table. Opening her mouth to ask the girl what she wanted to do now, she snapped it shut at the sight that meant her eyes.

Aimee, her eyes closed, slept, her head pillowed on her crisscrossed arms.

Cara smiled. She walked over, reached down, and picked the child up in her arms. Aimee was as light as a feather. With ginger steps, Cara carried the girl into her room. A rush of warmth poured through her when Aimee snuggled closer.

When she reached the bed, Cara settled Aimee on the pillow before she lay down beside her and wrapped her arm across the girl. She pressed a gentle kiss to Aimee's forehead, lay down, and closed her eyes. The soft lull of Aimee's breathing eased her into a soft sleep.

"No! No! Leave me alone."

Cara woke to the Aimee's shrill scream. The girl thrashed on the bed, and Cara cursed herself for not reinforcing the protection spell. She placed her hand on the girl's head, closed her eyes and entered Aimee's dream.

Aimee stood on top of a high-rise building, her eyes wide with fear. The lass took baby steps backward as Deidra advanced toward her. Aimee stopped. She had nowhere else to go except off the top of the skyscraper.

Cara materialized behind the child before she stepped over the edge, wrapped her arms around Aimee, and pulled her close. *"'Tis okay, Aimee. I'm here,"* she whispered words of reassurance in the child's ear.

Shock and anger raged like an inferno inside her. With a narrowed brow, she glanced at Deidra. *"Ye'll never learn, will ye?"*

Deidra's eyes flashed. She shot Cara a black layered look. *"You again? Why don't you go away and leave us alone?"*

"Me? Leave ye alone?" Cara shook her head. *"Ye're the one intruding. Ye wilna get what ye're looking for with Aimee. That I promise."*

Deidra lips curved into an evil smile, her fangs visible from the corners of her mouth. *"I will. Mark my words, guardian, she will belong to me."*

"Over my dead body."

"That can be arranged."

"Then arrange it, but until ye do, stay the hell away from her," Cara replied, her voice laced with steel. She glanced at Aimee and smiled. *"Let's go home, doll."*

In the next instant, Cara and Aimee were home in Aimee's bedroom. Aimee jumped into Cara's lap, and wrapped her arms around Cara's waist. Her wee body trembled. Cara caressed her hair. "It's okay. We're okay, honey."

Aimee pulled away. "Who is she, Cara?" she asked in a voice that trembled.

"She's a verra bad woman, Aimee."

"She tries to get me to do things I don't want to do."

"What kind of things?"

Aimee put her head down, but Cara lifted her chin with a slight nudge of one finger. "Aimee, I can help ye, but ye have to trust me."

"I do, Cara, I do trust ye, but Mrs. Denton told me I need to be careful what I say to people."

Cara frowned. "Now, why would Mrs. Denton tell ye such a thing?"

"Because the child has special powers that even her own daddy refuses to acknowledge."

Cara stiffened and spun at the sound of Mrs. Denton's voice in the doorway.

Mrs. Denton glanced at Aimee and smiled. "It's okay, baby girl, we can talk to Cara." Mrs. Denton turned to Cara. "You're like her, aren't you?"

Sensing that at least one moment of truth was upon her, Cara nodded. "Aye. When I first arrived here, I sensed the power that Aimee possessed just by looking at the photographs on the wall. Aimee inherited them from her mother, didn't she?"

"Yes."

"I thought as much.

"Aimee is in danger, isn't she?"

Once again, Cara nodded.

"You will protect her, won't you?"

Cara stood and proclaimed, "With my life, if needed. Please, Mrs. Denton, trust me."

"I do." Mrs. Denton glanced toward Aimee. "Show her, Aimee." With those words, Mrs. Denton inclined her head in Aimee's direction. "She knows the story and will share it with you. If you have any questions, I'll be downstairs."

Aimee jumped from the bed and walked to the closet where she opened the door and disappeared inside. Moments later, she emerged, walking slow and careful toward her bed. In her hands, she held a wooden box that she set down on the bed in front of Cara. "Mrs. Denton gave me this box. She said it was a gift from my mother."

Cara gasped when she looked down to find the markings of the Tuatha De Danann carved on the lid of a small oak chest. She traced the figures with her fingertips before she glanced at Aimee. "Do ye know how she got this?"

"Mrs. Denton told me that the box was passed down from my great grandmother to my grandmother to my mother. It was their…what did Mrs. Denton say?"

"Their heritage?"

Aimee bobbed her blonde curls. "Yeah, that's it."

"Aimee, I know ye have special powers."

Aimee nodded and shrugged. "Yeah, sometimes I see things."

"Like what?"

"I see things that haven't happened yet, even things that have. People who have died come back to talk to me."

"Ye have the gift of sight."

"That's not all." At Cara's encouraging look, Aimee continued, "If I concentrate real hard, I can move things from one place to another. Mrs. Denton says I'll only grow more powerful with time, but I need to learn how to control what I have now before that times comes."

"She's right. I find it hard that yer daddy doesna know."

Aimee smiled. A conspiratorial gleam entered her eyes. "He knows. He caught me using my powers once. He was real mad at me, and told me I couldn't do things like that, that even though I was special, it had to be our secret. No one else was to know."

"He's protecting ye. There are people who would try to take ye away from him."

Aimee tensed. Her brows furrowed, and her lip trembled in fear. "You won't do that, will you?"

"No honey, I wilna. Ye belong with yer father."

Aimee smiled in relief then turned her attention to the box. Opening the lid, she pulled out an old book, its edges worn and torn with time. "It's my family's diary. Mrs. Denton has been reading it to me. A lot of the words I don't understand, but she tells me that it's my birthright and I shouldn't be afraid of what it says. I should learn it, use it, and live by it until the time comes."

"What time?"

"Mrs. Denton didn't say." Aimee handed it to Cara. "Take it. Read it."

Cara stretched out her hands to take the fragile offering, but hesitated. "Are ye sure?"

"I'm sure."

Cara took the book and held it to her chest. "I'll take good care of it."

Aimee grinned. "I know that."

Cara stretched across the bed and grabbed Aimee in a hug. For one so young, she had the intelligence of the ages.

Chapter Fourteen

In the living room, Cara dropped into the recliner and leaned her head against the cool leather material. She pulled her feet up and tucked them beneath her.

Her eyes shifted to Lisa's diary on the table beside her. She drew a deep breath then reached for the book. She slipped her fingers between the pages. It opened to Lisa's last entry dated three days before her death.

January 17, 2005

This entry will not only be my longest, but my last.

My time on this plane is ending. My visions have told me this. I cannot tell Jake. He would try to protect me, but no one can change their destiny, no matter how hard they may try.

A person must live every day as if it were their last, and be thankful for what they have been given.

And I am. I am grateful for my life. Jake will blame himself when the time comes, but he will recover. I've been granted the foresight of his future and it is bright. He'll find the love of a great woman. She will be his redemption. I hope that, in his stubbornness, he understands what has happened and what must happen for him to live again.

And then, I look at my precious daughter, Aimee Alysse. She is beautiful and very powerful. The essences of my ancestors, the powerful Druids of the Celtic lore, lie dormant inside her, more powerful, more destructive than any that have come before. I've prayed she be granted a teacher who will show her how to use this glorious power.

Aimee Alysse's future is not within my sights. It has been forbidden. I have only been told that she has been chosen for some grand design. Of which I am not a part. I've had many years to adjust to this fact and lived my life to the fullest. I'm not afraid for me, nor do I fear for Jake, only for my child.

I pray the Gods of the Tuatha De Danann know what a precious gift I am entrusting into their care.

Aimee Alysse—know that you are loved from this world into the next forever. Have patience with your father. He believes, but needs a little nudge once in a while.

Regardless, he loves you and will always love you...just as I will.

A chuisle, a chro go Síoraí.

Lisa "Ceara" Bradshaw

Tears spilled across Cara's cheeks as she read Lisa's final words. *A chuisle, a chro go Síoraí...my pulse, my heart forever.*

She closed the book and held it to her chest.

Lisa Bradshaw shouldered many responsibilities as a loving wife, mother, and a powerful princess of an old magical race from Cara's home country, Scotland.

Cara glanced up to find Mrs. Denton in the doorway.

"She knew she was going to die."

Mrs. Denton nodded and walked across the room. As she moved closer, her image wavered and changed from the elder housekeeper to the beautiful, young woman Cara had seen in Aimee's pictures.

Cara blinked then rubbed a hand across her eyes. Her heart stampeded in her chest.

Was this really happening?

Cara lowered her hand, and lifted her eyes. She sat forward, prepared to stand, but Lisa Bradshaw waved her back.

"No, please, don't get up." Her eyes twinkled. "Yes, I knew I was going to die, but it was my cross to bear. I couldn't tell Jake. He would have tried to stop it." She laughed. "No one can change destiny."

"Stubborn man, isn't he?" Cara asked, trying to smile, although as hard as she could, she couldn't get past the uncomfortable situation. "Look, Lisa, I didn't come here to take yer place—" Cara's words caught in her throat when Lisa held up a hand.

"I know. Your destiny has brought you here."

"You know about me?"

"Of course." Lisa grinned. "And I now know that you are my daughter's protector, my husband's redemption, and you will love them both for eternity."

"If you know so much about me, then how can ye say that I'm Jake's redemption? If he took issue with yer powers, my being an immortal warrior wilna set well."

"You'll make him see and believe. More importantly, he'll love and be loved."

"What makes ye think I love him?"

"I can see it in your eyes when you speak his name. I hear it in your voice even when you call him stubborn. Despite his flaws, you love him."

Cara shrugged, uncertain how to reply. "But he doesna love me."

"You don't think so? You forget, as Mrs. Denton,

I've seen how you react to each other. There's a powerful bond that exists between you."

"That's the curse of the guardians."

"Curse?"

"Aye, the bond. If a guardian bites a human, they're bonded for an immortal lifetime. How do ye think he'll react to that? I dinna give him any choice in the matter."

"You didn't have to. Jake is not like ordinary men. He's unique. When he gives his body, he's already given his heart."

"But I bit him before—" Cara flushed. How embarrassing to talk to a man's dead wife about sex with her husband.

"There had to be some attraction that allowed you to get close enough to bite."

"Ye make…" Cara stopped, waving her arms wide. "…all of this out as if it is part of a normal day." She shook her head. "But it isna. It's a nightmare. I know in my heart that Jake wilna be as accepting of my past as easily as ye appear to be."

"But I know Jake. He loves you, and love overcomes all. Don't you know that?"

"At the moment, I doona know anything."

Lisa reached for Cara's hand and gave her a reassuring squeeze. "You'll figure it out." And with that, Lisa stood up straight, changed back into Mrs. Denton, and turned to leave the room.

"Why are ye here? As Mrs. Denton?"

Mrs. Denton turned around and smiled. "I made a pact with the gods."

"What kind of pact?"

"The kind that allows me to watch out for Jake and

Aimee until their protector arrives. As long as I kept my identity a secret from the two of them, I could stay, but I sense that silence has nothing to do with it anymore. My time is limited."

"Ye've been teaching Aimee."

Lisa nodded. "To understand the future, she needs to know of her past, and why she has been given these special powers."

"But she is only seven-years-old," Cara insisted. "How can ye expect that wee child to comprehend the evil in this world?"

Sadness burrowed deep in the depths of Lisa's eyes. "Aimee is an intelligent child."

"But still a child," Cara stated. "'Tis no' fair that she must lose her childhood."

Lisa flinched at the bitterness in Cara's voice. "We have all been forced to make sacrifices, as well you know." She inhaled. "I would wish a happy childhood for my daughter, yet it is not meant to be. By no choice of hers, she has been drawn into this war. We must give her the knowledge and the courage to survive the battles."

Cara's stomach knotted at the truth of Lisa's words. "I'm sorry," she said in a sincere voice.

Lisa smiled. "Don't be. You will be good for Jake and Aimee, and I wouldn't trust anyone else."

Chapter Fifteen

Cara collapsed against the front door. She closed her eyes and released a deep, agonized sigh.

Jake's heart twisted at the exhaustion in her posture. He ached to draw her into his arms and ease the tension that filled her stance, but first he needed some answers.

Where had she been? What had she been doing?

When he woke, the sheets on Cara's side of the bed were cold. When he searched the house, he discovered it empty except for Aimee and Mrs. Denton, both asleep in their beds. For the past hour, he sat in the dark and struggled with the indecision aroused by her absence.

"Hey there," he said. Annoyance sharpened his voice.

The heavy lashes that shadowed her cheeks flew up, and a soft gasp escaped her lips. She straightened. Her gaze searched the darkness.

Jake rose from the recliner, walked across the room, and flicked on the wall switch beside the fireplace. Light flooded the room.

She tilted her chin. Her lips curved into a slight, tentative smile.

"Jake! Ye scared the hell out of me." She slipped the jacket from her shoulders and turned to hang it on the wall rack. Her hands hesitated, and her knuckles whitened as the grip on her jacket tightened. She drew a sharp breath, spun around to face him, a stiff smile pasted on her lips. "What are ye doing up?" she asked as she stepped into the room.

The sleek, skintight black leather outfit accentuated every curve of her body, and his heartbeat ramped into overdrive. He cleared his throat. "Waiting for you. Where have you been?"

A flicker of fear entered her eyes. She lowered her lashes hiding the emotion from his sight, but only for a moment. She recovered and shrugged. "I had some errands to run."

His gaze raked over her body then he glanced toward the wall clock. His eyebrows shot up in surprise. "At four o'clock in the morning? Dressed like that?"

"Jake—" He held up a hand to silence her.

Anger fired the edge of his control. His jaw clenched, his eyes narrowed. "Oh, let me guess. Another friend's daughter was running around the cemetery and you had to run to the rescue," he remarked in a cool, composed voice, although his insides churned. His eyebrows rose. "Oh, and before you answer that, I thought you didn't have many friends here?"

Her hands clenched into fists at her waist. He'd pissed her off. Her fury revealed itself in the rosy color that brightened in her cheeks and the vivid emerald sparks in her eyes.

"I think it might be best if we wait until morning to have this discussion," she said through clenched teeth. Her voice trembled with barely controlled anger. She swiveled on her heels and headed from the room.

He rushed after her, grabbed her arm, and spun her

around to face him. "It's already morning. I think now is a perfect time."

She swallowed hard and lifted her chin. Fortitude lit up the depths of her eyes. "Doona do this," she warned in a voice tight with strain.

"Do what? Am I supposed to forget that the woman who shares my bed runs mysterious errands in the middle of the night dressed like a—"

"Doona say it." Her voice lowered. "Stop it, Jake. Please stop!" she begged.

"What are you hiding, Cara?"

Cara stiffened as though stung by his words. "I have nothing to feel guilty for."

"Then why won't you talk to me about it?"

"It doesna concern ye."

Jake's brows drew together in an affronted frown. "How can you say that? I thought we had something special, Cara."

"Let me go, Jake."

Jake stood in fear-choked silence. He couldn't do what she asked. He couldn't let her go. Her sweet fires, her shimmering warmth were as crucial to him as the air in his lungs. He fought for her in much the same way he would fight to breathe.

But any hope of victory slipped further from his grasp until it became difficult to breath. His chest compressed in a suffocating vice. Somehow, he had known he would lose, but he hadn't known it would come this soon and hurt this much.

The pain of loss enraged him.

"No!" he snarled and tightened his grip on her. "Talk to me, damn it! Don't walk out of here like what we shared never existed."

Cara jerked her arm from his grip. "There is nothing to talk about," she said in a nasty tone.

He recoiled at the animosity in her voice.

A snarl curled her lips, and then she spun around and disappeared through the patio doors.

Jake cursed under his breath.

A tumble of confused thoughts and feelings assailed him, and he wandered around the room. Cara's presence floated around him, a charge of electricity that brought the hair on his arms and legs upright.

He only intended to talk to her, to demand answers. Instead, he snapped and charged her, unable to think beyond the moment and the two emotions that clung to him like a second skin, desire for Cara O'Leary and the fear of losing her.

Nice job, Jake.

This woman tormented him. Awake, or asleep, it didn't matter. Just the thought of her generated an inappropriate bodily reaction at inappropriate times.

He couldn't let her go. Not like this.

He stormed out the patio doors where Cara disappeared a moment ago and came to an abrupt stop. She stood near the rail, her head tilted toward the sky. Her cheeks glistened of tears in the moonlight. As if she knew he stood there, she swallowed hard.

"I canna do this, Jake."

Her words struck an angry cord inside him. He scooped her into his arms and carried her through the house to his bedroom where he dumped her onto the mattress.

"What the bloody hell do you think ye're doing?" she yelped.

Jake dropped beside her. His legs framed her hips

and his hands grasped her wrists and yanked her arms over her head.

He stared down at her. "I don't understand the power you have over me. When I'm asleep, you taunt me. When I'm awake, the memory of you torments me. I don't want to lose you without seeing it coming. Here I am, Cara. Right here. No Dream. If you want to mess with my mind, do it to my face. If you want to have sex with me, do it in the flesh."

Not giving her time to respond, Jake lips covered her. His hands slid to her face and he cupped her cheeks while his weight lowered to rest on his forearms. She lay still at first, as if she fought her reaction to him...to his touch, and yet, mere moments later she whimpered in his mouth.

He deepened the kiss and made love to her with slow, sensual slides of his tongue. Her scent, her taste, her very presence filled him, and pushed him to take more. And he did. He didn't hold back.

Satisfaction filled him. Her fingers drifted up his arms and laced together behind his neck. Proof, she no longer held back. Proof he was breaking her, not the opposite. This woman might dominate him in sleep, but not here, in this waking world.

An insatiable hunger twisted his gut. He cupped her ass, lifted and molded her hips against him. He moaned at the sweet pressure against him.

Her hand slipped beneath his shirt. She caressed his back. The skin-to-skin contact scorched him, and he craved more.

Without removing his lips from hers, he shoved her top up. His fingers located the front latch of her bra and, with a quick flick, he snapped the material apart.

He trailed his lips along her jaw, and neck, even as he filled his palms with her breasts. Impatient, Jake wanted her shirt gone. Instead of taking the time to remove the barricade, he slid downwards, his mouth found her nipple and, he suckled.

Cara moaned and arched her back. Her fingers slid through his hair. Her response drove him onward and he swirled his tongue around the hardened peak. He took his time to lick, suck and tease first one nipple, then the next. Her body writhed beneath him in arousal.

When he lifted his head, his gaze caught hers and locked. In her passion filled eyes, he found more than lust and desire, more than the arousal they shared. Lord help him, the emotions in the depths of her emerald eyes moved him.

He stared at her, wondering why she reminded him of his wife, why she did to him what only Lisa had done. Though there were no real answers to be found, her gaze held innocence, beauty, and honesty. She didn't plot against him. Intuition told him that she was pure truth, and with that realization, Jake knew he couldn't do this...not like this.

He murmured an apology, and rolled onto his back. He covered his face with an arm, and willed the rage of his body to calm. Everything inside him screamed to go back to her, to take her, to prove that he was man enough for her, but he couldn't force her.

Not like this.

****

Cara scrambled to fix her shirt and bra, her cheeks flushed with the realization of just how close Jake came to losing control. If he hadn't stopped...well, she wasn't sure she would have.

With her clothes in place, Cara sat on the edge of the bed and stared over her shoulder at Jake. At the wild array of hair that framed his face beneath the muscular forearm that rested over his forehead.

Her gaze traveled the length of his body, coming to rest on his bare stomach. A thin trail of hair led from his inverted navel to his waistband before disappearing into his pajamas.

Cara diverted her gaze, pulled her knees to her chest, and wrapped her arms around them. If she kept looking at the man, her mind would not be on talking. The urge to climb on top of him and kiss him again was too strong.

She couldn't put it off any longer. "We need to talk."

Jake removed his arms from over his eyes. He stared at her, his dark eyes intense, potent and unreadable. With an agile motion, he jumped off the bed. He paced the room a moment then stopped at the window. With his back to her, he ran a hand through his hair.

"I'm sorry. I don't know what came over me."

"I do," she said in a soft voice.

Jake turned to face her and fixed her in a potent stare. His eyes contained a hint of dark shading beyond their natural blue color.

"Then tell me. Tell me why I can't stop seeing your face. Everywhere I look, everywhere I go, and you're there. I sensed your absence in bed tonight. That's what woke me up, and when I didn't find you—"

She swallowed and fought the panic that welled in her chest. His emotions reached out and wrapped around her, an odd connection that made her understand exactly what he felt.

"I'm no' who I appear to be."

"Then who are you?"

"Maybe ye should be asking what I am."

He cut her off with a swipe of a hand. "Don't be foolish."

"I'm no'," she insisted.

Jake's eyes widened and his teeth clenched. A muscle jumped in his jaw.

Cara continued, unafraid.

"I was born in Ireland in the year 1232. I was married to a wonderful man named Braedan O'Leary and we were expecting our first child. We were on our way to my parent's house to share our news when we saw the fire." Cara got lost in the memory. "The reivers who killed my parents also killed my husband. When I woke up, Semias, the Druid from the city Murias, stood before me. She told me—"

"Stop this, Cara."

She glanced at him. A look of intense disbelief filled Jake's features. Her lips twisted into a sad smile.

"Ye know there are people out there who are different than some. Even if ye deny their presence, ye canna change their existence."

He shook his head. "I don't know what you're talking about?"

"I think ye do." She hesitated for a brief moment, then continued, "Before I was born, I was chosen...destined, if ye will, by the Celtic Gods of the Tuatha De Danann. When I lost my family, I lost the ties that connected me to the mortal world. I received immortality amongst other powers that I use to fight the evil of the world."

Jake walked to the bed where he sat on the edge and looked at her, his brows drawn into a deep frown.

He didn't say a word, just let her continue.

"I'm no' crazy, Jake."

"I've heard of the tales of the Tuatha De Danann and of the guardians they created."

"From Lisa?"

He nodded. "She was special."

"Lisa had the magical powers of the Druids, and those same powers were passed to yer daughter. That alone has put Aimee in a great deal of danger."

The words Aimee and danger together in the same passage didn't set well with Jake and he jumped to his feet. "There is no connection between my daughter and the Tuatha De Danann, Cara," he insisted through clenched teeth.

"Did Lisa ever tell ye why the guardians of the Tuatha De Danann were created?"

"To fight some evil that would resurrect from the dead."

Cara nodded. "That evil is here, in Santa Monica, Jake, and it goes by the name of Deidra Sidhe. She portrays herself as a woman. She is the one responsible for the murders in this city."

Jake jumped to his feet. "You knew this, and didn't tell me?"

"Mortals canna fight Deidra. She's an evil Vampryss who feeds off the blood of humans. Right now, she creates her own army and prepares to take over this world. If she succeeds, she'll destroy everything. It's my job to stop her."

"Cara," he said her name as if in warning.

"Listen to me, Jake. The guardians were simple

people chosen before the day of their natural birth to become immortal beings, protectors of the world's population. They were granted the supernatural powers needed to fight and defeat the creatures of the night: vampires, shape shifters, werewolves, and ghoulies." He grunted. She ignored him and continued, "It is believed that the talismans of the Tuatha Dé Danann would be held and protected by these four guardians. Four talismans, four guardians, would be used to fight the demons of the world. Each talisman resurrects a power unknown to its carrier."

"And how do you know of this?"

Cara sighed.

She would have to spell it out for him. She pushed aside her shirt and showed him the mark that Luna had placed on her shoulder the day she was granted immortality and strength.

Jake stood and walked over to take a closer look at the tattoo. He shrugged. "I've seen this when..." he stopped, running a hand over the tattoo, tracing the intricate design. "I thought it was damn sexy."

The tattoo was simple. Creeping vines of a willow tree stood in the forefront with moonlight shining through the branches. Another moon was embossed in her flesh above. In the center was the slight imprint of a man's face.

"It's the *Mark of Luna*. I received the mark on the day I died and resurrected as a guardian."

Jake's eyes widened. His hand jerked away as if on fire and he stared into her face. "Do you expect me to believe that you're a guardian?"

"I tried to tell ye, Jake."

Jake dropped his hand. His expression grew hard

and resentful.

"You didn't try hard enough," he said, his tone vicious.

She walked toward him, her hand outstretched. "That isna fair."

"What's not? That I found out the woman living in my home is more than seven hundred and fifty years old. She's an immortal vampire slayer and has been watching over my daughter." He held up his hand to stop her advance. "I believe you, Cara. Everything you say, but I won't allow you to influence my daughter, and I'll not allow you to put her into danger."

"Ye have no say in it, Jake. Deidra has chosen her." She shook her head. "I doona know why, but she has."

"I'll take Aimee away from here."

"Ye wilna be able to hide, Jake."

His eyes widened as if startled by another thought that flashed through his mind. "And us? How do we, you and I, fit into this? Or were you playing me to stay close to Aimee?"

She shook her head. "It wasna like that."

"Look," he hesitated and ran a hand through his hair. "Lisa taught me all about the paranormal crap in the world, but what I don't understand is you and me? Why can't I stop seeing your face? You're always there." He pointed to his head. "In my head."

She cleared her throat. It was time to come clean.

"I bit ye," she answered. "I crossed the line, and there's no going back from that. I lose everything I am, and you and I are bonded for life."

"Bonded? What the hell does that mean?"

"Look at it as being married under the eyes of your

God."

"I didn't ask for that. What makes you so different from this Deidra Sidhe who destroys people's lives?"

She cursed under breath. Anger boiled her blood.

"Now ye know why I dinna tell ye. I knew ye would react this way. Can ye blame me for wanting to hold onto the moments with ye as long as I could?"

"What did ye expect, Cara? You didn't give me any choice in this."

Cara drew a deep agonized breath. "Jake, I understand if ye never want to see me again, and I'll respect yer wishes, but there is a reason I'm here."

"Of course there is. You're here to screw up people's lives. Well, mission accomplished."

"No, Jake. It's Aimee. Deidra Sidhe wants the power she has harnessed inside her. The bitch wilna stop until she gets it."

Jake's brows narrowed. "You brought her here."

Cara shook her head. "Deidra was drawn to Aimee by her power. She'll try to use it to bring Ághmach back from the underworld. Believe me, ye doona want him on this plane. Ághmach makes Deidra look like a pussy cat. If he returns, they'll recreate the first evil cabinet, the Camarilla. There wilna be any stopping them from taking over the world."

Jake rubbed a hand across his face before he looked up at her. His glare burned through her, and she cringed at the look of betrayal in his eyes. "I want you to leave."

"I canna."

His face hardened, and he raked a disgusted look over her. "You will leave, Cara, or I'll physically throw you out myself."

A sick feeling settled into the pit of her stomach. "Jake—"

"Now!" Jake hissed that one single, brutal word, tearing her heart from her chest.

Chapter Sixteen

Cara flinched at the arctic contempt in his eyes. He spun away from her. Icy fingers of terror crawled over her body.

"Jake." His name, wedged in her throat, sent spiraling pain across her chest and between her shoulder blades. She swallowed hard, past the panic that welled in her throat.

"Ye canna mean that." She bit her lower lip. Her gaze followed him as he paced the floor.

He swiveled around and strode toward her. He towered above her for a long moment, his expression grim, eyes deadly, and then he drew a deep breath. He grabbed her arm and escorted her from the bedroom into the living room.

"Oh, but I do," he whispered, grinding the words out between his teeth. With a ruthless shove, he pushed her toward the front door. "And I want you out of here tonight." He turned away.

She rushed after him and placed her hand on his arm. "Please doona do this. I am the only one who can keep Aimee safe."

He glanced at her hand on his forearm. The line of his mouth tightened a fraction more and he jerked away. He swung around and gripped her arms in a vice-like grip. With a sharp jerk, he shook her. "I'm her father. I can protect my own child."

And with those words, he thrust her from him. She stumbled and would have fallen but her hand caught the back of the couch. After she regained her footing, she walked toward him.

She couldn't back down. This was too important. Aimee's life counted on her being strong, unbendable. "Ye canna protect Aimee. No' against Deidra. She's more powerful than ye can imagine. Right now, she only enters Aimee's dream, but it wilna be long before she..." she hesitated and shook her head. She refused to think of what might happen then. "I can stand between them. Keep Deidra from Aimee's dreams."

"You're crazy."

"Mayhap, but ye've got to trust me."

His mouth twisted into a cynical grin. "Trust you? I don't need you to protect my daughter, Cara. I will keep her safe, even if it means I have to protect her from you."

"Protecting her body is different than protecting her mind. Aimee fears her dreams. I can create a mental block that keeps Deidra out of Aimee's head."

"Enough!" He ran long fingers through his hair in frustration. "No more, Cara. I've heard more than I care to."

He held up a hand for silence. She bit her lip.

"Now, I want you to leave *my* home."

She rushed forward. "Listen to me."

"Now!"

She cringed at the determination, the unbending resolve of his stance.

Defeated, she lowered her head. "Okay, I'm leaving." One last ditch effort, she begged him with her eyes. "But, Jake, if ye need me, or Aimee needs me—"

"We won't," he interrupted. He walked to the door, opened it, and waited for her to pass through. When she didn't move right away, he jerked his head toward the door in impatience. "Goodbye, Cara."

With slow steps, she walked toward the door. When she came abreast to where he stood, she stopped.

"Ye will need me. If nothing else, trust in that. I'll be nearby," she whispered, gulping back her tears.

"Don't," he hissed in a tone vicious, unyielding.

Like a blade, his tone pierced her heart. She glanced into his face. His eyes were filled with hatred. Heartache twisted through her and left her shaken.

Choked by the lump that clogged her throat, she nodded and stepped across the threshold. Once again, she hesitated. Without turning, she said, "Take care of her, Jake." She swallowed. "And yourself."

The door slammed behind her.

A swift breeze from the action ruffled her hair.

She flinched at the finality.

Outside, she slumped against the door and yielded to compulsive sobs that shook her. Wild laughter clawed at the back of her throat, but she maintained just enough self-control not to give in. She knew, with certain humiliation, that if she did, the laughter would mutate into the raw sounds of excruciating heartache.

A loud crash sounded on the other side of the door followed by shattering glass. Cara whipped around and reached for the doorknob, prepared to rush in and make certain he was okay.

Her hand hesitated above the handle. After a brief moment of indecision, she clenched her fingers into a tight fist and stepped away.

As much as she needed to stay and protect Aimee,

she couldn't do it.

Not this way.

Releasing the deep breath she held, she brushed the tears from her cheeks. With one last look at the door behind her, she headed off the porch and down the driveway.

She had to find Deidra before the Vampryss got to Aimee, but first, she needed to seek shelter. The moon began its slow descent from the sky. Bright oranges and yellows flickered on the horizon.

She needed to move fast.

****

Jake stared at the glass shards on the floor, mesmerized by the prism of colors that radiated from them like a kaleidoscope.

The broken pieces were a reflection of how he felt in that moment. Shattered. Broken. Alone. After Lisa, he never thought he'd find another woman he could care about.

He had, and he'd sent her away.

Dropping to the recliner, Jake cradled his head in his hands. He had no choice. Despite his feelings for Cara, Aimee always was and always would be his number one concern. He promised Lisa he would protect their daughter, and he planned to honor that vow.

When Cara told him Aimee's life was in danger, he nearly lost it. And when she'd informed him that he was incapable of protecting her from this…this…evil bitch, well, he'd taken offense.

Even now, in the silence that raged around him, he reflected on the events over the last few weeks.

The Santa Monica murders. Was it true? Was this

Deidra responsible? And Aimee's nightmares. Did she haunt his daughter's dreams?

Lisa possessed powers...unusual, supernatural powers, but he loved her. He understood how important her heritage was to her, but that didn't mean he liked it. He accepted Lisa, and everything that she was. That his daughter inherited her mother's powers became apparent when his daughter turned six months and retrieved her rattle from the shelf without leaving her crib.

So what made the present any different than the past?

The harder he tried to ignore the truth, the more it persisted.

Aimee, his daughter, once told him Cara saved her from the bad woman in her dreams. When she screamed out in her sleep, she cried for Cara. Not him. Cara claimed that only she could help Aimee, save her from this evil, and in his heart, he knew Aimee would accept no other.

A flash of grief ripped through him and heaviness pressed on his chest.

His gaze shot to the front door.

What had he done?

"Daddy?"

Jake glanced toward the hall. Aimee, her hair tousled, stood in the entrance. Her balled-up fists rubbed the sleep from her eyes.

When she took a step into the room, he jumped to his feet. "Don't move, Aimee," he shouted.

Aimee's eyes widened and she jerked to a stop.

His heart broke at the dejected expression on her face. He held up a hand.

"Stay there, honey. There's glass on the floor," he explained in a softer voice. In four long strides, he reached her and swept her into his arms.

Her head dropped to his shoulder. "I love you, daddy."

Jake squeezed her. "I love you, too, baby."

She raised her head and glanced around the room. "Where's Cara?"

He grimaced at the fear in her voice. Did she already know what he'd done?

"She's gone."

Aimee looked into his face. His heart skipped at the terror in the depths of her blue eyes. "She's coming back, isn't she?"

Jake carried Aimee to her room where he laid her on the bed. He sat beside her and brushed the tendrils of blonde hair from her cheek. He bent over and kissed her cheek.

"Go back to sleep, Aimee," he whispered, pulling the covers up and tucking them around her.

"No, daddy! Cara's got to come back. That mean lady…she'll come back for me. I know she will. She's a monster."

"Stop it, Aimee! There's no such thing as monsters."

Aimee's eyes filled with tears. "There are, daddy." She jumped up on the bed and wrapped her arms around Jake.

Jake hugged her close. Sobs racked her small body and struck him like a knife in the chest. He caressed her hair.

"It'll be okay, honey. We'll be okay." He murmured into her hair.

Victoria Noxon

"You'll find Cara and bring her home." Aimee pulled away and looked up at Jake, her expression hopeful.

The word "home" hit a cord in Jake. Aimee considered Cara a part of their family. And why not? In the short time that Cara stayed with them, she wormed her way into his daughter's heart, and if he were honest, his own. He suddenly realized that no matter what Cara was, she was a part of him.

"Hush, baby."

"Promise me, daddy. Pinky swear that you'll find Cara and bring her home." Aimee held up her pinky to Jake. "Swear."

Jake couldn't say no and wrapped his pinky around hers. Aimee gave their joined fingers a little shake.

He gave her a small smile. "I swear. Now, please get some sleep."

"Will you stay with me until I fall asleep?" Aimee asked.

She yawned. He lay her down and pulled the blankets around her neck.

"I will, baby. I promise."

And daddies always kept their promises.

Didn't they?

But at what cost to him as a man?

Deep down, Jake knew Cara wouldn't hurt Aimee, nor would she physically hurt him, but what about his heart? Did he send Cara away to protect his daughter or was that only an excuse to avoid heartache?

Chapter Seventeen

Physical and emotional exhaustion consumed Jake. The lingering effect of the roller coaster ride he'd been on for the past three days. It began with Cara's eviction, followed by Aimee's night terrors only to end with three more murders.

He arrived home twenty minutes ago after a horrific day at Angstrom Cemetery. There was no doubt in his mind that the three teens had gone to the gravesite to party, but what happened next was anybody's guess.

Every muscles in his body ached, and his nerves stretched taut with tension.

He eased under the spray of the steaming shower. Reaching for the soap and the washcloth, he held it under the showerhead, manipulated the items together and waited for the cloth to lather. Spinning around, he tilted his head back and let the spray spill over his back while he massaged the sudsy fabric over his shoulder, behind his neck, then down his chest.

He imagined Cara's hands gliding across his shoulders, her long, auburn hair brushing against his skin, and her sparkling, emerald greens eyes. His breath caught in his throat as the scent of apple blossoms filled his nostrils.

Rage erupted in his veins like a firestorm, and his gut churned into a violent volcano that exploded into a

163

fiery inferno. A part of him understood that sexual frustration was a good percentage of what fueled his anger, but, *damn it,* he missed her.

Only three days had passed since he made Cara leave, but it seemed like a lifetime. Even though, he spent hours upon hours convincing himself it was the best for all of them, doubts plagued him.

Her face disrupted his dreams and filled his thoughts during the waking hours.

But something else changed in his night-time world of dreams. Not only did he envision Cara, he dreamt of blue flames and demons. They were so real he often woke up shaken, drenched in sweat.

Did they hold some deep, special meaning?

Aimee hadn't spoken to him except for a few curt words over the past few days. She was still angry, and yet, he knew that once he kept his promise and brought Cara home, she'd be fine. Until them, he gave her space. And if he didn't find Cara, well…in time, his daughter would get over it and realize that life was a challenging journey full of disappointments.

He would have preferred she learned it later in life, and not at this tender age, but unpredictability was part of existing.

Regardless, he prayed he located Cara before he dropped dead of exhaustion. Par for the course, he supposed. A father's work is never done.

He spun around, faced the shower's spray and watched the soapy suds shift down the drain. He needed sleep. Even four hours of shuteye would do him a world of good, but every time he closed his eyes, Cara was there. The warmth of her body snuggled against him left a lasting impression.

During the day, he immersed himself in trying to solve the murders of Santa Monica.

So far, he'd been batting zero in his efforts to apprehend a suspect. Every murder the same, occurring at night with no witnesses. Other than those belonging to the victims, the department had been unable to find a single fingerprint or solitary footprint at the scenes.

In fact, half the force, including him, walked around in a nauseated state over the brutality of the murders.

The coroner determined that a metal implement, such as an ax or knife, had not been the weapon of choice. The torn flesh lacked any metal fragments prominently found in tools made of iron or steel.

Jake frowned, turned off the shower, and whipped the curtain open. He shivered at the blast of cool air that hit his heated flesh. After he grabbed a towel from the hook on the wall, he wrapped it around his waist and stepped from the tub.

This case dominated his life. Captain Dawson ordered a skin and fabric analysis of the latest victims in the hopes that it might result in a specific cause of death. The more they had to go on, the better, but as far as everything stood right now, they had squat…not even Cara.

Thanks to him.

****

Cara strolled along Fifth Street. Taking a deep, unsteady breath, she moved toward the road that would take her to the warehouse near the wharf. She'd been on her own again for the past three nights, and her cramped quarters at the boarding house made her tense and anxious to escape. She hoped a nice long walk would help ease the tension.

A white road sign read Grandiose Marina and pointed to the paved street to the right while a beaten wood one read Barker Plant & Warehouse and indicated the dirt covered road to the left. Cara forced her thoughts away from her rag-tag room and her inner turmoil to the vampires she hoped to find at the plant. Perhaps, they would lead her to Deidra.

She veered to the left. A warm, sultry breeze swayed the palms trees lining the drive. The road turned out to be at least a mile long, but Cara didn't mind.

The road narrowed, and gave way to what appeared to be a bayou of sorts. In California? She shook her head and glanced around. Palm-covered islands dotted the wetlands into clumps on both sides of the road. The roads, pitted and marred with potholes, made her grateful for the bright moonlight that lit her way.

The road widened and smoothed out.

She sighed in relief at the sight of the wharf a quarter of a mile away.

She wasn't surprised to discover that it looked deserted. In fact, the walk had taken longer than expected which meant the vampires that occupied the shadows had probably gone out hunting themselves.

Crap! Without another thought, she rotated and began the long trek back to where she started.

Her mind wandered, traveling back to the days spent at the Bradshaw household. She missed Jake and Aimee. The laughter and joy she experienced while she lived in their home coursed through her veins, and she ached to experience it again.

She hadn't been able to connect with Aimee since she left Jake's house, nor had she any luck finding

Deidra's hide-a-way.

Helplessness and a sense of hopelessness washed over her, and left her drained.

It was time.

With her left hand, she reached inside the pocket of her jacket and pulled out her cell phone. She flipped it open and scrolled through her contact list. Her eyes searched for one name, Cameron MacLean, the youngest Síoraí Guardian. Exhausted, she ran the fingers of her right hand through her hair even as her thumb on her left pushed the autodial button.

Through the earpiece, she heard the instrument dial then connect.

A low, female voice answered on the second ring. "Hello."

Cara recognized Aiyanna's voice. A white witch, Anya was well liked among the guardians, especially by Cameron since he'd married her. The two met and bonded a little over eight months ago, just after their last clash with Deidra.

Deidra kidnapped Aiyanna's sister, Cheyenne, and tried to use the power of the two white witches to release Àghmach from the underworld. The guardians freed Cheyenne and nixed the plan, but their attack brought Deidra to Santa Monica and after Aimee Bradshaw.

"Hey, Anya," Cara said, adding a soft lilt to her voice.

"Cara, is that you?" Surprise echoed in Anya's voice.

"Aye, 'tis me." Without preamble, she continued, "By any chance, is Cameron home?"

Anya must have recognized the tone in her voice.

167

"She's back, isn't she?" she asked. There was a bitter edge of cynicism in her tone.

"Aye, she's back. And she's after a wee girl's power. I've tried, Anya, but I canna find her. I'm afraid—" Cara's voice broke and faded to a hushed stillness.

"Hold on, Cara. I'll get him for you."

After a few moments, Cameron's deep voice came on the line. "Hey, Cookie. I hear the bitch is back."

A long-standing joke, Cameron liked to call her Cookie because she received the Cauldron of Dagda as her Talisman. It held the feast of the centuries, and the prophet's held that no one shall go hungry. Cara-Cookie, she never figured out the relationship, but it made him happy. To Cara, it lost its taste appeal a hundred years ago.

She ignored the banter. "I need help, Cameron," she said in a serious tone.

"Where are ye?" She could almost picture his serious expression and rigid stance as if primed for battle.

"Santa Monica, California. Deidra's here and doing what she does so well…killing. She's after the powers of a seven year-old girl, Aimee Bradshaw."

"I doona understand what she would gain from a child that young."

"Aimee is a descendent of the powerful Celtic Druids, and, as such, has inherited her dead mamma's powers."

Cameron's whistle echoed through the ear piece. Both knew just how powerful the Druids were. After all, the Druids trained the guardians and taught them to use their powers in preparation for this war with the

Vampryss.

"Let me get in touch with Fallon and Devlin, and we'll be there as soon as we can. Can ye hold on until then?"

"I doona know what Deidra's plan is, so ye need to hurry," she rushed out, hoping she didn't sound as desperate as she felt.

"Cara?"

"Aye?"

"I've go' to ask this. What is yer connection with the child?" he asked in a low, composed voice.

"I'm her friend." Cara replied. "We met through her father."

"Och, I see," he responded with quiet emphasis.

"What do ye see?" Her tone rose. "Look, Cameron, I doona know why ye're asking—"

"And I doona know why ye're getting so defensive."

"There's nothing to tell. Even if there were, I doona believe it's any of yer business."

A soft chuckle radiated through the phone. "Tsk! Tsk! Yer temper sure hasna changed any."

"Cameron? Will ye help me or no'?"

"Cara, ye know I'll be there. We all will, but ye know a little background music helps figure out what our next dance moves will be, especially since we doona know what we're walking into."

Cara's hand tightened around the phone. He spoke the truth. Not to mention, Cameron knew her so well, by the end of their conversation, he'd deduct that she had already bonded to Jake.

She released a deep sigh. "Aimee's mother is dead. The girl lives with her father who is a detective on the police force."

"And…" he prompted.

"He hit me with his car, took me to his house where I met his daughter," she spit the words out without drawing a breath.

"Ah, ha, I see," Cameron chuckled. "Breathe, baby, breathe."

"Doona patronize me, Cameron. Ye see nothing so doona try to put more into it than necessary."

"Ye've bonded with him, havena ye?"

"No," she said in firm denial.

"Liar!" Cameron said in a loud growl. "I sensed yer urgency about the girl, but there was something else in yer voice and then ye started talking about him."

"So ye're a mind reader now?"

Cameron chortled. "No' by a long shot, but I do know ye. We'll be there as soon as we can. Hang on, Cookie."

"Thanks, Cameron, and stop calling me Cookie."

His laughter echoed in her ear as he hung up.

"I hope ye make it in time," she whispered into the now silent phone.

Chapter Eighteen

The room scorned her, mocking her with endless isolation. For the first time in decades, Cara belonged, or so she believed until Jake threw her out on her arse.

The emptiness left a gaping hole inside her, and a terrible sense of bitterness assailed her. With no control over her own fate, she might as well accept the facts. She was a woman who faced the harsh reality of being alone now and forever.

When Jake told her to leave, she had no choice but to return to the boarding house she'd first stayed at upon her arrival in Santa Monica. Her room remained vacant during her absence, although if she were to hazard a guess, most of the rooms in the flea ridden firetrap were unoccupied.

Ensnared like a wild animal in a cage, she paced the small confines of the room and waited for the sun to go down. Three steps took her across the room with three steps back. A tiny cubicle, the room reminded her of a prison cell with four walls the color of putrid oatmeal and a creaky russet colored floor.

The room itself stood empty except for a small limp bed where the springs pushed through the mattress, a mismatched bureau table, and an equally off-colored chair. This place wouldn't be considered a five-star hotel. By her estimation, it wouldn't qualify as much of a mud hole.

The sun would set in less than an hour.

She gazed around the dingy room. On the opposite side of the front door, another door led to the bathroom. The door proved to be more of a hindrance then an avenue of privacy. A thick coat of paint jammed up the frame and made it impossible to open at times.

As one of the two rooms occupying the top floor of the three-story building, the view from her window was impressive at night. The city lights brightened the skyline for miles.

If only she could enjoy the sights during the day. Since the window faced westward, she had to cover the glass with a thick black blanket to keep the sunlight out. The other day, overcast skies allowed her the slight freedom of peeking outside during the day, a sight she hadn't been able to appreciate in more than seven hundred years.

Cara wandered to the bed and sat. The springs squeaked beneath her weight. Blowing out a quick breath, she lay down, shoved an arm over her eyes, and settled down for a quick doze.

A loud siren pulled her from the dream world where Jake and Aimee greeted her with open arms. Red lights flashed in her room. She blinked. Her heartbeat thudded against her breast.

How long has she been asleep?

She swiped a hand across her eyes and wiped away the residual traces of sleep.

What the bloody hell was that noise?

She jumped to her feet and rushed to the window.

On the street below, blue and red lights of fire engines and police cars illuminated the area. The wailing echo of sirens blared a warning. A man, dressed in a neon orange vest, stood in the center of the road and detoured traffic with a bright flashlight.

The smell of burning timbers rose up around her. The acrid smell burned her nose and throat until she gagged. She swung around to the door. Her heart skipped a beat. A faint grayish mist seeped into the room from the fissure beneath the door.

And then she heard it…a loud crackling as if someone crumpled paper in their hands. She spun back to the window, praying that the adjacent building was on fire, but the bright reddish-yellow glow that flared up from below did not come from next door. Instead, the blaze radiated from the floors below her.

She hurried across the room where she whipped the door open and gasped at the smoke choking the hallway. It rolled into the room, burned her lungs and stole her breath.

She slammed the door shut to obstruct the smoke's progress into the room. She rushed to the window and glanced at the street.

Water shot from the fire truck hoses, aimed at the floors below her. There was no way down. The fire escape, just like the rest of the building, wouldn't hold the weight of a mouse, let alone a human.

Rescue workers hung yellow ribbon blocking the crowd from entering the danger zone. The people's eyes fixed on the building, their mouths open in a stunned "O", their faces masks of concern.

She could jump and risk an injury that would heal in a few hours. But then, how would she explain that to those on the streets. Injury was always a risk, especially in her fight against evil, and even now, she would risk it just to live. To hell with the Tuatha De Danann and that bitch Vampryss.

Her hands gripped the bottom of the window seal and she prepared to jerk it upward.

She hesitated, thought of Jake then shook her head. She couldn't do this. The bond that sealed their fate was more than spiritual, and she feared he would he would suffer the consequences of her actions…whatever they may be.

So, she decided to do it the old fashioned way, and rushed to the bathroom door. She gripped the handle, twisted and gave the door a sharp yank. It didn't budge.

She yanked again.

Still nothing happened.

"Damn it," she cursed and kicked at the wooden door. "Ouch," she shouted as a stab of pain shot through her big toe. The door rattled on its hinges, but didn't open.

"Ye piece of crap," she shouted. "Open."

Once again, she yanked, pulled and tugged on the handle, hoping for any sign of movement. Her eyes burned from the smoke that filled the room, and tears of frustration spilled down her cheeks.

Just as she was about to give up, the door whipped open. Unprepared for the abrupt release, she lost her grip on the handle and shot backwards where she sprawled across the bed. She grimaced when a spring penetrated her thigh.

Not wasting any time, she jumped to her feet and raced into the bathroom where she grabbed a bath towel from the hanger. She tossed it into the bathtub and flicked on the tap. Once the liquid soaked through the cloth, she wrapped it over the top of her head and returned to the front door.

Cara braced herself for the blaze of heat on the other side. Drawing in three agonizing breaths, she held the last one, and then threw open the door.

She shuddered as it slammed against the outer wall with a loud crash. She hurled herself toward the stairs. Heat fanned up the stairwell. The ancient wood panels crackled and shifted against the intense inferno that consumed them.

Cara stumbled down the first flight of stairs. Flames licked their way along the walls. Above the sound of the hissing fire, a faint cry resonated from the room across the hall. She glanced at her exit and then back to the door. Perhaps it was just the steam from the pipes escaping.

She covered her mouth with the towel and took a deep breath punctuated with several uneven gasps. The heat of the fire had long since dried the moisture in her towel.

She needed to get out of here. There wasn't much time before the timbers that supported the building structure collapsed.

And then she heard the sound again...faint but audible. She swallowed, lifted her chin, determined not to let anyone die in this garbage dump. She staggered to the door and placed the flat of her palm against the wood. Cool to her touch, she twisted the knob and shoved the door open.

Her eyes squinted. She strained to see through the smoke filled room.

"Hello, is anyone here?"

"Over here. Please help me," a female voice choked.

Cara rushed in the direction of the cry. A petite

dark-haired teenager, barely a hundred pounds, huddled in the corner. Her cheeks smudged with sooty powder.

"Is anyone else here?" Cara asked in an anxious tone. The smoke tickled her voice box, and she coughed.

The girl shook her head. "It's only me. My mom ran to the store an hour ago. Please get me out of here."

Cara cringed at the panic-stricken expression on the girl's face. Her determination faltered, and she fought hard against her own tears of fright.

Instead, she clenched her jaw to kill the sob in her throat and spoke with quiet, but desperate, firmness.

"What's yer name, sweetheart?"

"Janie."

"Okay Janie, I'm going to get both of us out of here, but I need ye to listen to me carefully."

The petrified girl nodded.

"I know ye're scared. I am, too, but I'm going to have to carry ye down the steps. I need ye to be as still as a rock. Do ye understand?"

Again, the girl nodded.

"Good girl." Cara settled her hands beneath the girl's knees and around her shoulders, and then hoisted her up in her arms. "Why doona ye take the towel around my neck and cover yer face?"

Cara cradled the girl against her chest and headed for the doorway.

In the hallway, a spray of water doused the fire that spread up the stairwell and smothered the fire on the ceiling.

A moment later, a fireman appeared. The water sprayed a continuous stream behind him, protecting his back.

Cara stumbled forward and shoved Janie into the fireman's arms. "Take her out of here," she shouted then coughed when the acrid smoke filled her lungs. "I'm right behind ye."

The man turned on his heels and sprinted down the stairs. Cara followed close, but just as she rounded the final flight, a loud crack sounded on the wooden boards beneath her feet. She saw the astonishment on the fireman's face as the wood split and separated. He took the final steps two at a time until he reached the lobby floor.

At the first crack, the fireman with the hose backed out the front door before the building collapsed.

At the doorway, he spun around and glanced back at her, his face a mask of horror.

"Go!" she yelled, knowing there was nothing he could do for her.

"I'm sorry," he shouted back. His face pinched and he raced out the door. A slight explosion from the back of the building rumbled through the hallway like a mini-earthquake and slammed the door shut behind them.

An omen?

The stairs in front of her splintered and collapsed. She held onto the railing until that, too, gave way and she fell. Her stomach dropped as she fell twenty-feet to land in a heap on top of the pile of rubble that used to be the stairs. Flames licked at her legs and she brushed out the fire that scorched her clothing.

She crawled to her feet, scowling at the stab of pain that flared across her ankle. At least she was alive. She stumbled to the door, holding her breath.

The door refused to open. Cara's fingers fumbled

with the locking mechanism, struggled to turn it, only to discover it wasn't locked. Looking down, she saw the reason. A piece of wood from the ceiling jammed against the bottom of the doorframe.

Her lungs expanded and she gagged, choking on the smoke that scorched the back of her throat and entered her lungs. Coughing, she twisted at the handle again then jerked back.

It budged a little then stuck.

Panic besieged her. She tried to draw a tiny breath, but the fire fumes filled her lungs.

By the gods, she couldn't breathe.

Her strength waned, and her body grew weak until her legs betrayed her. No longer able to support her own weight, she collapsed on the floor overcome by the black smoke trapped in the room.

The fire closed in around her, reaching out to take her in its arms. The flames whispered to her and called her name. Her lungs filled once more with the bitter, stinging cloud of smoke, and her vision blurred.

As she slipped into the blackness around her, she imagined Braedan coming toward her, his hands extended.

She smiled, ecstatic to be going home.

He reached her side and pulled her into his arms.

"It isna yer time, love," he whispered. His breath ruffled the hair around her ear, sending shivers up her spine.

Disappointment stabbed through her and she swallowed the pain that swelled inside her.

And then, he wrapped his arms around her and picked her up in his strong embrace. He pressed his lips to her cheek.

"Be happy, love," he said in the deep, baritone voice she'd always loved. "And live."

In the next instant, her mind slipped away, and she was sheathed in blessed darkness.

Chapter Nineteen

By the gods! Someone was beating the crap out of her!

A steady rhythm of thumping assaulted her chest, pressing her back against a solid concrete wall. Then the pounding paused, replaced by a soft pliable object over her lips. A puff of air entered her lungs...then another. Her chest rose after each breath, and then the rapid succession of wallops started all over again.

She struggled to wake up. Her eyes fluttered and she drew a deep breath. The air entered her lungs, filled the smoke damaged organs, and filtered through the tissues to begin the healing process. Her body jerked. She choked and coughed, washing the poisonous gases from her lungs.

Cara opened her eyes, and looked into the kind blue eyes of a man with brown hair. Her eyes watered, but she caught sight of his blue paramedic uniform.

His brows flickered in concern and he watched her with a critical squint. After a moment, he smiled in relief.

She tried to sit up, but he pushed her back down. "Take it easy now. We're going to take you to the hospital and have you checked out."

Cara waved her hand in front of her. "I doona need a hospital. I'll be fine," she whispered in a hoarse voice.

She spoke the truth. Her lungs would heal, as well

as any other injury she might have sustained in the fire.

"Ma'am—"

Cara raised an eyebrow at the designation, observing the young man with tolerance. "The name's Cara, and I'm no' going to the hospital."

He gazed at her with a bland half smile. His brows creased with worry. "I would be derelict in my duties if I didn't advise you to seek medical treatment."

She bit her lips to stifle a grin, and then patted his arm. "Ye've advised. Am I correct in assuming I can deny treatment if I doona want it?"

He nodded. "That's your right, Cara, but you swallowed a lot of smoke in there."

Cara glanced over his shoulder at the boarding house. She cringed at the pile of smoldering wood and ash. *Damn! Now she'd have to find another place to live.*

Then another thought struck and her eyes shot back to his face.

"Janie? How's Janie?" she asked. Her words came out in a rush that at first, the man looked confused.

Then his eyes brightened in comprehension. "You're the lady who saved the girl?"

She shrugged and rolled her eyes. "Is she okay?"

He smiled in reassurance. "She'll be fine. She suffered some smoke inhalation, but *is on her way to the hospital* with her mother."

Cara ignored his stressed reference to the hospital. She didn't need the hospital. In fact, she felt better already.

She sat up, rubbed her eyes and pushed herself to her feet.

"Are you sure you don't want to go to the hospital?

It wouldn't look good of us to let our hero drop over now, would it?"

She giggled at the label and swiped her hands across her pants to brush off the residual soot and grime. With a deep sigh, she shook her head in defeat. The thick layer of grayish dust that coated her from head to toe seemed to be a permanent fixture for the moment.

"Honestly, I'm fine." She lifted her eyes as a man in a pair of black jeans and a white polo shirt made his way through the crowd toward her. The rich outlines of his shoulders strained against the fabric. Tall, attractive, this man had a beautifully proportioned body, but he wasn't Jake.

He appeared familiar, but Cara couldn't remember where or when she'd seen him before.

And then, something clicked a cord in her mind, a memory of the night on the beach when she deceived Jake into thinking she had no place to go. Jake had been speaking to this man the moment before he left the circle of emergency and police personnel to come for her.

The man stopped in front of her. He reached out, caught her hand in his, and gripped her in a tight clasp.

"I'm Detective Matt Russell. I've been assigned to investigate the fire." He waved his hands in front of him. "Just as a preliminary, can I ask you a couple of questions?"

"Sure, but I'm no' sure how much assistance I can be."

He grinned. "Anything you can tell me would be appreciated."

She shrugged. "I was asleep. If it werena for the

sirens, that place would have been my grave."

His eyes widened at her frankness. He tilted his brow, and looked at her in indecision. "I'm sure the firemen would have gotten you out before that happened." He glanced at the paramedic who packed up his equipment. "Isn't that right, Joe?"

Joe hesitated and shrugged matter-of-fact. "As a matter of fact, I'm not sure about that. From what I heard, Cara, here, carried a teenager out of the fire by herself. She passed her over to Gregg on the steps, but before she could get out, the stairs collapsed." He glanced at her, his brows drawn down into a frown. "No one knows how she managed to get out of the building. Gregg thought she was a goner."

Both sets of eyes locked onto her as if they expected her to divulge some secret trick to escape a fire when all seemed lost.

She shrugged and grimaced. "How am I supposed to know?" There was no way she would tell them about Braedan...no way in hell.

"Anyways, when they brought her to me, she was clinically dead. It was touch and go for a little while. I almost didn't bring her back."

Matt's gaze swept over her before he returned to her face where he studied her with a curious intensity. "Well, she seems to have suffered no ill effects from the episode."

Cara laughed to cover her annoyance. "Would ye mind no' talking about me as if I werena standing right here?"

Matt grinned like a boy with his hand caught in the money jar, and a slight pinkish flush crawled up his neck into his cheeks.

"Sorry," he said, his tone apologetic. "But I'm real glad you're okay." He smiled, and then winked.

To her annoyance, warmth filled her cheeks.

"Hey, Matt, where's Jake tonight? Taking the night off?" Joe asked as he bent over to pick up the equipment from the pavement. "He needs one. That man's been working non-stop for the past month," Joe commented over his shoulder while he shoved the gear into the back of the ambulance and slammed the door. He turned back, his eyes fixed on the detective.

Cara hesitated. Her stomach clenched into a tight ball. Jake? Was it possible? She held her breath and waited for Matt's response.

"Home with his little girl, I would imagine. I saw him at the precinct an hour ago. He got a call. She wasn't feeling well."

An icy fear twisted around her heart. Fearful images of Deidra and Aimee formed in her mind. Panic welled in her throat.

What was wrong with Aimee?

She forced her insides to settle down and imposed an iron control around her emotions.

"Are ye talking about Jake Bradshaw? And his daughter, Aimee?" Cara asked, trying to keep her tone as neutral as possible.

Matt spun around to face her. "Yeah, you know them?"

"Aye, we're old friends. Is Aimee okay?"

"I'm sure she fine. It was just a little stomach ache. Jake was going to go home and take care of her."

Cara released the breath she hadn't realized she held. "Oh, okay."

Matt glanced into her face. "Are you all right?"

Cara twisted the corner of her lip into a semblance of a half-smile. "Fine, except—" She looked at what remained of her building. "I'm not sure where I'm going to sleep tonight."

He laughed. "There's a shelter three blocks over on Twelfth Street. I'm sure they'll provide you with a room for the night."

With a slow twist, she turned and walked away. "Thank ye. I'll give it a shot."

Matt followed. "Hey, what's your name?"

"Cara O'Leary."

He jotted her name on his pad. "Thank you, Cara. I don't think I have any questions right now, but if I do, will I find you at the shelter?"

She spun around to face him. "I'm thinking that will be the place. At least until I can find an apartment," she said with a crooked smile.

Matt nodded. "Take care and good luck. I hope things work out for you."

She swiveled and turned her back to the two men.

"Me, too," she murmured, although her confidence waned.

****

Jake walked through the door a little past nine. He felt a little guilty about the lie he'd told his partner. Aimee wasn't really sick, but he used that as an excuse to get out of investigating the fire at the Merriness Boarding House. That firetrap should have burned down a long time ago. Matt could handle it without his help.

He dropped his keys on the table and walked through the living room into the kitchen where he flopped down at the table and settled his head in his hands.

"Mr. Bradshaw?"

Jake lifted his head at Mrs. Denton's questioning voice. She stood in the doorway, her eyes serene.

"Can I get you anything? Something to eat, perhaps?"

He shook his head. "No, thank you. I'm fine." He smiled. "What are you still doing up? Wasn't today bed day?"

She nodded and suppressed a chuckle. "It was a trying day." Her expression turned serious. "I got up to check on Aimee."

Jake stood, his heart jumped into his throat. "Is she okay?"

Mrs. Denton nodded in reassurance. "She's fine, sir, but she sure misses Ms. O'Leary."

Jake grimaced at the soft reminder and dropped back into the chair. "I know Mrs. Denton. I made her a promise that I would find Cara and bring her back, but…"

"You're afraid."

His brows shot up in surprise, momentarily speechless. He glanced at her and saw no recrimination in her expression, only a perception that ran deep.

"Why do you say that?" he asked in a sharp voice, sharper than he intended and he quickly apologized. "I'm sorry. It's just that I don't know what you mean."

Mrs. Denton shrugged. "Ms. O'Leary is a wonderful woman. She fits in here well, and she's good for you and Aimee."

"Yeah, well, she's not all she seems to be," he remarked under his breath.

Mrs. Denton sat in the chair opposite him. She

reached across the table and placed her wrinkled hands over his. She smiled. The creases around her eyes softened. "She's more than you can ever imagine, and you haven't begun to break the surface. But I know one thing, Mr. Bradshaw. You have to give her a chance for both you and your daughter."

Mrs. Denton patted his hand and stood.

At the door, she turned and smiled. "Mrs. Bradshaw loved you, and the two of you made that beautiful little girl sleeping in the other room. She wouldn't want you to give up on life because of her death. That wasn't your fault. She would want you to live, to be happy, and love again. Create a new life for you and your daughter."

And then she was gone, leaving Jake alone to think about her words.

****

By the time Jake went to bed, exhaustion overtook him. He slept and dreamt of an auburn-haired beauty with emerald-green eyes.

He sat on the edge of his bed. Cara stood before him, tall, proud, and so breathtakingly beautiful. His name whispered from her lips, husky and low, a promise and a breathless cry of pleasure at the same time.

He stretched out his hands intending to grip her around her waist and pull her on top of him, but she sidestepped his grasp, and knelt in front of him. His fingers tangled in the silken ginger ends of her long hair.

Her hands closed around first one of his boots. With a soft tug, she slipped it off his foot. The other boot followed, and then she removed his socks until only his skin lay beneath her caressing touch. Her fingers slipped beneath his pants and rubbed the calves of his legs.

Slowly, she worked her fingers back down to his ankles once more, prickling his skin lightly with her nails, smiling when his legs goose-bumped in response.

She rubbed her palms up the outside of his jeans, hesitated a moment to look into his eyes. The tip of her tongue slid from between full lips, teasing him. Her hands then moved up, sweeping past the hard evidence of his desire without touching him. He stifled a groan of protest.

She pushed him back on the bed and straddled his thighs. There was no hesitation when she reached his belt buckle. With quick movements, she undid the clasp and separated the leather straps. Her fingers unbuttoned the snap of his jeans, and then reached for the zipper. The echo of the zipper's teeth separating rang out in the room.

Jake's indrawn breath made a raged sound as Cara's fingers slid into the openings between his skin and briefs. His hips undulated beneath her, urging her hands to touch him. He shuddered heavily at the first touch of her fingertips on his hard, naked flesh. He closed his eyes and enjoyed the sensation of her hands around his hard member.

And then, his body chilled, as if she'd doused him in cold water.

His eyes opened. "Cara?"

Without looking away from him, she stepped into the darkness that lay beyond the shaft of moonlight that poured through the window.

"Cara," he called.

No response.

She reappeared. Her naked body shimmered against the pale light. His eyes traveled the length of her beauty. His body hardened painfully at the sight of the hardened tips of her breasts and the pale triangle at the apex of her thighs. His breath came in with a harsh sound and went out on a husky sigh.

"Come here, sweetheart," he murmured.

Suddenly, the twinkle in Cara's eyes disappeared and her expression stilled and grew serious.

"Jake!" A wintry blast of fear ran through him at the panicked tone of her voice. "Aimee! Go to Aimee! Now!" she said again, her voice more urgent this time.

Chapter Twenty

Aimee huddled under the covers and clutched Tillie Bear to her chest. A loud tapping noise boomed in her bedroom. No rhythm, no beat, just a dull, nonstop rap much like the sound of kids beating their pencils on the wooden desks at school. She cringed, hating the sound. Mitch Leroy liked to do that in Social Studies class just to make Mr. Abrams mad.

She pinched her eyes shut, and pulled the pillow over her head.

The banging continued for another few minutes before it slowed, then stopped. She breathed a sigh of relief, reached for the covers, and inched them down.

She stole a quick peek into the dark room. Black shadows moved in the corner, crossing the room toward her. She whimpered and yanked the blankets back over her head.

Monsters!

Her tummy jumped and her breath caught in her throat. She shivered, opened her mouth to shout for daddy, but her cry couldn't get past the tears that clogged up her throat.

And then, a slight pressure, a soft caress ran down the length of her back. She held herself stiff against the touch.

"It's going to be okay, child," a sand-paper voice whispered. Chills oozed like ice water down her back.

She couldn't move, paralyzed in fear. Her body, although stiff and leaden, trembled in a state of panic. A scream rose in her throat, only to escape as a tiny squeak.

She swallowed hard. Frightened tears slipped down her cheeks.

A freezing, slimy hand slipped beneath her body, followed by another. Her body rose from the mattress. She drew a deep breath on a sigh and gagged at the odor of rotten meat that burned her nose. She brought Tillie to her nose and pressed the stuffed animal into her face to block the unpleasant smell. Nausea swirled her stomach, and she wanted to throw up.

A strange, weightless sensation overpowered her as if she floated on a cloud. Dizziness swept over her. Her limbs weakened. She could barely think, let alone move.

What was wrong with her?

And then, as quick as the sensation hit, it passed.

Strange noises filtered through the air. At first, it started as a loud whoosh, followed by painful cries and soft whimpering sobs. The noise grew until she thought her eardrums would break.

Heartbreaking emotions reached out, wrapped around her, and suffocated her. She'd read about this in her mother's diary. The feelings probed the edges of her terrified mind, entered, and delved deep—searching, questing, and craving a power as it fed off her fears.

Blazing red and white lights flashed and spilled through the material of the blanket around her.

She cried out and tried to turn her mind way from the sights and sounds that assaulted her. Thoughts of Cara eased her, but only for a time as she hid within herself with memories of the woman who always saved her from the monsters in her dreams.

Where was she now?

Cara. Her mind called out in a small frightened voice. *Where are you? I need you. Please help me.*

In the next instant, Aimee realized something was wrong. She wasn't home anymore, and Cara wasn't going to rescue her this time.

The monster's arms tightened around her, and lowered her onto a hard, solid, cold object. She lay still, her eyes clamped tight. Tears spilled down her cheeks. Her shoulders convulsed with sobs.

She wanted daddy.

****

Jake tossed from side to side. His body burned with desire for Cara. The images in his dreams were so vivid, her touch so real, and then she disappeared a moment before her voice pierced his eardrums.

"Jake!" she shouted in panicked urgency. "Aimee…Go to Aimee…Now!"

Just as her warning faded, Jake jerked upward, his eyes wide. His heart thudded against his breastbone in a panicked state of undefined horror.

He glanced out the window on the opposite side of the room. The moon's light filtered through the curtains…still dark outside. He ran a hand over his eyes.

"Jake!" Cara's voice echoed again in a tone more insistent than before.

It was just a dream…just a dream, wasn't it?

"Go now!"

The vibrancy in her demand sent prickles of dread up and down his spine. The hairs on his arms stood at attention as if an electrical current had been exposed nearby.

He didn't know how, but this was no dream.

Jake whipped back the covers of the bed and jumped from bed. Instinct urged him forward.

Without hesitation, he rushed out the door and down the hall where he whipped Aimee's bedroom door open and ran inside. He came to an abrupt stop. His body stiffened in shock. His stomach churned with anxiety. Beads of sweat formed on his forehead, and he breathed in shallow quick breaths.

Her bed was empty, his daughter gone.

The curtains blew in from the window that had been shut when he'd gone to bed.

His gaze searched room. He ran across the room, whipped open her closet door, but Aimee wasn't inside. Spinning around, he raced through the house where he swung doors open in his frantic search for his daughter.

"Aimee! Aimee, where are you?" he shouted.

By the time he returned to Aimee's room, his voice had grown hoarse. He dropped onto Aimee's empty bed and ran his fingers through his hair. Tears spilled from behind his eyelids and a lumped formed in this throat.

"Mr. Bradshaw, what on earth is wrong?" Mrs. Denton asked as she walked into the room. She gazed around the room, then back at him. Her brows dipped into a frown. "Where's Aimee?"

His mouth moved, but the words wouldn't escape. He ran his hands through his tousled hair, no longer able to avoid the undeniable and dreadful fact.

His daughter had been kidnapped.

Chapter Twenty-One

"We have the child, Your Majesty."

Deidra Sidhe smiled at the short, stubby, ashen-faced minion who bowed in front of her. With a slight tilt of his head, he nodded to the corner where a female held a bundle in her arms. She passed her a quick glance before her attention returned back to the man in front of her.

She shook her head. Times sure have changed. Back in the days of the Camarilla, her male followers were all broad muscled men. The pale color of their skin accentuated their beauty. She didn't know what happened to her race over the past thousand years, nor was she ever likely to discover the one guilty of tainting her line.

She brushed a hand in front of her and waved him away. He hunched over, sure to keep his head low and backed away. At the door, he stood and rushed out of sight.

Deidra dropped onto her chair and closed her eyes, savoring this monumental victory. Two days ago, she learned the whereabouts of the magical child, but feared the woman guardian would hinder her plan to sneak in and capture the girl. That one always seemed to show up when Deidra was in arms reach of her prey.

So, patience and a well-thought out plan had been needed. By her orders, her followers searched for the guardian. They were ordered to trail the guardian, but not confront her. When they discovered her location, they were to report that information to her.

And *Ághmach be honored*, they did exactly as directed and provided her with the exact location of the guardian...a run-down boarding house on the east end of town. Armed with this knowledge, she wandered along the beach until she found a recluse asleep under the pier.

She used her mind and commanded him to set the building on fire, which he did without argument.

Deidra snickered. These humans were pathetic creatures and so easy to control.

Her intentions to detain the guardian had worked. Her minions snuck into the girl's unprotected home and stole her.

Her strategy worked far better than imagined.

While her human set the blaze, she strolled along the pier. What was it they called that...ah yes, she had an alibi. As she passed by one of the shops, her eyes had been drawn to a square picture box in one of the window shops. An image of the towering inferno flashed across the screen.

No one could have escaped that fire, not even a guardian.

"One down, three to go." She giggled. "I wonder how the gods like their precious guardians now."

She returned to the present and glared at the minions who'd slunk into the corners. "Make sure the child is placed in with the medium. Tell Elena to keep her calm. A child who's scared to death is of no use to me. We have nine days until solstice."

****

"Calm down, Jake!"

Jake took a deep breath. He clenched his hands at his sides and suppressed the urge to strangle Matt. It was so easy for him to sit there and tell him to calm down, but it wasn't his daughter. Matt had no idea what he was going through…the anguish, the guilt, and the anger. He'd failed Aimee.

A barrage of police trekked through his house. Every once in a while he caught the subtle looks of sympathy from the officers. They dusted for fingerprints and looked for any clues that might lead them to the person responsible for his daughter's disappearance. His gut told him they would come up empty.

He jumped up from the sofa and waved his hand toward the window in agitation. "Matt, my little girl is out there somewhere. I've got to find her. I promised Lisa—" His voice broke, and he swallowed hard.

Matt placed a hand on his shoulder. "We will find her, Jake. I promise."

"Detective Bradshaw?"

Jake spun around to the lieutenant who walked into the room. "Did you find anything?" he asked.

The other man shook his head. "I'm sorry, sir."

The pain from those words seared through him, and he nodded. "Thank you."

"We're done inside for now. It's pretty dark outside, so we'll have to come back tomorrow and check the grounds."

Jake nodded again. The lieutenant passed a quick glance toward Matt and backed from the room.

In less than ten minutes, the police officers had vacated the premises. Jake dropped back to the couch and released a frustrated breath. His eyes filled with tears.

Matt sat in the chair opposite him. "Jake, I'm sorry you have to go through this, but we will find her and put the people who took her away for a very long time." He hesitated. "Look, I know it won't be easy, but you really should get some rest."

Jake snorted. "Rest? How do you expect me to sleep when Aimee is out there with no one to protect her?"

Matt stood and slapped him on the shoulder. "Jake, there's nothing you can do tonight," he insisted. He walked toward the door. "I'll give you a call tomorrow."

Jake glanced toward the wall clock, and then over his shoulder at Matt, his mouth twisted into a grimace. "It is tomorrow."

"I know." Matt's lips curved into a cynical grin as he reached for the door handle. His hand hovered for a second before he spun around. "Hey, before I forget, I met a friend of yours tonight."

Jake really didn't care to talk about anything other than Aimee, but decided to humor his friend. "Oh yeah, and who was that?"

"A lady by the name of Cara," he said, pulling his notepad from the pocket of his jacket. He flipped it open and continued, "Cara O'Leary." He glanced up at Jake with a smile. "She's quite the looker, my friend, even though she was quite the mess."

At the mention of Cara's name, Jake's heart palpated in his chest and his nerves jumped. He shot to his feet. "Where did you see her?" he asked in an anxious voice.

Matt's eyebrows rose in surprise. "She was in that fire earlier tonight," he replied.

"What?" Jake shouted and strode toward Matt. "Is she okay? Was she hurt?"

"Whoa, slow down, man. She's fine. You remember Joe, the paramedic?" Matt asked. At Jake's nod, he continued, "He told me when they brought her out, she was gone. They were lucky to bring her back."

Jake's shoulders slumped in relief.

"That lady was the hero of the night. She rescued a teenager from the fire, handed her over to a fire fighter before the stairway collapsed beneath her. Honestly, they thought they'd be taking her to the morgue, but somehow she got out of that building."

Jake ran for the door, intent on heading out in search of Cara, certain that she would help him find Aimee. "Is she at the hospital? Where did they send her?" he asked and grabbed his jacket from the rack.

Matt shook his head. "She refused medical treatment. Told us she didn't need a doctor, mumbled something about being a quick healer."

Jake's shoulders slumped in dejection. He walked back into the living room, dropping his coat across the back of the chair. "Do you know where she went?"

Matt nodded. "The fire destroyed the building, and she had nowhere to go so I directed her to the city mission on Twelfth Street, but she headed off in the opposite direction." His eyes widened as if struck by another thought. "Funny, she seemed real concerned about you and Aimee. At the time, I told her you were both fine, but now—"

"What?"

Matt shook his head. "Nah, she wouldn't have had

the time…"

"Time for what? What are you talking about, Matt?" Jake's eyes widened and his body stiffened in shock. "Are you suggesting that Cara kidnapped Aimee?" he asked with deceptive calm.

Matt tilted his brow and looked at him, an uncertain glint in his eyes. "At first, perhaps, but I don't see how it would be possible."

"Cara wouldn't do that, Matt."

"How do you know for sure?"

"Because I know Cara." Jake brushed a hand across his face. "Keep me posted on the investigation, will ya?"

"I will."

And then the soft click of the door closing indicated that Matt had left. Jake collapsed on the couch and closed his eyes. His fingertips massaged his temples.

A soft *clunk* split the silence of the room. He opened his eyes. Mrs. Denton stood over him, her eyes haunted. The aroma of fresh brewed coffee filled the air.

"I thought you could use this," she murmured and pointed to the steaming coffee on the table. "Find Cara, Mr. Bradshaw. She's the only one who can bring Aimee home," she begged in a voice that trembled.

Jake's heart skipped. He opened his mouth, but snapped it shut at the realization she'd already left the room.

Aimee…Cara…

How the hell was he going to find them?

God help him.

Chapter Twenty-Two

Aimee gripped the edges of the blanket, pulled it around her, and let the darkness embrace her. Fear curled around her and tightened her chest, making it hard to breathe.

She sniffled. Her body tingled from the cold of the person's arms around her, an icy pressure that felt much like being surrounded by two blocks of ice.

She was freezing. Her mind recoiled in panic, drawing back, trying to hide in the shadows.

The last thing she remembered was saying good night to daddy on the telephone, and then Mrs. Denton reading her a bedtime story. She'd fallen asleep just as the prince put the shoe on Cinderella's foot.

The next thing she remembered was loud taps, followed by a raspy babble. She'd opened her eyes, and that was when she first saw the dark figures in the corner of her room.

Warm tears spilled down her cheeks.

The voices of both men and women echoed around her, but the sounds were muffled by the covering over her head.

And then, she was spun around in the person's arms, and she bounced along the path they took her.

Aimee wanted to scream, "*Where are you taking me?*" but the words remained trapped in her throat.

After a few moments, she stopped moving. A loud

creaking noise pierced her eardrums, and her insides jumped. Numbing horror hit her in waves.

A soft light filtered through the material over her head. Brilliant lights, in a spectrum of black and white colors, surrounded her. She cried out, and turned away, squeezing her eyelids shut.

She moved again. Within a few seconds, she lay on a rickety surface that wobbled beneath her weight. She whimpered, afraid to lower the blanket from her face.

The cold arms disappeared.

Aimee remained still and motionless. The footsteps faded, followed by the loud creaking noise again. She covered her ears with her hands.

Her clamped lips imprisoned a sob.

A soft scuffle, more footsteps, and this time, they drew closer. In a fit of panic, she shoved the blanket down and took a quick glance around the room.

An old woman shuffled across the room toward her. Before she reached the cot, Aimee sprung to her feet and bolted toward the door.

A hand settled on her shoulder, and she choked on a scream.

"It's okay, child," a gentle voice reassured. The hand moved from her shoulder, down her back, and caressed her in small circles. "I'm not going to hurt you."

Aimee stopped her frantic attempt of escape at the soft spoken tone. She drew a deep breath and turned to face the woman with gray hair, gentle eyes and a tender smile that held a lot of emotion—sorrow, regret, comfort.

The woman nodded in reassurance and knelt on her knees in front of her.

"Who are you?" Aimee asked, her voice strangled by tears.

"My name's Elena, honey. It looks like you and I are going to be roommates for a while."

"But I don't want to stay here. I want to go home and see my daddy."

Aimee yielded to compulsive sobs.

Elena pulled her into her arms and held her while she cried. "I wish I could take you home, child," Elena responded. "But I'm afraid I'm just as stuck as you."

"Why are we here?" Aimee asked, and then hiccupped.

****

Keeping her arms wrapped around the child's slight frame, Elena drew back to examine Aimee's tear-stained face. Her insides twisted at the petrified expression on her face. She'd come to terms with her fate, but it wasn't fair to this innocent little girl.

Elena didn't want to alarm the girl with the truth. The less she knew the better it would be…for both of them.

"I'm not certain why we're here, but I'm sure we'll find out soon enough." She smiled. "So, what's your name?"

Aimee's brows pinched in question. "I can't tell you."

Elena frowned. "Why not?"

Aimee's eyes widened. "You're a stranger. I'm not supposed to talk to strangers."

Elena laughed. "Yes, I am, and your parents would be proud of you for not responding so quickly." She winked. "I'm sure they wouldn't mind. After all, it looks like we'll be spending some time together."

The girl's lips puckered. "My mom's dead."

"I'm so sorry, child." Elena gave her another hug. "I wish I could bring her back for you, but I can be your friend, can't I?"

"I guess so. My name's Aimee."

Elena smiled in relief. Baby steps. "Hi Aimee." She led Aimee to the cot where they both sat. Elena grabbed the girl's blanket and tucked it in around her. A brown teddy bear fell out of the folds, and Aimee snatched it up, cuddling the stuffed animal under her chin.

"What a cute bear. Does he have a name?" she asked.

"It's a she, and her name is Tillie Bear," Aimee responded, squeezing the bear tighter. "My mother gave her to me when I was a baby."

"Your mom must have loved you very much."

She nodded. "My daddy told me that she didn't want to leave me. That it was an accident."

"Oh, honey, I'm sure your daddy is right."

"My daddy's always right." Aimee sniffled and swiped her hand across her nose. She glanced around the room. "Where are we?"

Elena followed her gaze and shrugged. "I haven't quite figured that out yet." She looked at Aimee's thick, fleece blanket. Thank God these creatures had the sense to bring it along. A child that age needed to keep warm. "I do know it gets cold in here, especially at night. I'm glad they brought your blanket with you."

Aimee held out the corner. "We can share."

Elena's heart melted at the offering. She snuggled beneath the blanket. Between the blanket and Aimee's warm body, the heat spread through her limbs and warmed the blood in her veins.

"Thank you," she breathed.

"You're welcome." Aimee tilted her neck. "Who are they, Elena?"

Elena grimaced. Perhaps, she should share a little bit of their situation, but not too much.

"They are very bad people," she said then hesitated. "Do you believe in magic?" At Aimee's indecisive look, Elena continued, "It's ok if you don't, Aimee." With one arm, she waved it in a circle. "This is what this is all about. You carry a magic inside you. They want to claim it."

"Is that why you're here, too?"

Elena nodded a bit surprised Aimee didn't deny her allegation. "I can speak to people not of this world. They're either dead or, as I have recently discovered, I can talk to those of another realm."

"What are they going to do with us?"

Elena pulled Aimee close in a tight embrace. Her chin rested on top of the girl's blonde curls. "I don't know, Aimee. Why don't you lie down, close your eyes, and try to get some rest? I'll be right here."

Aimee closed her eyes and leaned against Elena's breast. In less than ten minutes, her small body grew limp. Elena breathed a sigh of relief when her even, deep breathing echoed in the small room.

"You've done well!"

Elena glanced up. Deidra stood above her. Her hands rested on her hips.

"Go away!" Elena muttered.

Deidra's eyes narrowed at her tone. "You do not need to worry, I will not stay long. I wanted to check on the child." Her eyes moved over Aimee and she nodded. "I see you have already grown attached to her. It is good."

"Let her go," Elena begged. Aimee stirred, but she didn't wake up. "What good is she to you? She's only a child."

Deidra smiled. Elena cringed, hating the sight of her yellow pointed fangs.

"That is of no concern to you. Just keep her happy, Elena."

And with those parting words, Deidra disappeared into thin air.

Elena hated when she did that, too.

It gave her the creeps.

Chapter Twenty-Three

Three days, sixteen hours and twenty five minutes...

That's how much time had passed since Aimee vanished. And it had been twice that long since Cara walked out of his life.

Two days ago, he began his search after dark. Hadn't that been what Cara implied? That the evil Vampryss sought his daughter's powers, and she only came out night? Hunted during the twilight hours?

Now, with his daughter's life in jeopardy, how could he not accept Cara's claim?

Jake's hands gripped the steering wheel in an iron-clad grip. His knuckles whitened with the strain. The lights of Santa Monica Boulevard flashed bright, his visions blurred. The sleepless days and nights played havoc with his senses, but he refused to give up his search. He couldn't.

"Detective Bradshaw, come in." Dotty Campbell's high-pitched feminine voice radiated from the squawk.

Jake reached for the mike and pulled it to his lips. "Go ahead, Dot."

"A body's been discovered near Palisades Park. There's a squad on scene and four others en route. As of last report, officers have the suspect cornered."

When he started these excursions at night, he'd asked dispatch to keep him abreast of all activities that occurred after dark. So far, he'd responded to three domestic violence cases and a vagrant who peed on the front lawn of the Civic Center.

His pulse quickened as the word 'murder' replayed in his mind. He glanced at the nearest street sign and breathed a quick sigh. "I'm on my way, ETA less than five minutes," he responded.

He tossed the mike to the floor, stretched his arm over the passenger seat, grabbed the emergency vehicle LED light from the back seat, and set it on his lap. With his finger, he hit the window switch and waited for the window to roll down then slammed the beacon on the roof of the car. He pushed the switch on his dashboard and the red and blue flashing lights blared to life.

He raced through the streets, cursing the vehicles that didn't move from his path fast enough.

Blinking police lights identified the crime scene. He pulled along the curb. His eyes surveyed the area. A procession of lampposts lit the concrete sidewalk. A three-foot high stone fence bordered the walkway on the backside. Beyond that barrier lay a heavily wooded area swamped by tall oak and pine trees.

A halogen floodlight from one of the police cars cast light into the darkness as the militia of officers skirted over the barricade toward a dark shadow veiled in the trees. They circled the figure but maintained an equal distance between themselves and the suspect.

Jake jerked the automobile to a stop, slammed the gear shift into park, and leapt from the car. His hand instinctively reached inside the pocket of his jacket where he gripped the butt of his revolver and pulled it free.

On the street side of the wall, Jake hesitated. He

studied the suspect, troubled at the oddly primitive warning that sounded in his brain. Something wasn't right. A peculiar sensation sent chills spiraling up his spine. His heartbeat raced a rampant pace, and the harder he tried to ignore the truth, the more it persisted.

Their suspect was a woman.

He observed the woman's black gown in vivid detail, noting the distinct crease in the material that surrounded her breasts. Black dress, black shoes, and a black veil covered her head and face. She blended in with the darkness around her, and if it weren't for the moonlight, she would be difficult to see.

Jake squinted in an attempt to discern the woman's facial features, but she stood quiet with her head lowered, her chin tucked into her chest. Jake thought he saw a lock of black hair peeking from beneath the head wrapper, but it could have been the shadows.

His mind flooded with questions and his eyes widened. Was this the creature Cara spoke of? The evil Vampryss? Did this woman have his daughter?

The sergeant on the woman's left advanced toward her, his revolver held out in front of him. "Stand still, lady!" he ordered. "Don't try any funny stuff!"

The suspect remained docile and immobile.

"That's a good girl," the officer said as he reached for the suspect's right wrist.

And then all hell broke loose.

The woman straightened. Her cowl slipped back to reveal her face. Jake gaped in bewilderment at the ruby red lipstick that accentuated full lips. High, exotic cheekbones highlighted the woman's delicate bones. Her pale chalky, austere complexion contradicted her back attire.

And then her eyelashes rose to reveal two blazing red orbs, scarlet eyes imbued with a fiery intensity.

Bewildered, Jake's eyes widened. Red eyes! The woman had red eyes!

The suspect straightened, grabbed the sergeant's right arm and the front of his shirt. She lifted the thrashing body of the officer into the air, and raised him above her head.

Transfixed by the swiftness of the attack, the assembled officers shot back a few steps.

The figure in black twisted, pivoted, and slammed the hapless sergeant into a tree, driving the man's face into the tree trunk. Jake, from where he stood twenty feet away, heard the clear, crunch as the bones in his face splintered.

The woman whirled and with a vicious swipe backhanded a second officer, knocking the uniform to the ground.

A patrolwoman with a shotgun stepped forward and fired at point blank range. The suspect took the full brunt of the blast in the chest.

The woman's torso snapped to the right. She staggered back two steps, but, within seconds, she regained her balance and sprung at the officer. Her right forearm brushed the shotgun aside and her left hand clamped onto the officer's neck. With a swift jerk upward, she lifted her in the air. The police woman tried to strike the suspect with the shotgun.

The surrounding officers rushed forward.

The suspect avoided the patrolwoman's frantic efforts to kick her. Her left arm flicked back and forth, and the officer went limp. She tossed the policewoman aside with a disdainful sweep of her arm then faced the charging officers.

They froze in their tracks when the woman smiled and two long fangs protruded from her top lip. Their faces reflected their indecision as they glanced at each other for a brief instant before they turned to face the suspect.

Four of the officers raised their firearms and let loose with several rounds. The air filled will smoke and the thundering explosions of discharging weapons. They emptied the chambers and the firing ceased. The air filled with the sound of hollow clicks.

The suspect swayed for a moment, then hurtled toward the ring of police. They recoiled and ducked when she leapt over their heads. A pair of patrolmen jumped at the woman's feet, but she sent them sprawling to the ground with a deft, flashing kick of her feet.

And then she flew over the stonewall fence and landed on the sidewalk. The police officers followed and swarmed around her. In an attempt to pin her to the ground, they all rushed forward and jumped on top of her.

She flung them away.

Jake started toward the fight, sidestepping the bodies that flew in all directions around him. Uniformed bodies of the Santa Monica police department kicked, cursed and screamed at their attacker. Several clubbed the suspect with their weapons. All to no avail.

The object of the onslaught seemed to be immune to the rain of blows, and continued to move to the north. Her steely fists arced right and left. She downed officer after officer, crushing a nose, smashing a throat, or breaking a bone.

A burly patrolman pounced on the suspect's back. He looped his brawny arms around her neck. The figure reached her right hand over her shoulder, gripped the officer by the collar, and yanked the patrolman up and over her back. With a sickening thud, the officer's head came into contact with the pavement where he lay still and unmoving.

Jake stood less than six feet away from the woman, his revolver clutched in his right hand. He raised the weapon. A few other officers reared back, also waiting for a chance to fire, but the cluster of officers prevented any of them from getting a good shot. The suspect burst free of the horde. Only one officer blocked the woman's path to freedom. A shotgun raised, he rushed forward. He held the empty firearm by the barrel. With a mighty burst of energy, he swung the weapon like a club. The stock slammed into the suspect's face. The eerie figure's head snapped to the left and then bounced back. She brought both of her fists up and in, boxing the officer on the ears.

The patrolman's face caved inward. Nausea flared in Jake's stomach. As the officer toppled to the ground, the suspect took a step around the patrol cars.

Jake pushed himself out of his stupor and rushed forward.

"Freeze!" he shouted and aimed his weapon.

The suspect halted in midstride and glanced over her left shoulder.

Her red orbs bore into his eyes, and he released the safety on his revolver. "You are under arrest! Drop to your knees with your hands behind your head."

She smiled. Her tongue caressed the sharpened

points of her teeth. And then she did something that threw him off guard. She winked. "I recognize your scent. I have something you want, but will never see again," she murmured.

Jake's heart dropped. Aimee!

"Where is she?" he shouted.

"Come and find her, if you dare."

Anger flared through him at the challenge. Beside him, he heard a gun shell shoved into the barrel of a shotgun, and the rifle cocked. He spun around to stop the officer, but was too late.

The magnum rifle thundered and recoiled, and he knew the sharp shooter hit his target, knew the gun centered on the suspect's head.

Jake's glanced at the woman. The ebony figure reacted as if stung by a pesky mosquito. She swatted at her left ear as if she brushed aside an annoying, buzzing insect. Then she executed an extraordinary leap and vaulted onto the hood of the nearest patrol car.

She looked back once. Her flaming red eyes mocked them all.

In a daze, Jake's eyes followed her.

She swiveled and bounced to the far side of the patrol car and took off at a fantastic speed in the direction of the northwest corner of Promenade Place. Several officers raced after her.

Jake stared at the gun in his right hand, bewildered. What in God's name had happened? How was it possible that one woman could take on LAPD's finest, be shot at close range, be punched, kicked and bludgeoned, and still live to flee into the night? How could anything human sustain such punishment and live? He glanced up and surveyed the carnage, the littered bodies. Agonized groans filled the air. A few of the fallen were lying in pools of their own blood.

A blonde patrolwoman ran up to Jake. "Detective! We need ambulances! Can you get on the horn and call for help?"

Jake nodded and holstered his gun. He turned and hurried to the nearest car, wrenched the door open and slid inside. As he picked up the microphone and opened his mouth to speak, a strange chill erupted along the length of his spine. His hand dropped to his lap. He shivered and looked out through the windshield.

One of the downed officers thrashed and convulsed on the pavement. Jake licked his dry lips and struggled to compose this jumbled emotions.

He recalled Cara's words. *That thing will keep killing unless it's stopped.*

Oh God!

That monster had his daughter, and now more than ever, he needed Cara's help.

He swallowed hard and raised the microphone to his mouth.

Chapter Twenty-Four

Cara strolled along the ocean's edge sidestepping the water as it *whooshed* on shore. Her gaze swept around the area. To a stranger, she might appear the casual tourist enjoying a quiet midnight stroll. Only she knew the truth of what she sought.

Answers.

The three bloodsuckers she vanquished an hour ago provided her with none despite her painful interrogation. Their silence fired her determination, and she vowed to fight the despair that settled heavy on her shoulders.

Girding herself with resolve, she stiffened her shoulders. *They would not defeat her!*

Too much lay at risk.

"Cara!"

Her name floated like a whisper across the breeze and brought her to a standstill. She tilted her head and strained to listen above the swish of the water.

And then it came again. "Cara!"

She spun around and stared across the beach. Her heart skipped, and she drew a quick breath of astonishment.

Jake jumped two feet from the pier to the sand. He straightened. His eyes met hers across the distance.

As if he were afraid she'd disappear, he sprinted toward her, his gaze fixed on her.

She took a step toward him, but faltered. The memory of that night and his hostility washed over her.

What was he doing here?

Ten feet from her, he stopped. Uncertainty filled his expression. His eyes were sharp and assessing as they traveled over her.

"Are you okay?" he asked in a tone that held concern. His eyes searched her face. "Matt told me about the fire."

Cara nodded. "I'm fine."

He inclined his head in a deep gesture and cleared his throat. His chin dropped, and he spun around to face the water. His hands tucked into his pockets.

She swallowed hard and squared her shoulders. "Why are you here, Jake?"

When he didn't immediately answer, she walked over to him and placed her hand on his arm. "Jake?"

He glanced at her. Remorse filled his expression. "I'm sorry. I behaved badly."

Damn right he did, but so had she.

"I wilna disagree with ye on that, but I dinna give ye any reason to trust me," she said.

His mouth curved with tenderness. He faced her and opened his arms in invitation. "Let's not play the blame game. Come here."

Her vision clouded with tears, and, without hesitation, she stepped into his embrace.

His arms surrounded her. She buried her face into his shoulder and inhaled his masculine piney scent.

He pressed his lips to her forehead. "Thank god I found you." His whispered words brushed her hair.

She stiffened at the undertone of fear in his voice. Something wasn't right. She withdrew from his arms, retreated two steps, and looked into his baby blues.

"What's wrong?"

"Aimee—" he started then paused.

Her stomach twisted. "What's wrong with Aimee?" Nausea twisted her insides while she waited for his reply.

"She's gone." He ran a frazzled hand through his hair. "I should have checked on her when I got home from work, but I didn't. I was so exhausted and went to bed. You were there, in my dreams. I heard you. You told me to wake up, to go to her. When I got to her room, her bed was empty." His voice broke. "I don't know where to begin looking, but I believe Deidra has her." He swallowed. "You have got to help me find her."

Cara closed her eyes. A deep, stabbing pain sliced through her heart. Her throat tightened, and she bit her lip, turning away. He hadn't come looking for her because he missed her. He needed her to find Aimee.

She brushed aside the selfish feelings of hurt and disappointment. Aimee needed her, and she needed to focus on that.

"How long has she been gone?"

"Almost a week," he muttered, turning away. He ran a rugged hand through his hair. She sensed his anger and frustration. "Damn it, why didn't I check on her?"

Cara placed a comforting hand on his shoulder. "Ye canna blame yerself, Jake. It wasna yer fault. Deidra would have found a way to get to her."

"I sent you away. I thought I could protect her myself, but I couldn't. I let Aimee down and reneged on the promise I made to Lisa to keep her safe."

She grabbed his hand and gave him a reassuring squeeze. "We will find her."

"I've looked everywhere. Do you know—?" His voice broke. He kicked the sand at his feet.

Cara understood his unspoken question and shook her head. "No' yet."

His eyes filled with terror. "She told me that she had something I wanted. I didn't want to believe it was her." He shuddered. "She's the devil incarnate, evil, and she has my daughter." His voice choked.

Cara jerked in surprise. Her eyes widened. "Ye've seen Deidra?" At his nod, she grabbed his arm. "Where?" she demanded.

"Palisades Park. Two nights ago, she took out half the police force in less than ten minutes."

She stretched up her hand to caress his cheek. Her eyes moved over his face. "Are ye okay?"

Before he had the opportunity to answer the question, a deep, harsh voice emulated from behind them. "Would you look at what we have here?"

Cara tensed and spun around in a circle to face the group of five men who emerged from the shadows. The pasty white color of flesh on four of them designated them vampire while the stench of wet cat identified shifter among them.

She glanced at Jake. "Guess ye canna find any peace and quiet around here," she commented. Her eyes moved back to the group, landing on the shape shifter on the far left of the group. "What are ye doing with this bunch? Crossing the line?" she asked, keeping her voice light.

The shifters' eyes widened and his cheeks burned red as if angered.

In the next instant, Jake jumped in front of Cara, and tried to push her behind him. She loved his sense of honor, but stood her ground. "Jake, ye doona know how to handle these guys."

"Handle what, Cara, this bunch of hooligans?" Jake reached for his badge prepared to use scare tactics. His hand froze when one of the hooligans smiled, displaying a set of sharp pointed eye teeth. "What the hell are you?"

The largest vampire stepped forward and smiled. "Your worst nightmare." He glanced at Cara. His lips twisted in a grim smile. "I don't think Felix appreciates your insinuation."

Cara giggled. Her gaze flicked to the shifter. "My apologies, Felix. I dinna mean to wound yer sensitivities, but 'tis hard to understand how one of yer kind can desert his own just to hang out with vamps. Doesna say much for yer taste level."

Once again, Jake attempted to push her behind him.

"Please, Jake, stay out of this," she murmured under her breath. Her stomach dropped at the angry expressions on their faces.

Cara pulled two wooden stakes from her jacket pocket and rushed forward. Using a kick boxing maneuver she'd seen on the television, she leapt through the air, kicked up one foot, then the other while twisting her body in a circle. Each foot connected with the chin of a vampire. The impact sent them spiraling backward.

She landed on her feet, spun around, and tossed a stake at each one of the vampires, striking them in their hearts. Bodies exploded and shattered into a cloud of gray dust that sprinkled and blended with the sand.

From the corner of her eye, she saw Jake battle the shifter. A barrage of body blows sent the cat wobbling.

For the moment, Jake appeared to hold his own against the shifter so she turned to a vampire.

Kicking off the ground, one...two...three cartwheels brought her to stand in front of him. She yanked both hands up. With a flick of her wrists, two knives slid from pockets inside each sleeves. She sliced him across his throat. She didn't wait for him to disintegrate before she turned to face the last vampire.

Jake and the shape shifter continued their fight. She flipped over until she stood in front of the final vampire. His brows rose. She smiled. In the next instant, she kicked up her foot where a blade appeared from the black toed tip of her leather boot and sliced the vamp across the chest. Another twirl and she caught his neck.

Without waiting for the explosion, she turned to face Jake and the shifter who continued to swap blows. Both men breathed heavy.

Cara strolled up behind the shifter, tapped him on the shoulder. When he spun around to face her, Jake lurched forward to capture the shifter's arm which he yanked behind his back.

She smiled.

"'Tis over." She shook her head. "Ye really shouldna hang with vampires. They offer no protection whatsoever."

"What. Do. You. Want?" he gasped, each syllable sharp as he drew a breath.

"Where is Deidra?" she asked in a calm voice.

At the mention of the Vampryss' name, the shifter

snarled. "Go to hell!" His nose lengthened to form a large snout. She balled her hand into a fist and pummeled his face. The act stunted his transformation.

He growled and started his change again. First, his face, then his hands changed into furry paws with sharp claws. Cara grabbed him around the throat, and applied a bit of pressure to his windpipe. He fought against Jake's hold. His body twisted and jerked, but she maintained her grip.

"Where is she?" Cara snarled out the question. When he didn't respond, she pressed harder, stifling the shifter's air supply.

He coughed. "I don't know what you're talking about," he wheezed.

"Ye know exactly what I mean. Where's the bitch ye work for?"

The shape shifter choked on a laugh. "I'm looking at the only bitch I know."

Worthless. She wasn't going to get any information, at least not any valuable information, from the cat. Grabbing the knife from the sleeve of her jacket, she sliced the shifter's throat.

She released her hold, watched the animal's body drop, and transform back into his human body.

Stepping back, she raised her gaze to Jake.

"What the hell were those guys?" Jake asked, gasping for breath.

His deep voice simmered with barely controlled astonishment. The sudden vibrancy of his voice caught her off guard.

"Four of them were vampires and…" she inclined her head to the naked man on the sand. "that was a shape shifter. It's unusual that vampires and shifters hang together, but there's been more and more of these mini-clusters over the years."

"How did you learn to fight like that?"

"The Druids." She glanced at him. His blue eyes impaled her, a gleam of interest in their depth.

Heat stole into her cheeks, and, in a self-protective gesture, she folded her arms across her chest. She grimaced when a burning pain shot the length of her arm. Her gaze shot to her arm.

"Damn it," she cursed aloud.

The shifter managed to get in a good swipe before she killed him. A two-inch long gash marred her forearm.

At her garbled curse, he rushed forward, and grabbed her hand. He angled her arms to view her injury in the moonlight.

She winced.

"Hey! Watch it, will ye?" she cried.

"You're hurt," he announced in an anxious voice.

"No shit, Sherlock, and yanking it about like that doesna make it feel any better."

He pulled her across the beach. "We're going to the hospital to get you stitched up." Jake urged, his brows drawn in concern.

She dug her heels in and forced him to stop. "What is it with ye and hospitals? I am no' going to any hospital. I'll be fine."

"Debatable."

Chills coiled around her spine at the feminine voice that echoed behind her.

Cara pasted a twisted smile on her lips. She swung around and inclined her head toward the woman in black.

Chapter Twenty-Five

Deidra's eyes widened as if caught off guard by Cara's presence. Her lips twisted into an arrogant grin, and she nodded. "Nice to see you remember me."

Cara snorted, and then pressed her lips together in anger. "For now, but as soon as ye're gone, see how long it takes me to forget." She snapped her fingers. "Deidra who?"

Movement appeared in her peripheral vision.

Jake.

"Stay back, Jake," she muttered in a sharp voice.

He stiffened and came to an abrupt halt.

Deidra laughed, a short hoot that created a regime of goose bumps racing up Cara's back. "I thought you were dead, guardian."

Cara heard the disbelief in Deidra's voice.

"It looks like ye thought wrong," she said in a low, composed voice.

Deidra shot a heated look at the minions on her right. She scowled when they shrunk back into the shadows.

"Screwed ye over, did they?" Cara laughed at the tell-tale action then shrugged, shaking her head. "'Tis hard to find good help these days, isna it?"

"You were supposed to die in the fire."

Cara's eyebrows shot up, her mind filled with a bitter awareness. "So it was *ye* who set that building

222

afire?"

Deidra wrinkled her nose. "If it were me, we wouldn't be having this conversation."

Cara crossed her arms across her chest. "But ye had someone do yer dirty work?"

Deidra refused to answer, but the beginning of a smile tipped her lips. A faint light twinkled in the depths of her glowing eyes.

Maybe she hadn't done the deed herself, but she was the one responsible.

Cara waved her hand through the air and gave an inpatient shrug. "It doesna matter, but ye can answer one question for me." Deidra raised her brows. "Where is the girl?" she ground the question out between her teeth.

Deidra threw back her head and burst into laughter, a humorless sound that grated on Cara's nerves. It didn't last long for she turned hard and passionless eyes to Cara.

"Why don't you come and get her?" Deidra asked in a sharp voice that held a challenge.

Cara took a step forward. "Ye doubt I would?"

"You and this..." Deidra looked pointedly at Jake. Her lip curled in disgust. "human?" She spat out the last word as though it burned her tongue. "He couldn't stop me the other night. What makes you think he'll be able to help you now?"

"Leave him out of this. This is between us."

Deidra's eyes moved past Cara then jumped back to her face. "What? None of the others decided to join you? Doesn't that figure, eh?"

Cara quirked an eyebrow in question.

"It's so sad to be deserted, especially at a time

when you need them the most. Men. That's what they all do, you know? It's in their nature. You should shove them all in a ditch."

"Ye mean ditch them, doona ye?"

Deidra shrugged unconcerned. "Ditch them. Shove them in a ditch. Push them over a cliff. It makes no difference. They're all the same."

"Oh, is that what ye did? Shove or did ye push yer man over a cliff?" Cara smiled when Deidra's eyes flashed a fury red. "Och, did I touch a nerve there?"

"Wow, what's all this? Man bashing time. Would you like me to leave and let the two of you do your thing?" Jake's voice rang out behind Cara. She jumped, startled.

"That might be a good idea," Cara encouraged. She had been so involved in their verbal sparring she'd forgotten Jake was there.

Deidra's eyes moved over Jake. A gleam of interest appeared in her ruby eyes. "Oh no, please don't rush off on my account." Deidra passed a quick look over Cara. "Where are your manners, guardian? Didn't you tell him that we're old friends? We go way back."

"Ye're no friend of mine."

"I'm hurt." Deidra flung out her hands in an animated gesture of despair. "Are you going to introduce us at least? I didn't catch his name the other night, although I believe I have something he wants. I smelled her on him."

"Ye won't be around long enough, so why bother with the introductions?"

"Cara, this isn't the time for a cat fight," Jake muttered.

"I am not one of those mangy creatures." Deidra

glared at Jake with eyes that took on a luminous crimson glow.

Jake turned his attention to Deidra. "Where's my daughter?"

"Jake, shut up!" Cara said in a frantic whisper.

"Daughter?" An appreciative smile graced Deidra's face. "Ah, now I'm beginning to understand." She turned to Cara, a black brow rose in curiosity. "Your sympathy for these pathetic humans is touching, howbeit a bit misplaced."

"She is only a child. Let her go."

"I think not. I am not done with her." Deidra shrugged. "Enough of this talking small."

Cara laughed at Deidra's misuse of modern slang which merely succeeded in pissing the witch off more. The Vampryss took a step forward. A growl rumbled deep in her throat.

Suddenly, she stopped. Her eyes widened, and then dilated as if focused on something over their shoulders.

"It looks like we're just in time for the party."

"Nice! I like parties. The wife doona let me get out much." A second voice reaffirmed.

Cara didn't turn around. The deep tenors of Devlin McNeil and Cameron MacLean, both guardians, eased the tension from her shoulders, and a bubble of relief burst over her.

Without taking her eyes off Deidra, Cara tossed a comment over her shoulder. "It's about time ye guys showed up." Cara smiled at Deidra. "See, I wasn't deserted. What's yer excuse?"

Deidra's eyes flamed red, and her face turned a mask of rage. "You will never find the girl. She's mine," she said in a harsh, raw voice.

With those words, Deidra's image wavered, faded in and out until she dispersed into a faint reddish mist that drifted into the sky.

"Fraidy cat," Cameron commented with a chuckle.

"Careful, Scot, Starr wouldna like being compared to the likes of her," Devlin said.

Starr, a talking cat, otherwise known as a familiar belonged to Aiyanna MacLean, Cameron's wife.

"Hey, where the hell did she go?" Jake asked in a voice full of confusion.

Cara turned and patted him on the arm. "No' to worry. She does that. Ye'll get used to it."

"To what?"

"Hey, Cookie, did we scare the big bad bitch away?"

Cara turned to face the guardians who saved her hide. Devlin, Cameron and the third and final guardian, Fallon, stood side by side. It always amazed her that she was the only woman chosen by the gods to become a guardian. But truth be told, she considered herself lucky to have all three of them as her friends.

What caught her attention was the fact that they held hands. Fallon had the power to transport through space, but for him to do so, he needed direct contact. Holding hands was the most natural choice, but she had to admit, the sight of the three muscular built, hunky-looking men holding hands presented quite the hilarious picture. She coughed and sputtered until she could no longer control the laughter that gurgled up into her throat.

Confusion lit up their faces.

"What the hell is so funny, lass?" Devlin asked. His brows shot up in surprise.

She took a deep breath punctuated with several uneven gasps. It took a few moments before she could regain her composure enough to speak. "I knew ye guys liked each other, but never thought I'd see ye holding hands." She stared at Fallon and Cameron. "Do yer wives know?" she asked then giggled at the flush of pink coloring their cheeks.

In the middle, Fallon lifted his hands and released the others as though they had the plague. "Let go!"

Cara giggled.

"Cara, ye're such a jerk," Devlin commented, although she saw the twinkle in his eyes.

"Why, thank ye, Dev. 'Tis good to see ye, too."

Jake stepped forward. "Cara, where did that woman go? And where did these guys come from?"

"Jake, that isna a woman. It would benefit ye greatly to remember that."

"But—"

She nodded toward the three men. "Jake Bradshaw, I'd like ye to meet Devlin McNeil, Fallon O'Callaghan and Cameron MacLean."

The three men stepped forward to shake Jake's hand.

"Cara." A weak and tremulous whisper entered Cara's thoughts.

"Sh!" she whispered, waving her hand to silence the men. She stepped away from Jake's confused expressions.

Using only conscious thought, she spoke, hoping Aimee heard her. *"Aimee, where are ye?"*

Mindless of Jake and the others, she stepped away from the group.

"Leave her be," Devlin murmured.

227

"Aimee, where are ye?"

"I don't know," the child cried. *"Cara, when are you going to come and save me from the bad lady? It's dark here, and I'm scared."*

Cara's heart broke at the fear in Aimee's voice. *"As soon as I can, but I need to know where ye are."*

"I don't know." Aimee sobbed.

"Do ye have any clue where they might be holding ye?" Cara asked. Her tone remained composed, but her inner voice wanted to shout at Aimee to calm down. *"I know it is hard honey, but think. Have ye heard them speaking?"* she encouraged, keeping her pitch soft.

"They keep saying it'll be all over when the moon is full. What's going to happen then?"

"I doona know, honey, but I promise I'll be there before anything happens to ye."

A jolt of electricity coursed through her body. The spark began at the tip of her toes and raged through her body where it ended at her scalp. The force of the bolt was enough to send her body hurling backwards.

Strong arms caught her before she hit the sand. She glanced up into Cameron's smiling face.

He set her on her feet, but kept an arm around her waist until she regained her footing.

"What would Anya think if she were to find out that ye're throwing yerself into my arms? Tsk! Tsk!"

Cara shook her head. "She can have yer arse. I doona want ye," she mumbled.

Devlin stepped forward. "What did ye hear, Cara?" he asked in a calm voice. His gaze remained steady and fixed on her face.

"What the hell just happened?" Jake asked, rushing over to Cara. She glanced at him sideways. Concern laced his features.

Taking a deep, unsteady breath, she stepped back. "Deidra dinna like my intrusion into her space and sent me on my way, but I'm okay," Cara patted Jake's arm in reassurance. She turned to Devlin and explained. "The girl I told Cameron about. Well, she's in trouble, but somehow, she was able to connect with me on the spiritual plane."

"Are you talking about Aimee?" Jake asked.

"What did she say?" Devlin demanded, ignoring Jake's question.

"She's someplace dark, and she's scared, but she's okay for now. Devlin, what can Deidra do on a full moon that requires a young girl?"

"What powers does she have?"

"She's a descendent from the Druids, clairvoyant with a powerful magic mixed in."

"Stop it!" Jake's tone rose to a bellow which halted the guardians' conversation. "Would you stop talking about my daughter and tell me what the hell is going on?"

At Jake's frantic tirade, Cara whirled around. She stopped, near to bursting with stunned realization. Her eyes studied his face.

"It's ye," she blurted in a voice she didn't recognize as her own.

He frowned and jerked back a step. His gaze swiveled around the group before landing on her.

"What are you talking about?" he asked, his tone hesitant.

"I've been trying to stay in touch with Aimee by connecting our psyches." Her gaze shot to Devlin then returned to Jake. "Even after I left yer house, I tried, but

I havena heard so much as a peep from her. I started to believe that Aimee's powers lay dormant, and that was the reason I couldna link up with her. I doona believe that's the case."

"What are ye thinking, Cara?" Devlin asked.

"It's Jake." She turned to the group. "Doona ye see. Aimee's powers *are* dormant. It's the father-daughter bond, Jake and Aimee's blood ties, and his presence here, right now that allowed me to hear her."

"Cara?" Cara heard the question in the way Jake said her name and turned to face him.

"Aimee inherited a powerful magic from her mother, but that's not the only power she's received." She placed her hand on his chest; felt his heart beat beneath her palm. "And that magic, she's received from ye," she whispered.

Jake's jaws clenched and a muscle ticked in his neck. "I don't have any power."

She smiled. "For Aimee to carry such a powerful inner light, she had to have inherited her magic from both of her parents." Her brows drew together in a deep frown as another thought hit her. "Is there something ye're no' telling us, Jake?"

Suddenly, Jake stilled, and his face paled. He hunched over, his arms resting on his thighs.

Cara knelt beside him. "Jake? Are ye okay? What is it?"

He straightened, sighed loudly, and shook his head. "I don't know what you're talking about, Cara. Yes, I knew Lisa could do things no one else could, but I've never—" He stopped. His eyes traveled the circle as if gauging their reactions.

"Perhaps ye are unaware of yer abilities, but I have

no doubt ye possess them. That is how I was able to communicate with yer daughter. And now that Deidra knows I can do that, she'll try to stop me." Cara turned to Devlin. "Dev, when is the next full moon?"

He rubbed his chin, looking thoughtful. "Six days."

Cara nodded. "Then we have six days to find Aimee, and we better hurry. If Deidra discovers that Aimee's power is only at its strongest when she's with her father, there's no' telling what she'll do."

Chapter Twenty-Six

After the incident on the pier, Jake invited them back to his house. All were welcome to stay as long as it took to return his daughter home where she belonged and vanquish the evil Vampryss from this world...preferably in that order.

"Wow, what a place," Fallon commented. His eyes widened as he glanced around the living room.

"Thanks," Jake replied. He tossed the keys on the table and faced the group. "Please make yourselves at home. There's plenty of food in the fridge. Help yourself."

"Hot damn," Cameron and Fallon shouted at the same and headed in the direction Jake pointed.

Cara groaned. "You probably shouldna have offered yer food to those two. They'll clean out yer entire kitchen."

Jake shrugged. "No matter."

Devlin stepped forward. "I want to thank ye for extending yer hospitalities to us."

"I just want my daughter back."

A loud crash followed by an even louder curse echoed from the kitchen. Devlin scowled. "I best go check on the two gluttons afore they trash yer place."

Devlin left the room, leaving Cara and Jake alone. His eyes caressed her, trailing up and down her body. A flash of heat flared into her cheeks at his perusal.

"Can I talk to you privately?"

Her gaze swiveled around the room. "Shoot."

He shook his head. "Not here." With an incline of his head, he nodded in the direction of his bedroom.

"Sure," she said and followed him as he led the way.

As they walked down the hallway, Mrs. Denton emerged from her room. She rubbed her sleepy eyes. She saw Cara and her face brightened with a smile. "Thank God."

Cara wrapped her arms around the elder. "We will find her," she whispered in her ear.

Cara pulled away and glanced into Mrs. Denton's teary eyes.

"Mrs. Denton," Jake addressed the woman.

"Yes, sir," she said as she glanced at him.

"There are three gentlemen in the kitchen," Jake said. "They'll be our guests for a while. They're welcome to anything they want."

Mrs. Denton nodded. "I'll go see to their needs." She passed a quick glance to Cara, spun on her heels, and headed down the hall.

Jake twisted the knob to his room and stepped aside to allow Cara to enter first.

Once inside the room, he closed the door with a soft click. "Now will you tell me who those guys are and how they suddenly appeared on the pier?"

Cara stared at him, startled by his rugged appearance. Dark circles colored the flesh under his eyes, a sign that he hadn't slept in days, and a shadow of facial stubble darkened his face. But the pain in his eyes yanked her heart strings.

She sat down on the side of the bed and closed her

eyes, uncertain how this conversation would start let alone how it would end. Her pulse pounded a furious beat and she could barely catch a decent breath, but somehow she managed to say, "They're friends, Jake, very good friends. And aye, they're also guardians."

He walked to the window where he pushed the curtains aside and stared at the sun as it rose in the east. "Are they like you? Do they have powers? Strengths like you?" He glanced over his shoulder. "Are they stuck in the house until the sun goes down?"

Cara rose and moved to his side. Staying off to the side where the curtain blocked the sun's rays, she rested a hand on his arm. "Devlin is the only one who's like me. He canna move around in the sunlight, either."

"What makes the other two so special?"

"I'm no' certain. Cameron and Fallon changed when they fell in love."

"I don't understand. What's that got to do with anything?"

She drew a deep, unsteady breath, and stepped away.

He closed the curtains and turned. She felt his eyes follow her motions as she walked to the wingback chair in the corner. She fell into the chair and pulled her feet up beneath her. Only then did she look at him and shrug. "I doona know what one has to do with the other. I only know that they met their mates, bonded, and then fell in love."

"Bonded like you and I?" At her nod, he asked, "Then why can't you walk during the daytime?"

Cara shrugged. "Perhaps it's different for me because I'm a woman. I doona know. I only know that love changed them. They can walk outside during the day, eat real food, and make babies. In fact, Fallon and Lizzie just had a baby boy."

"But where did they come from?"

"Well, let me see. Fallon and Lizzie live in Michigan. Cameron and Aiyanna live in Virginia, but I'm no' sure where Devlin hangs his hat."

"Why are they here?"

"On the night I left yer house, I broke down and called Cameron for help." She giggled at the memory. "He laughed at me." At his raised eyebrow, she explained, "It takes a lot for me to seek their help, and they know that. I normally wilna ask. The guys like to tease me about my stubbornness." Realizing she rambled, she stopped and bit her lip.

"But how did they get here?" Jake asked. "One minute, we faced that woman alone, and the next, they were there. How?"

"One of Fallon's special abilities."

He held up his hands. "Maybe I don't want to know about that. Please tell me the truth. Can they help find Aimee?"

Cara looked him in the eyes. "I wouldna trust anyone else," she said, without blinking.

Jake nodded.

She swallowed hard and lowered her eyes. Her hands clenched in her lap.

His footsteps crossed the room, but she refused to look up at him. He placed his hands on her shoulders and gave her an affectionate squeeze. "I'm sorry."

His voice filled with tenderness. It didn't help. She took several deep breaths in an attempt to calm her racing pulse.

And then he pulled her into his arms and held her

tight. "I'm so sorry for everything, Cara." His whispered apology brushed her hair.

She released a sigh, leaned back a little so that she could look into his eyes. Warmth flared in their blue depths, as well as a plea for understanding.

By the gods, she did understand.

"I'm sorry, too, Jake. I should have told ye at the get-go what was going on, but I was afraid."

He frowned. "Afraid of what? Me? I would never hurt you."

She smiled. "I know that. I was terrified of the way ye would react. I spoke to Mrs. Denton. She told me about Lisa."

Anger flashed in his expression, and he gritted his teeth. "She had no right."

She turned her gaze to his chest and shook her head. "Doona be angry with her. She cares about ye and Aimee, and only thought to help." Her eyes came up to study his face. "Ye're verra lucky to have her. I hope ye know that."

He sighed. "I know," he said, drawing her back into his arms.

Cara pulled herself from his arms. "Jake, what happened at the beach?"

He frowned. "What do you mean?"

Her lips curved into a gentle smile. "When I mentioned that ye were my connection to Aimee, ye grew so still and paled. Did ye remember something?"

Jake sat on the edge of the bed and dropped his head in his hands.

Cara knelt on the floor in front of him. Her hands moved up and down the length of his forearms in a soft caress.

"We'll find her, Jake," she reassured.

He lowered his hands. Her heart skipped at the look of misery in his expression.

"I want to believe you, Cara. I do, but—" His words dropped off, his voice choked, and he swallowed.

Cara stood, moved to his side and sat.

"Jake, tell me about ye and yer life."

He frowned, staring at her in confusion. "Why? This is about finding my daughter, not about me."

Cara shook her head. "Ye're more involved in all of this than ye realize." She smiled. "More than a father-daughter relationship exists between the two of ye. Maybe if we can figure out how that fits into all of this, it'll help us find Aimee."

Jake snorted. "I have no magical powers if that's what ye're thinking."

"We doona know that for certain, now do we?"

Intense disbelief flared in his eyes, and he jumped to his feet, his arms folded over his chest. "Oh, come off it, Cara. You cannot be serious."

She stood, walked over to him, and placed her hand on his arm. "Please, Jake. Trust me. Tell me about yer parents. Did ye notice anything different about them?"

He ran his hands through his hair. "I didn't have parents. At least none that I can remember," he said in a stilted tone.

"I'm so sorry, Jake," she murmured.

His mouth tightened. "Don't be. I got over it a long time ago."

Despite his words, it was apparent it was still a painful topic.

He held her gaze. His eyes narrowed. "Look, I

don't remember much of my childhood."

"Nothing?"

"What little I remember, I don't like to talk about."

"I know this is an emotional topic, but, please, talk to me." She pressed a soft kiss to his cheek, then leaned back to capture his eyes. "Where did ye grow up?"

"I was dropped on the front steps of the Orange County Orphanage when I was five." He shrugged. "No one wanted to claim me."

"I'm sorry, Jake," she said again.

"Don't pity me." He gritted the words out from between his teeth, and the look he gave her was cold and frightening. A sick feeling settled in her stomach. She couldn't blame him for being angry, but she needed him to come clean.

"All of that is what made ye who ye are today. I doona pity ye, but it looks as if ye're feeling sorry for yerself." Cara knew she was being harsh, but he needed a swift kick in his ass. She tensed when he cocked an eyebrow at her, a bitter grin on his lips.

"Even the sisters at the orphanage didn't want me there. They sidestepped around me, looking at me with disdain." He shook his head. "When I was eight, I heard Sister Angelique telling Father Joseph that I was the devil incarnate. He needed to send me away before I destroyed them all." He chuckled harshly. "Needless to say, I became a rebellious teen."

"There must have been a reason they believed ye were the devil incarnate. What happened? Try to remember, Jake. It could be important."

She swallowed the pain that swelled inside her at his vacant stare. It was as if he were suddenly assaulted by a barrage of memories he'd kept buried.

Suddenly, his eyes widened, and he turned to gape at her. "I don't—" his words broke off.

"Jake? What is it?"

"I was only five. I thought it was my imagination."

"What?"

"I could do things...move objects without touching them." He walked to the bed, flopped back down, and shook his head. He gazed at her with a bland half smile. "Blue lightning. I remember streaks flashing through my head, and then, the other night," he paused. "I thought it was a dream."

Everything became clearer.

"Don't ye see, Jake? Part of the power Aimee carries inside her, she inherited from ye. That combined with Lisa's magic makes your daughter a verra special lass."

"I was only five years old, for Christ's sake. It wasn't real." Doubt filled his eyes. "It wasn't real," he repeated, his voice troubled.

"Yer powers dinna go away, Jake. As a child, the treatment ye received at the orphanage was so traumatic that ye buried them deep inside ye. That's why ye told Aimee no' to show her powers, because of what they did to ye. Ye wanted to protect her."

"But I didn't remember..."

She sat beside him. "Subconsciously, ye remembered."

He wrapped his arms around her, and his eyes met studied her with a curious intensity.

"What happens now?" he asked in a hoarse whisper.

Cara caressed his cheek. "We have faith in our abilities to bring Aimee home."

Chapter Twenty-Seven

His chin dropped to rest on the top of her head while his hand stroked her back in a soft rhythmic motion. Her cheek rested against his broad chest. She closed her eye, drew a deep breath and savored his fresh, clean masculine scent.

By the gods, she'd missed him.

As if he read her thoughts, he pressed his lips to her cheek.

"I missed you," he murmured against her skin. Her skin tingled where his whispered words splayed across her skin. Goose bumps ran a path up and down the spine of her back.

And then his lips covered hers in a deep, devouring kiss that left them both breathless. His tongue slid between her lips and caressed the inside of her mouth. A low growl escaped from the back of his throat when she rubbed her tongue against his.

She had very few inhibitions when she was with him.

Without removing his lips from hers, he spun around and settled down on the edge of the bed where he pulled her between his legs. His eyes smoldered with fire when they met hers.

****

The harder Jake tried to ignore the truth of his past, the more it persisted, and a cold shiver spread over him.

His mind burned and his blood soared with the unbidden memories.

"Jake."

Cara's tone held a degree of warmth and concern. The sweet lilt of her voice wrapped around him and drew him from his reminiscence. His hands reached for the button of her top, and began the slow, sensual process of unfastening each one.

He would have to face the boy from his past, but there would be time for that later. Right now, he vowed to live in the moment and savor Cara's return to his arms.

He pressed his lips to the naked skin of her stomach. She tugged on the hair at the nape of his neck, and moaned deep in her throat.

His lips trailed a path up her belly and between her breasts as he rose from the bed. He stood to his full height and pressed his lips against hers. His hands rested on her shoulders and, with a quick downward swipe, he shoved the shirt off her shoulders. He made quick work with her bra and the remainder of her clothing. His breath trapped in his throat at her beauty.

When she reached for him, he sidestepped around her. "No, let me," he murmured in a husky tone.

In the space of a heartbeat, he stood before her naked. With a sensual smile, he lifted her into his arms and placed her in the center of the bed. He came down on top of her. His knees rested between her thighs, his weight braced on his elbows.

Her responses, the soft little purrs, nearly overpowered his desire to take it slow and easy. His hand explored the soft lines of her waist, her hips, sliding upward to cover her breast. Her nipples firmed under his touch.

She writhed beneath him, driving him frantic with need. He kissed her again, a long, hot, wet kiss that made passion pound through his heart, chest, and head.

He drew his mouth from hers. He slid down the length of her body. His lips caressed the fragrant valley between her breasts. She gasped. His hands stroked, caressed, and teased. When he couldn't wait another second, his lips covered her breast, and he suckled one nipple into his mouth. The rosy peak grew to pebbled hardness.

Her back arched against his mouth, and she reared off the mattress.

Jake's restraint slipped away, and he shook with uncontrollable need. His desire to taste her overwhelmed him. His hands stroked her flat stomach and he moved lower until he touched her inner thighs. His fingertips pressed into the soft skin of her thigh, and he gently eased her legs further apart. He leaned down and kissed around the soft triangle of curls that shielded her warmth from him.

She jerked. Her hands grasped his head. "Jake, doona do—"

"Yes," he murmured in a hoarse voice, pushing her hands away.

And then his mouth covered the heat of her womanhood. Her hips rose from the mattress. Her nails dug into his shoulder blades. Jake shifted and eased a finger inside her. His tongue rubbed the delicate nub hidden between the folds.

Cara's reaction damn near snapped his control.

She cried out his name. Tremors ravaged her body, and he spread her thighs wider in anticipation of his possession.

He rose and knelt between her legs. "You are so beautiful," he whispered in a husky demand. He covered her mouth with his, forcing her to lay still by holding the sides of her hips while he placed himself in position.

He hesitated at her threshold for only a second then eased inside her.

Jake ground his teeth against the incredible pleasure that exploded inside him, and drove forward with one powerful thrust. Her hips rose to meet him. He stopped and drew a deep breath. She was so hot and tight. He ached to slam into her again and again until he found release, but that would defeat his intention of making slow, sensual love to her.

He kissed her brow, then the bridge of her nose, and finally captured her mouth for a long, passionate kiss. His hand moved between their joined bodies and he stroked her core.

He started to move, slowly at first. Her moans of pleasure echoed in the room and urged him to pick up the pace. He thrust inside her, again and again. She lifted her hips to take more of him. Her nails dug into his butt as if demanding more.

He obliged.

Jake buried his face in the crook of her neck and clenched his teeth against the white-hot pleasure that consumed him. An unbearable pressure built inside his loins.

Cara gasped as she found her release. Her nails dug deeper into him and held him. Her muscles clenched and unclenched around him, igniting Jake's own release.

With a low groan he thrust forward, a kaleidoscope of colors filled his vision, and his body shuddered.

He collapsed against her with a groan of satisfaction. The scent of their lovemaking filled the air between them. Jake's heart hammered in his chest and he tightened his hold on her.

He hurtled back to earth as reality struck. He never wanted her to leave. He wanted her to stay with him, build a life, and, more importantly, love him.

She was a guardian, an immortal warrior, created by the gods to fight vampires.

How could he ask her to stay?

Chapter Twenty-Eight

Cara tucked the feathered pillow beneath her chin. An hour ago, she'd left Jake in the kitchen with the guys. She needed a little quiet time to reflect on her actions over the last couple of days.

Every night, she searched for any clue that might reveal Aimee's whereabouts, but every night, she came back empty-handed.

Why Aimee? What did the evil Vampryss have in store for the innocent child? Where were they? Would they get to them before Deidra had the opportunity to put her devious plan in action? And what was that?

Ceaseless, inward questions hammered at her and chilled her blood. She closed her eyes, hugged the pillow tighter, and forced herself to calm down.

"I will find ye, Aimee. I promise," she whispered to the empty room.

Just as she hit that pivotal point of sleep, Aimee's voice slammed against her subconscious.

"Cara!"

Cara's inside knotted at the panic in the child's tone. She kept her eyes closed, hoping to enhance their spiritual connection.

"Aimee, where are ye, lass?" she asked, using only her thoughts to communicate.

"I'm here, Cara."

And then, their connection solidified, and Aimee's

vision appeared on the inside of her eyelids. The blood pounded through Cara's veins in excitement, and she released a sigh of optimism.

Thank the gods.

The child stood in a room surrounded by concrete white walls. Her pajamas were torn, splattered with dirt and grime, her hair matted, but, otherwise, she seemed unharmed.

Cara resisted the urge to rush across the space that separated the two domains and grab the child in her arms.

"Aimee, are ye okay?" Cara asked, in an anxious tone.

"I want to come home." Her bottom lip extended into a pout. *"When are you going to be here?"*

Aiyanna's stomach knotted at the look of desperation in Aimee's eyes. *"I'm looking for ye, honey,"* she assured. *"But can ye tell me where they're holding ye?"*

"A cemetery."

Startled, Cara's eyes widened at the female voice. Her gaze shot to the poorly lit area above Aimee's head where the face of an elderly woman appeared. She stepped forward, and draped an arm across Aimee's shoulders.

"Who are ye?" Cara asked, keeping her voice neutral even as her insides swirled with caution.

Elena smiled at the girl and squeezed her shoulder in reassurance before she gazed at Cara.

"My name is Elena. Madame Elena," she said. *"You must be Cara."*

Cara nodded in response. *"I am. What are ye doing here?"*

Loud footsteps echoed in the hall outside the room. Elena glanced over her shoulder. When she looked back at Cara, apprehension lit up her eyes.

"She's coming. I can hear her," she whispered, in an uneasy voice.

A sense of urgency filled Cara. *"Madame Elena. Do ye know what she plans on doing with Aimee and ye?"*

Elena nodded. *"On the night of the full moon, Deidra plans to use Aimee's powers and bring Àghmach back from the underworld."*

Cara frowned. *"She canna do that unless she has someone to bridge the—"* she paused. Her gaze shot to Elena's face.

"I'm a medium."

An ominous sense of foreboding spilled through Cara. *"So she has spoken with him?"*

Elena nodded. *"Yes, she has. He is the one who told her about Aimee and her powers."* Her shoulders stiffened, and her tone changed. *"You must go. Leave now!"*

The door to the room burst open and created a ripple that flung Cara from that realm.

Cara gasped aloud and sat up straight. She kicked her legs over the edge of the bed.

"Oh, no!" she cried. She tossed the pillow on the floor and jumped to the floor.

Whipping the door open, she ran from the room and sprinted down the hall as fast as a racecar sped around the track. All eyes turned toward the doorway when she entered the kitchen.

Drawing a deep breath, she forced air into her lungs. Her gaze shot around the table.

Devlin must have recognized the panic in her expression. He jumped up and rushed to her side.

"Cara, what the hell is the matter with ye?"

"I…know…what's…going…to…happen." Each word a panicked gasp.

"Cara, slow down. What are ye talking about?" Devlin grabbed Cara's upper arm and led her to the table.

Jake, his brows creased in concern, held out a chair, and waited for her to sit. He then placed his hands on her shoulders as if to keep her shaky frame from slithering to the floor.

She gasped a few more times. Her gaze moved toward Devlin. "We have got to find them, Dev. They're running out of time."

"Cara!" he said, her tone stern. "Calm down. What do ye know?"

"I spoke to Aimee. She isna alone. Deidra has also taken a medium by the name of Madame Elena. She's holding them both until…"

Cara let her words fade away, but Devlin finished "…the night of the full moon."

Cara nodded. Her hands clenched.

"What happens then?" Jake asked.

"The *Ligint Saor* connotation."

Jake shook his head. "What is that?"

Cara looked up into Jake's face. "'Tis an ancient Gaelic spell that's been used to release an evil spirit from the restraint of their prisons."

"How does it work?"

"First they'll connect to Ághmach through the medium's gift of speaking with the souls of people no longer living. But that will only bring an apparition of his self to this plane, no' his body. Then Deidra will need to harness Aimee's energy and use that to draw him across the barrier that separates his world from ours."

Jake stuck his hands in his pockets, his face ashen. "How?" he choked out.

"Ághmach is a verra influential creature. He doesna need a body to draw it from her."

No one mentioned that neither Aimee nor Elena would survive such a feat. The words remained unspoken, but the reality existed. Only the guardians knew that no human could survive the intensity of that kind of magical shift.

They glanced at each other in muted silence for what seemed like an eternity.

And then the phone rang.

Jake cleared his throat. "That's me," he said, moving across the room. He grabbed his cell phone off the counter, glanced at the number, and flipped it open.

"Yeah," he muttered into the receiver.

Silence.

"You have got to be shitting me."

More silence.

"I'll be there as soon as I can," he said into the receiver. He turned to the group then snapped the phone shut. "I don't understand any of this. I thought that once this bitch had what she wanted, the killing would stop. Well, she has Aimee, and this Madame Elena. What else does she *fucking* want? When will it end?"

"It wilna end, Jake. At least, no' until Deidra has been taken from this world." At the confusion in his eyes, Cara continued, "Deidra needs to feed. She feeds off the blood of humans. It's what keeps her alive.

Jake snorted in disbelief. "Are you telling me that this woman is also a vampire?"

"She isna a woman in any sense of the world. Doona forget that." Fallon commented as he stepped forward to join in the conversation. "Deidra Sidhe is the creator of all things evil. She's dangerous and very deadly, but she needs human blood to survive."

"Well, last night, she ate supper at Mission Cemetery. A sixteen year old boy was ripped apart."

Cara jumped forward. "Wait a minute…" Looking at Jake, her eyes held his. "Ye said cemetery?" At his nod, Cara looked at Fallon, Cameron and Devlin. "Elena told me that they were being held in a cemetery."

Before the words had even left her mouth, Fallon and Cameron rushed forward. "It looks as if ye're going to have company on this one."

Jake nodded and headed out the door. The other two guardians followed behind.

"Jake," Cara called. When Jake stopped, she ran up to him and pressed a kiss to his cheek. "Be careful," she murmured in his ear.

When she stepped back, she saw Fallon and Cameron's wide grins. She pasted a scowl on her face. They scuffed their feet on the linoleum, and their eyes shot to the ceiling as though to say they didn't see a thing. And yet, the smiles remained plastered on their faces.

As she walked by, she nudged Cameron in the ribs, "Watch out for him," she whispered.

****

At the cemetery, Jake steered his car through the maze of police officers and rescue squad workers. As he stepped from the car, Matt hurried over to him. Fallon and Cameron left the car and walked to the other side of the crime scene.

Matt watched them for a brief moment before he focused his attention to Jake. "Who are those guys?"

"Friends," he commented then glanced toward the officers that milled around an area. He inclined his head toward them. "What do ye have?"

"Since when do you bring friends to a crime scene?" At Jake's raised eyebrows, Matt shrugged. "Steven Lynch, sixteen-years-old. He lived about three blocks from here. He and a friend, William Marton, cut through the cemetery on their way home from a party."

"But there was only one victim?"

Matt nodded. "Yeah, we caught a break on that one, although I'm not certain how much of one. William Marton survived. He ran home and called us, but he's in rough shape. His report makes no sense."

"What did he see?"

"That's the problem. He claims he saw a black shadow, shaped like a woman. She jumped out from behind that tree over there," he remarked, nodding toward a large oak. "She picked Lynch up with one hand around his neck and stuck her other hand clear through his chest."

"A woman? Was he sure about that?" Jake asked, but inside his stomach clenched. He already knew the answer. *Yeah, it would be a woman.* "It's probably the same woman that took out half the force at Palisades Park."

Matt's brows rose, and then he chuckled. "I heard about that bullshit. My take on that story was that someone was covering up a fuck-up."

Jake shook his head. "It wasn't a bullshit story. I was there, Matt, and *it* was a *woman*."

Matt's lips twisted. "It must have been a hell of a strong woman." He shrugged, doubtful. "I still say it was an ax."

It was obvious to Jake that Matt didn't believe him. Apparently, Matt hadn't read the reports. So be it. He slapped his partner across the shoulder. "Thanks, I'll go take a look around."

Jake started to walk away, but stopped when Matt placed his hand on his arm. He glanced at his friend's face.

"Hope you got a strong stomach," Matt said.

Chills spiraled up Jake's spine at the intensity in the other man's lowered voice. He tapped his stomach. "Cast iron. It has to be with the amount of shit I've been seeing lately."

Not waiting for a response, he spun away.

The closer he walked to the scene, the more his stomach churned upside down. He gagged. The kid lay on his back. His lifeless eyes stared toward the sky. His mouth was wide open as if he'd been screaming at the time of his death. Blood painted the headstones, trees and a large pool formed under Lynch's body.

The boy's neck bore deep gouges on both sides, and his throat looked like it might have been crushed. But the neck was nothing compared to the boy's stomach; his intestines had been ripped from his abdomen and scattered across the ground.

Jake stared at the mess in total disgust. When bile rose in his throat, he spun away from the sight. He searched the crowd for Fallon and Cameron only to discover they were nowhere in sight.

Where the hell did they run off to?

His cell phone rang. He reached inside his jacket pocket and pulled it out. Not recognizing the number on the caller id, he flipped it open, and put it to his ear. "Bradshaw."

"Hey, Jake, it's Fallon."

Jake started and glanced around the area. "Where are you guys?"

"We're scoping out the place. There are some really strong vibes out here, but nothing we can put our hands on."

"Aimee?"

"Jake, when ye're done with yer investigation, go home. We'll meet ye there."

"Hey look, man, if you know something about my daughter—"

"At this point, we've go' nothing," Fallon interrupted. "Ye do yer job, and let us do ours." The phone went dead in his hands. Jake slammed it shut and tucked it in his pocket.

"Damn it!" he muttered under his breath.

****

In the brilliant afternoon sunlight, Mission Cemetery, devoid of malignant gloom, expressed a pure and untouched cheerfulness, despite its purpose on earth. Fallon and Cameron walked through the gravestones. Twigs and dry grass crackled beneath their shoes.

When a squirrel chattered at Cameron from a nearby tree, he raised his head, pursed his lips, and prattled off a response.

He glanced at Fallon who looked at him as if he'd lost his mind. After a moment, his lips quirked and his dark eyebrows arched. "Ye know how to speak squirrel?"

Cameron chuckled. "What? Ye doona know how?"

"Ye're a jerk, man!" Fallon commented.

Cameron laughed. "So I've been told on many occasions. And I'm sure ye wilna be the last one to do so." Something sparkled from the dirt, catching his eyes. He knelt and scrutinized the mound. "Hey, Fallon, check this out."

Fallon stooped beside him. A shiny silver object emerged from the pile of dirt. He plucked it from the ground and held it up to the light. As he studied it, he pressed his tongue against his teeth and made a clucking sound.

Just as suddenly, he stopped, and turned to Cameron, his mouth tight and grim.

"What is it?" Cameron asked.

Fallon shrugged. "If I were to hazard a guess, I'd say it's a magic charm."

"What's it used for?"

Fallon twirled the object in his fingers and stood. "It's used by medians to contact the dead."

Cameron shook his head and stood, his gaze skimming over the object in Fallon's hand. "How would ye know that?"

Fallon's eyebrows raised a fraction of an inch in humorous surprise. "Do ye forget that my Lizzie is a spiritualist? She's learned the craft very well since the last time ye've seen her."

Cameron smiled.

Suddenly, a soft melody floated across the breeze. Both men dropped to their knees and hid behind a large, oak tree.

A young woman with blonde hair and a slender figure in jeans and a flannel shirt, strolled toward one of the mausoleums. She carried a large satchel under one arm. She glanced over her shoulder. The area must have looked clear to her for she disappeared through the door of the crypt.

Cameron lifted his nose in the air and drew a deep breath. Since he'd regained his human soul, his sense of smell beat out all others. "Roast beef, mashed potatoes, and...hmmm..." He sniffed again, turned to Fallon. "Corn."

Fallon chuckled. "Nice," he commented.

Both men stood and looked at each other with cocky grins. Vampires fed off blood, not foods such as those Cameron described. So, that meant they fed humans...most likely, a child and a medium.

Fallon held out his hand to Cameron. "What say ye? Shall we go share the news?"

Cameron looked at Fallon's hand then into his face where Fallon grinned like a Cheshire cat who'd eaten the proverbial canary.

"Aye, but ye best no' try any funny stuff." Cameron muttered under his breath, placing his hand on Fallon's arm instead of in his hand. "I'll knock ye on yer arse."

Fallon chuckled. "Home, James," he said as he twirled a finger through the air.

Fallon looked at him strangely, and then shook his head. "Ye've been watching too many damn movies."

****

"Are ye certain?"

Fallon frowned his frustration. "By the gods, Dev, ye're a pain in the arse. For the fiftieth time, aye, we're

255

certain."

"Dev, who would they be feeding if no' for Aimee and the medium?" Cameron asked. "Think about it."

"I am thinking about it, but we canna rule out the possibility that we could be walking into a trap." Devlin's gaze switched from one guardian to the other and back again. "And neither should either of ye."

Fallon grunted and slapped his hands against his thighs. "No one saw us, Dev, no' even the lady who delivered the food."

Cara took a step forward. Determination flowed through her veins. "When can we leave?"

"Doona be in such a hurry, Cara."

"The full moon is in two days' time, Dev. We canna sit here on our arses and let this opportunity pass."

"Colorful language ye have there, Cara."

Cara crossed her arms over her chest, giving him her best "*to hell with ye*" look. She tapped her foot. "And ye still havena answered my question? When do we leave?"

The corners of Devlin's lips twisted with exasperation. "Cara, what is wrong with ye?"

Cara bit down on her lower lip. Her annoyance increased when she realized her hands trembled, and she tucked them into her jeans.

"What's wrong with me?" Her voice rose. "What the *bloody hell* is wrong with ye?" Her eyes shot around the gathering. "All of ye? She is just a wee lass." Tears filled her eyes. "We canna leave her in the hands of that bitch."

Devlin gripped Cara's arms in his and gave her a soft shake. "Cara, we're no' going to leave the girl there, but we canna walk into the middle of Deidra's camp blind. We need to devise a plan."

Realizing the truth of his words, Cara drew several deep breaths and stared into the elder's eyes.

"Then what's the plan, boss-man?" she demanded.

Before Devlin could reply, the front door opened, and then slammed shut.

"Hey, where is everyone?" Jake's voice echoed through the house.

His thumping footsteps rang out, coming in their direction. An instant later, he stepped into the kitchen where he came to an abrupt stop. His gaze darted back and forth between Cara and Devlin.

"What the hell is going on here?"

Chapter Twenty-Nine

The handle twisted and the heavy metal door of the room swung open. Rusty hinges squealed in protest and echoed in the small area.

Aimee stood in the center of her room. She gripped the sides of her pajamas in trembling hands. Her knees shook and insides churned. She choked back a terrified sob and fought the urge to throw up.

Elena, hidden behind the door, nodded and passed her a reassuring smile. With her own shaky hands, the gypsy held a rotted piece of wood over her head.

A man, his hair streaked with gray strands, ducked beneath the doorframe and stepped across the threshold. Inside the room, he stood to his full height and stared at Aimee with black eyes.

"Where's the other one?" he grumbled.

In a blur, Elena rushed forward and brought the wood down on the man's head. The tip shattered. Splinters of kindling rained across the concrete floor. The man dropped to his knees and shook his head as if to clear the fragmented pieces of confusion from his thoughts.

"Run, child," Elena screamed.

Even though they contrived this plan hours ago, fear held Aimee immobile. She shook her head. "No, I can't leave you, Elena."

The man groaned and struggled to stand.

Elena's eyes widened when he wobbled on one foot. She swung the weapon hard and knocked the man over the head again. This time he fell to the concrete floor unconscious. Elena glanced at Aimee, her expression pleading. "Aimee, please, you have to leave. You can run faster than I can. I'll hold them back as long as I can." Elena winked then smiled, softening her voice. "I know you're scared honey, but you'll be okay. Find Cara and come back for me. You're the only chance we've got." She nodded toward the door. "Go!"

Aimee nodded, jumped over the man's feet, and rushed out the door. In the hallway, she glanced down the corridor to the right then looked left. Both were empty. At the end of the right hall, sunlight lit up the hall, signaling a way out of this cellar. She dashed toward it.

Outside, she scurried through rows of grayish black headstones, oak trees and drooping willows. The branches of the last tree bent and swung around in the breeze, forming shadows that wagged like the arms of an enormous octopus.

She scooted around the creepy giant, covered her mouth with a hand to muffle the sob that rose in her throat.

When the monster lay behind her, she slowed. She ducked behind a tree to catch her breath, while trying to figure out where she was.

She peeked around the tree. Although she'd zigzagged around trees and headstones, the building she escaped from sat in the distance, but still remained visible. Above the trees behind the concrete shack, gray smoke shot into the bright sky. Like a frightened animal, she glanced around. After a moment, she

259

breathed a brief sigh as she recognized the smoke stacks of the Crescent Street Factory. Daddy drove by that place a lot when they went to visit mommy at the cemetery.

"Find her!" Deidra's shout echoed through the trees.

Aimee fell to her knees. Her heart hammered in her chest and she gasped with fear. Vibrant red orbs glowed from the shadows inside the doorway of the nearby building. It had to be Deidra's whose eyes flashed that angry cherry color. Several men stood together in front of the doorway. They backed away from her high-screeched pitch.

She was surrounded by bad people. Her only option: run, hide, and pray Cara found her before they did.

She inched away from the tree and crawled along the ground. When she could no longer see the building or Deidra, she jumped to her feet. She ran around headstones, rose bushes, and tall trees until she saw an area thick with brush and tall weeds.

Oh yes, she could hide in there easy.

She crawled on her hands and knees into the dark. The darkness was as scary as the trees with their animated tentacles. A soft glow of light through the branches gave her hope that she would find someone to help her on the other side.

She cried out when sharp pain shot through her kneecap. She looked down. The ground was littered with small gravel and sharp stones. There was no way around them.

On the other side of the rock inundated area, tall grass mingled with prickle bushes to slow her down more. Aimee rose to her feet and tramped through the bushes. Her chest burned and felt as if it would burst, and she breathed in shallow, quick gasps. She took a quick glance through the tree limbs.

Two men rushed across the pebbled drive, coming her way.

She rounded a large oak tree, and skidded to a stop before a large mound of dirt. Breathing heavy, she scooted behind it. Her tummy hurt, and she dropped to the ground, hiding behind the pile. After gulping in a few deep breaths, she crawled to the top of the pile on her stomach, peeked over, and looked for the men who followed her.

They'd separated. One of them moved through the trees. He didn't run. He walked at a slow pace, across the grounds and into the high grass. His expression blank except for cold rage, and his hand slapped at the weeds in his path. The other one had moved beyond her vision.

Aimee slid down the bank and rushed back into the high brush. The further she traveled, the higher the weeds grew, topping well above her head.

Crunching grass and crackling brush sounded behind her.

Aimee's heartbeat quickened. Elena had been right. Her smaller size let her go places they couldn't, but those bad men weren't going to give up.

Fear knotted inside her.

Aimee clawed through the bushes and sidestepped trees. Thorns caught her pajamas and scraped across her skin. Her arms covered by a gooey liquid that spilled down her arms. Tears streamed down her cheeks at the stinging pain, but she bit her lip to keep from crying out.

Her actions became more desperate.

She glanced up and found herself surrounded by more trees. Less than five feet away, a light filtered between the branches. She weaved through the maze of trees, only to come to an abrupt stop at the hedge where she almost crashed into a chain-link fence.

Tilting her chin, her gaze followed the six-foot barrier to the top. It rose above her, and she released a defeated groan. There was no way she could reach the top and scoot over before they reached her.

From behind her came the harsh whispers of two men. They must have met up in the woods.

Aimee continued her frantic scramble along the barrier. Through the diamond-shaped openings, mounds of rubble, piles of refuse and rows of rusted cars, some flattened, and others not, created a skyline against the city background.

Behind her, Deidra's men cleaved a path through the bushes, and urged Aimee onward. She jogged beside the fence. Her fingers clutched the cold metal. She shook it, tested it, and looked for any defect in the inflexible obstacle. She whimpered when it held fast.

Then suddenly, the wire separated to reveal a three-foot split in the rusty cable. Her pulse jumped and heart thudded. It was just wide enough for her. She tucked Tillie into the top of her pajamas. Using both hands, she gripped each side and tugged, creating the perfect portal for her to slip through.

With a quick glance over her shoulder, Aimee yanked Tillie from her top, and clutched her under one arm. She ducked her head, and squeezed between the metal chains.

Her ankle twisted. She moaned, sprawling head-first on the hard, graveled drive. She grimaced when the pointed tips of the stone pierced her right palm. Tillie cushioned her left.

She sat up quick.

And then she heard the soft *swish* of grass moving and a *clink* as something sharp, perhaps a knife, brushed the length of the link fence.

She gasped, panting in terror. They were getting closer.

Aimee clambered to her feet. She glanced along the fence row. The bushes rustled ten feet down. They had not yet reached the break in the fence.

She spun around and scurried down a dirt pathway between tall mountains of metal scraps and rusted household appliances.

Aimee's gaze took in the creepy graveyard of busted up refrigerators, washing machines, and squashed cars. Despite the uncertainty of her course, she didn't slow.

A dark cloud streaked in front of the sun like black smoke, releasing a light rain that sprinkled down on her.

She gasped for breath and paused beside a pile of scrap metal. Bending over, she rested her hands on her knees and swallowed while she attempted to catch her breath.

Snap! She twirled around and stared at a group of trash cans near the front fender of the car. And then, one of the cans shifted. Aimee's eyes widened and she jumped.

After a moment, a large rat, about the size of a mountain lion she'd seen on TV, scrambled from between two cans. It scuttled along the border of the mountains and disappeared into the crevice between a stack of crushed metal.

Then she heard the rattle and creak of the fence. They'd found the opening.

Like an overcrowded village, the junkyard was lined with streets. Aimee turned down a lane. On either side of her towered racks of crushed cars. She raced down the path. As she rounded a corner, her foot slipped on the wet ground, but she quickly recovered. A shuddering chill coursed through her. The squashed cars looked down at her. Their smashed, stacked headlights reminded her of cracked eyes.

Then she turned down another lane of dead cars. Here, the stacks of car skeletons formed a high fence on each side of the narrow pathway. The rusty frames crouched like creatures ready to leap.

She cut down another lane. Flattened cars surrounded her, and Aimee lost all sense of where she was or where she'd been.

Finally a long wide path presented itself, with more dead cars lying like metal corpses in the weeds, but at least she was out of those lanes of looming towers.

The cars in this area were in better shape. They sat side-by-side in rows, like a used car lot positioned in a circle on an open field.

One of these cars might make a good place to hide. They wouldn't be able to find her in one of them? Would they?

In the midst of the sea of old automobiles sat a rusty blue van. The dented door was open as if welcoming her inside.

She scurried into the old clunker and slipped

behind the wheel. Shutting the door, she leaned over the steering wheel to peek through the broken window. A metallic *clunk* at her right caught her attention.

One of Deidra's followers stood where she had moment ago. Red eyes flashed out of a pale, white face.

A moment later, the other man strolled up beside him. Both men stared at the mountain range of rubble, their gazes searching.

Aimee ducked and squeezed her eyes shut.

Please don't see me. Please don't see me. She chanted, cowering low in the front seat. The coarseness of broken safety glass on the seat rubbed against her and tore her jammies.

With her eyes still closed, she mentally called to Cara.

"Cara!"

Nothing.

"Cara, please help me!"

Behind her eyelids, Cara's face flashed. Concern furrowed her brows. *"Aimee! Are ye all right? Where are ye?"*

"The city junkyard. They're after me. Please help me!" Aimee gulped and then sniffled. *"Don't let them get me. They're bad, Cara. They want to hurt me."*

"Stay where ye are, honey. I'm going to send yer daddy right away."

Outside the window, their footsteps moved away, and then faded entirely.

"They're going to find me, Cara. I can't stay here," she replied in a small, frightened voice.

"Aimee, No! Ye need to stay where ye are!" Cara demanded.

Aimee flinched at the forceful tone of Cara's voice

and chose to block her out.

She needed to think.

They would come back, and then they'd find her. Could she take the chance of being caught? She waited for what seemed like forever, but, in truth, it was only a few seconds before she came to a decision.

She placed her hand on the door handle and pulled herself up to glance outside.

There was nobody in sight.

Aimee struggled to breath. Tears welled in her eyes, and she dropped back behind the decaying steering wheel, trying to decide what to do next.

Should she wait for daddy to come?

Would he come in time? She needed to get back to Elena. She promised.

She covered the door handle with her hand, and gave it a soft twist. The door opened. She shuddered when the corroded hinges squeaked. Her heart skipped and she jumped back against the seat. With her foot, she pushed it wide enough so she'd be able to crawl out. Her gaze moved from side to side. Seeing no one, she scuttled across the seat and dropped to the ground.

She closed the door. It made a sharp *click*, not very loud, but enough to make her jump and she looked around. No one came back. Aimee searched the horizon littered by a refuse of broken automobiles and backed away from the car.

Large hands dropped on her shoulders, sliding down to grip her upper arms in a tight grip.

A scream bubbled out of her throat.

The other man rounded the corner. "Just where did you think you were going, young lady?" he snarled.

Aimee froze at the intense look of fury on the

second man's face. Angry eyes glared at her from a round face, overshadowed by a pointed nose, angled cheekbones and a chin covered by sickles of dark curly hair.

Before Aimee could summon an answer, a noise drew their attention to the shadows between two cars. What began as a low rumble swelled into a loud deep, aggressive growl.

Both Aimee and the man jumped. Green, transparent eyes, almost demonic, appeared, and moved forward until a black snout and legs revealed the shape of an animal.

And then, the muscular shoulders of a pit-bull emerged into the alley. His head was as big as Aimee's upper body, his torso thick and tubular. Its growls turned into snarls; vicious fanglike teeth bare, and dripping saliva. A heavy metal-studded collar hung around his neck. A steel tag made clanking sounds when the dog trudged toward them.

The man holding her stiffened, as if petrified.

"Get back girl," he shouted, then shoved her behind him. "Stop it," he shouted to the other man, raising a finger to point at the dog.

The dog caught sight of the man behind him and spun around. It's long, pink tongue licked its long snout, and he headed toward him in a slow trot.

The man held up a hand.

"Stay!" he shouted in a panicked tone, but it did no good. The dog lunged. Its large paws landed in the middle of the man's chest and knocked him to the ground.

The man that held her spun around, yanked her arm, and pulled her out of the animal's sight.

Behind them, the man's cries of agony were overshadowed by savage growls and ripping cloth.

Aimee glanced over her shoulder. Through the busted out windows of a car, she glimpsed the man's red-streaked flesh as he tried to hoist himself from the ground. His bloodied limbs flailed as the pit-bull dragged him back down. His scarlet hand slid down the window, leaving a smeared red handprint across the broken glass.

Suddenly, the dog howled as if in pain.

As the man's screams faded, the growls of the dog subsided too until only silence remained.

Chapter Thirty

Moisture clung to the air like rose vines to a trellis. The light rain stopped, but the scent of more precipitation hung heavy in the atmosphere. Brief flashes of lightning lit up the sky in the distance.

Jake jumped into the alley between two towering walls of busted-up cars.

"Aimee!" he shouted in the hushed silence.

No answer.

Fallon stepped up beside him. "Hey, man, ye might want to keep yer voice down. We doona know what's hiding out here."

Cameron shrugged as if in nonchalance. "'Tis the middle of the day. Vamps are napping. Only humans will be out, and I'm sure we can handle them."

Fallon grimaced. "Aye, ye and I can handle ourselves well enough, but I'm no' certain about Jake there."

He'd made the comment in a low voice, yet Jake heard. "Hey guys, I've been in worse situations than this before. Don't worry about me. I can take care of myself." He drew his revolver from his coat pocket.

Cameron grinned and turned back to Fallon. "That'll work against humans, wilna it?"

Fallon nodded. "Aye, but have ye forgotten that these are real people. They havena been given a choice in this."

"And do ye forget that they can be just as dangerous as Deidra? They've been possessed, Fallon." Cameron stated and pulled the sword from the casing at his side.

"Possessed?" Jake asked as he walked over to stand between the two men.

Cameron glanced at him. "Humans overcome by evil. The fragility of their inner spirit provides the perfect opening for Deidra to jump into their psyche and take control. They have no choice but to obey her commands, and, more often than no', the possessed are more dangerous than vampires."

Stunned, the blood drained from Jake's face and his eyes widened. "She can do that?"

The corner of Fallon's mouth tipped. "Ye canna think of her as human. Female, aye, but she's a creature...a monster that has a great deal of power inside her. She wilna hesitate to use it to get what she wants."

Cameron nodded agreement. He rubbed his hands together. "Well, shall we?" he asked and spun around. He looked around the lot, up and down the rows of junk. When he turned to them, he scowled. "Bloody hell! I wish Cara were here. She'd be able to sense Aimee and lead us right to her."

"Well, she's not here. If you're not up to this, then go back to the house. I'll find her myself," Jake growled, forcing the words out between clenched teeth.

Fallon and Cameron jerked at the anger in Jake's voice.

"Back down, Jake," Fallon ordered in a stern voice. "We understand ye're upset, but now is no' the time to act like that. We will find yer daughter," Fallon assured.

"Why don't we split up? We can each take a section of the yard, and meet back here in an hour," Jake suggested.

Fallon shook his head. "Splitting up isna an option. Too many places to hide here, and we'd only be setting ourselves up for an ambush." He glanced toward the sky. "It'll be dark in a couple of hours. If we're no' out by the time the sun goes down, we risk an attack from vamps as well as those possessed."

"But—," Jake started.

"We stay together," Fallon interrupted, in an adamant tone.

Cameron nodded. "Fallon's right, Jake."

Fallon glanced toward the alleyway leading to the right. "Come on. Let's get moving."

They stepped into the pathway between the rows of corroded automobiles. Jake drew a deep breath at the mounds of trash that littered the grounds.

For more than an hour, they searched between rows of rusted, beaten down refrigerators, old washing machines and out of service cars.

They rounded a corner, and discovered the dead body of a man. His eyes were wide and staring from a pale, ashen face streaked with blood. His forearms were shredded as if he'd tried to protect himself, and his intestines spilled from a gaping hole in his abdomen.

Less than a foot away laid a very large, very dead black pit-bull. A knife protruded from its soft underbelly.

The man's neck lay at an odd angle, tilted nearly ninety degrees to the left. It was obvious that the bones in his neck had been snapped by the dog's strong jaws. The animal's teeth left puncture wounds in the man's carotid artery.

Jake threw his hands up in the air. "What the hell does this mean?"

Fallon slapped Jake on the shoulder. "It means that the dog took out one of our enemies. That's all it means. Doona read more into it than there is."

Jake's stomach churned and he forced the bile to return to his stomach. He'd seen much worse before.

He turned away from the sight.

A brown object on the opposite side of the alley drew his attention. There was something slightly familiar about the small mound. Taking a deep, unsteady breath, he walked across the lot.

With the speed of a freight train, the bile rose in his throat again. He froze at the fear coursing through him as he as he stood over the much loved familiar stuffed animal.

Tillie Bear.

"No!" he gasped, realizing a shiver of panic. He bent over a picked up Aimee's bear. His gaze shot around.

"Aimee!" he shouted. "Where are you?"

Cameron and Fallon rushed to his side.

"Hey, man, will ye keep yer voice down?" Cameron said. His eyes landed on the bear clutched in Jake's hand. "What's that?"

Jake held it up. "It's Aimee's teddy bear. She was here."

Cameron grabbed the teddy from Jake and held it up to his face. He lowered it, handed it back to Jake before he turned on his heels and walked around the area. After five minutes, he turned back to Jake and Fallon, shaking his head.

"She isna here anymore."

"We're too late," Jake murmured, dejected.

****

Cara paced the living room, just about wearing a path in the carpet from the couch to the chair, then back again. Her stomach fluttered with a combination of concern and apprehension. It had been more than an hour since Jake, Cameron and Fallon had gone to the junkyard in search of Aimee.

As soon as she received Aimee's mental call, she rushed to the kitchen where the guys sat around the table. It had only taken a second to tell them where Aimee could be located. She wanted to tag along, but, it would have been a suicide mission with the sun still high in the sky.

A rush of nausea overwhelmed her, and she paused, pressing her palm to her forehead.

By the gods!

It had to be her nerves that were making her feel ill...tense and jittery at the same time. She couldn't afford to be sick at a time like this. Aimee needed her. She had to be at the top of her game.

She dropped to the crouch and stared into the empty fireplace.

She pictured Aimee's face...her innocent expression and smiling eyes. In her thoughts, she relived the fun they had, the laughter shared on their special day, but, most of all, she remembered the love in the child's eyes when she spoke of her mother and father.

Cara snapped back to the present.

Why was this happening?

Dampness clung to her cheeks and she swiped her

hands over her eyes. They were tears born of the memories of a wee girl who pierced her heart with her innocence.

She jumped at the soft *thump* of an object landing in the center of the coffee table. Gasping at the sight of Tillie Bear, she wrenched forward. Her hands shook. She picked up the bear and ran her fingers through the muddy rag tag fur before glancing up into Jake's face. She wanted to cry at his dull, lifeless eyes.

"We were too fucking late." His tone was just as vacant as his stare.

Cara squeezed her eyes shut, shocked at the image of Aimee's terrified face behind her eyelids.

No! She screamed in her head, rejecting the vision.

She stood and stretched out a hand to Jake. He glanced down at her offering, shook his head, and spun away, heading out of the room. A moment later, his footsteps echoed down the hallway, followed by the slamming of the bedroom door

She started to follow, but stopped at the pressure of Cameron's hand on her forearm. She glanced up into the warrior's eyes.

"Give him a wee bit of time, Cookie," Cameron said in a soft voice. "I thought the man was going to pass out when we found that doll."

Cara's gaze moved to where Jake had disappeared a moment ago, realizing the truth of Cameron's words.

She moved away from Cameron and brushed a hand over her face. The memory of Jake's empty expression sent a stab of pain through her heart. Would he ever forgive her?

Stubborn man.

Even though he wasn't ready to accept it yet, he

needed her just as much as she needed him.

She didn't know what the future held for them, or even if there was a future, but, right now, in this moment, she was here.

And she wasn't going anywhere, at least, not until they found Aimee.

Chapter Thirty-One

Cara drew a deep breath and turned to Fallon and Cameron. "So what did ye find?"

Fallon grimaced. "A dead dog, a butchered man, and—" he hesitated, nodding toward the bear. "—that stuffed animal." He glanced toward the hallway where Jake had disappeared. "It hit him pretty hard."

"No sign of Aimee?"

Fallon shook his head. "None, I couldna even pick up her scent from the stuffed bear."

Cara spun on her heels to face Devlin who'd entered the room just as Jake left. He'd remained silent throughout the exchange.

"I'm thinking 'tis a good time to start coming up with that plan," she stated. She quirked an eyebrow at Devlin and dared him to deny her.

Devlin didn't respond right away. His brow furrowed as if in thought. After a moment, he glanced at Fallon, then at Cameron.

"Do ye boys feel up to another wee scouting expedition?" Devlin asked.

Fallon stepped forward. "What do ye go' in mind?"

"Cara's right. We canna wait any longer."

"I agree. What do we need to do?" Cameron asked.

"Do ye remember where ye saw the girl carrying the basket of food?" Devlin's gaze shot between the two other male guardians.

Fallon laughed. "Aye, I remember it well. Why?"

"Ye need to scope out that area again. My gut is telling me that the junkyard is nearby. If it is, then we can assume that's where they're holding the girl and medium. I hate to base my decision on an assumption, but chances are Aimee dinna travel far to get to that scrap yard."

Cara opened her mouth, but snapped it shut when Devlin raised an eyebrow. "Look, Cara. We need to know what we're up against, and, like me, ye're stuck in the house until nightfall. Hopefully, the guys can paint a more accurate picture of what we're walking into."

Fallon held out his hand in Cameron's direction and winked. "Come on, Irish. Care to hold my hand?"

Cameron grimaced and slapped his hand on Fallon's forearm. "Nay, I doona want to hold yer hand." His mouth twisted. "I just might have to have a wee talk with Lizzie. The way ye want to hold my hand all the time has me thinking, ye might be into the kinky stuff."

Fallon chuckled. "Think all ye want. Lizzie knows what I want. Hang on."

And then the two men faded away.

Cara lifted her eyes to Devlin. "Do ye think they'll find anything?"

Devlin shrugged. "I'm no' sure, Cara, but I agree with ye. Time is running out, and we've go' to find out where Deidra is holding Aimee. The guys will come back with answers. I'm sure of that."

Cara nodded. "I'm going to find Jake." She turned and started down the hall.

"Cara," Devlin called after her.

She stopped and glanced over her shoulder. "Aye."

"We need this confirmation. I couldna let ye guys go rushing in there over a basket of food. She could have been taking it to anyone on the grounds, maybe her family or the other workers." He shrugged. "Who knows?"

"But we could have checked it out sooner?" Cara insisted then shook her head. "It doesna matter, now, does it?"

Devlin didn't respond, and she spun away.

She walked down the hall, past Aimee's room. Movement inside drew her attention and she glanced in to find Jake sitting on his daughter's bed.

"Jake."

He glanced up.

Shocked at the furious look in his eyes, she recoiled.

"Leave. Me. Alone." He said each word a broken syllable.

Now was obviously not the time to talk...at least not rationally, and she turned away before he saw the tears in her eyes. Instead of facing Devlin or Mrs. Denton, she wandered down the hall to Jake's bedroom where she slipped inside, and closed the door behind her.

She walked across the room and dropped on the bed.

"Please let them find her," Cara whispered, clutching Tillie Bear against her chest.

Fear flooded her mind. With this fear, Cara thought of Jake. Had he lived the pain of watching his wife die and not being able to save her, only to suffer the same fate with his daughter?

Cara let out a deep breath she didn't even realize

she held and let the silent tears fall.

****

Jake wanted an explanation…a solution…anything that would help him to understand what was happening in his world. He stood outside his bedroom door, prepared to face Cara to get the answers he sought.

This was *his* house. No longer would he be a victim under his own roof—not any more. His daughter already held that title…something he vowed to correct. For the past few weeks, their lives had been controlled by the so-called gods of the Tuatha Dé Danann and those they *created* to protect them.

Yeah, right?

His heart pounded against his chest.

If he couldn't control what happened here, how the hell could he expect to control the obstacles beyond these four walls? The barriers that stood in the way of finding his daughter?

He opened the door and slipped inside the room. Cara lay across the bed. She faced the opposite way, but her body stiffened as if aware of his presence.

Her essence flooded over him like a charge of electricity, and, in the next instant, his self-control shattered.

Desire raged over him. Driven by passion, underlined by primal anger, Jake rushed across the room and dropped his hands on her shoulder. With a twist, he rolled her onto her back.

"What are ye doing?" she yelped, squirming against his hold.

Jake dropped to the mattress and straddled her waist. His legs framed her hips, and his hand grasped her wrists, pinning her to the mattress.

"Damn you for making me want you," he whispered.

"No' like this, Jake. Please," she pleaded. She twisted in his arms, arched her body upward and yanked her arms at the same time. He didn't release her. "Ye're upset about Aimee. I get that, but this isna—"

In the next instant, he covered her lips with his and muffled her words. He released her hands and slid a palm across her face to cup her cheek.

She held herself stiff, but within seconds, her sweet whimper vibrated in his mouth.

His hands explored her back, her waist, and skimmed over her hip. He explored her thighs then moved up to her taut stomach, traveling upward to outline the circle of her breast. Her nipples surged at the intimacy of his touch. He deepened his kiss, and made love to her with slow, sensual thrust of his tongue.

Cara's erotic scent filled his senses with pleasure, pure and explosive. Passion rose within him like the hottest fires.

Her fingers slid up his arms and caressed the hair at the nape of his neck. Hypnotized by her touch, he tingled under her fingertips.

His hand cupped her butt. He lifted her and tucked her against the contours of his own body. He groaned when she strained against him as if trying to get closer.

Her hand slid beneath his shirt. The warmth of her palm grazed his naked back. Her touch burned his flesh.

He trailed his lips along her jaw and neck. His lips moved across her cheek to her neck. At the base of her throat a pulse beat and swelled. He pushed her shirt up, slid her bra from his way and filled his palm with her breast.

He drew away and glanced into her face. Rosy cheeks and glazed eyes, she gasped for breath. Her chest heaved. The hot tide of passion swept over him.

And then, his mouth found the rosy peak of her nipple and he suckled. A moan of ecstasy slipped through her lips driving him onward, and he swirled his tongue around this hardened peak.

Cara moaned and arched against his mouth. Her fingers slid into his hair, and she tugged, holding him against her. He took his time to lick and tease as he moved from one nipple to the other.

When he lifted his mouth from her breast, his gaze caught hers. In her passion-filled eyes, he saw more than lust and desire. More than the arousal they shared.

And he felt ashamed.

He'd come here in anger…anger that he'd failed Aimee. It hadn't been Cara's fault, but, in some sick sense, he took his frustrations out on her.

She didn't deserve this.

Murmuring an apology, he rolled onto his back and covered his eyes with his forearm. He willed the sexual rage in his body to calm.

Blood pounded in his brain. Everything inside him screamed at him to make love to her.

But he couldn't. *No' like this.* Had she sensed his emotions?

A knock at the door sounded.

Jake lay still. His arms covered his face. He swallowed then cleared his throat.

"Yeah," Jake called, in a gruff voice.

"Sorry to bother ye, but the guys are back," Devlin said through the door. "'Tis time."

****

Cara scrambled to the edge of the bed. She yanked her bra and shirt into place. Over her shoulder, she glanced at Jake, his clenched lips, tense jaw, and the well-built forearm that rested across his forehead.

Her gaze traveled down across his stomach where his shirt settled high on his abdomen. A thin trail of dark hair led from his inverted belly button to the waistband of his faded black jeans. She swallowed and licked her lips, remembering where that line led.

She shook her head.

They needed to talk.

Cara diverted her gaze and pulled her knees to her chest where she wrapped her arms around them.

She cleared her throat. "Jake?"

Silence.

"Jake?" She asked again. This time, she placed her hand on his shoulder.

He jerked away, rolled to the edge of the bed, and dropped his feet to the floor.

"What the hell is wrong with ye?" she demanded. Agitation spilled through her veins. She jumped to her feet, swiping a hand through her hair. "Why are ye acting like a jerk?"

He dropped his head into his hands. "Don't do this, Cara. Not now. I can't deal with much more."

Fury almost choked her, and she stormed around the bed until she stood before him. He didn't even have the nerve to look at her.

"You? You can't deal with much more?" She could hardly lift her voice above a whisper. "What about me? Ye come in here like the fires of hell are upon ye, jump on me, and—". She swallowed. "I tried to stop ye, but ye wouldna listen. 'Tis no' my fault this happened."

He sat forward and listed his chin to look into her eyes. She took a step back at the anger in his eyes.

"No?" he asked in a harsh, raw voice. "Not just this, Cara. Everything…ever since you've arrived in my life, everything that I once knew is gone. How do ye expect me to act?"

"No' like an animal in rut." And then his words registered, and her eyes widened. "Are ye blaming me for everything that's happened to you?"

When he didn't respond, tears filled her eyes. Of course, he would blame her.

She cleared her throat. "Look, Fallon and Cameron are back. I'm going to see what they found out." She noted his set face, his clamped mouth and fixed eyes.

He stared at her, his blue eyes intense. Unreadable, but his inner torment sent an electrical charge through the air.

"I know ye believe ye canna trust me," she said in a low voice, moving to stand beside him. "Ye can. I never thought I'd say this to anyone, but there isna anything I wouldna do to keep Aimee safe…and ye."

Jake fixed her with a potent stare. His eyes held a hint of darkness that lay beyond their beautiful cobalt color.

"I find that hard to believe."

She swallowed and fought the apprehension that rose in her chest like a tidal wave.

"Jake—"

He jumped to her feet, cutting her off with a swipe of his hand. "I can't do this now, Cara. I just can't."

A flash of wild grief ripped through her. She fought hard against the tears that threatened to fall and tried to swallow the lump in her throat.

Victoria Noxon

Her determination faltered, but only for a moment.

She gulped hard, lifted her chin, and met his gaze, unafraid. "I guess that's it then," she said, before she spun on her heels. Without haste, but with hurried purpose, she left him standing in the center of the room, staring at the floor.

At the door, her hand twisted the knob, but, before she pulled the door open, she hesitated. "As soon as Aimee comes home, I'll be on my way," she said in a voice that trembled.

And with those final words, she walked out the door.

Chapter Thirty-Two

Tears streamed down Aimee's cheeks, and she ran into Elena's outstretched arms. The woman caught her and drew her beside her on the cot.

Elena glanced toward the door, prepared to shoot Aimee's deliverer an annoyed look. Instead, her gaze met the movement of the door as it closed with a *snap*.

"I'm sorry," Aimee sobbed, rocking back and forth.

Elena tightened her embrace across Aimee's shoulder and gave her a reassuring squeeze. "It's okay, child. You did the best you could."

"But they—"

"Aimee, stop!" Elena said in a sharp voice. She gazed into Aimee's eyes. Her voice softened. "You cannot blame yourself."

No matter how much Elena tried to calm her, Aimee was inconsolable. Deep sobs racked the child's insides, and the only thing Elena could do was hold her.

After ten minutes, Aimee's violent bout of crying eased, replaced by strong hiccups and quick, uneven gasps for breath. Ten minutes after that, Aimee's even breathing hinted that she'd fallen asleep.

Elena's heart broke for the child in her arms. She held back tears of disappointment. That had been their one chance to get help. She didn't blame Aimee. After all, she was only a child.

She held Aimee for two hours until footsteps echoed in the hallway. Elena stiffened when the handle of the door turned and swung open.

Deidra stood in the doorway. She stared down at the child sleeping on Elena's lap. Her lips curved into a cocky smile and she slapped her hands together. The sound echoed in the room like the crack of a whip. "Chop! Chop! It's time to get up!"

Aimee moaned, jerked upright, and rubbed her eyes. When her eyes landed on Deidra, she moaned in fear and pushed closer to Elena's side.

"What do you want now? Haven't you done enough to this poor child?" Elena demanded.

Deidra winked. "Oh, you haven't seen anything yet." She waved her hands through the air toward the door. "Come on!"

"Where are we going?" Elena asked.

"*Tsk! Tsk!*" She shook her head. "I don't want to ruin the surprise." In the next instant, her eyes flashed vibrant red. "Now, *move!*"

****

"So, what's the plan?" Cara asked as she walked into the kitchen.

Devlin, Fallon and Cameron looked up from their positions around the table.

Fallon pushed a diagram toward her and nodded. "The caretaker was kind enough to make us a Xeroxed copy of the cemetery layout." He pointed to an area on the paper record. "This is where they're holding the girl and medium." His finger slid about half an inch to the left. "And this is where the bitch is hiding."

"Are ye sure about that?" Devlin asked his brows creased in uncertainty. "Did ye actually see them?"

Cara's nerves tensed when Jake entered the room. He walked to the table, his movements stiff and awkward. She drew a deep, unsteady breath, ignored him, and walked around the table where she dropped into the nearest chair. He must have noticed her actions because he stiffened and crossed his arms over his chest.

Aimee was her sole purpose for being here now, and she had no patience, nor time, for his childish behavior.

Cameron stepped forward. "We're sure. We saw a few of her guards...human, of course. They were sure to stay out of sight, but they were there. No' to mention, we smelled them."

"So, what's the plan?" Jake asked, repeating Cara's earlier question.

"This is what I think we should do..." Devlin started, and for the next two hours, the five discussed their options.

****

"There's no one here," Devlin ducked beneath the threshold of the dark concrete building into the night air. He lifted his head and faced the group. His gaze landed on Cameron and Fallon. "This is where ye say they were being held. Are ye sure no one saw ye nosing around today? If they did, then they've skedaddled, and we may never find them."

Cameron crossed his arms over his chest, his brows drawn. "No one was around and we were sure to stay out of sight. What do ye think we are? Stupid?" he asked, in a sarcastic tone.

Devlin's jaw clenched and he waved his hand through the air as if in dismissal. "Then where the

287

bloody hell did they go?"

Suddenly, through the trees, sparks of electrical currents flashed across the atmosphere, lighting up the nearby skies with pink and purple flashes of light.

"Bloody hell! What's that?" Cameron asked.

Cara glanced at Jake. "What's over there?" She inclined her head in the direction of the light show.

"The Crescent Street Factory. They're a manufacturer of electrical supplies and equipment." His eyes widened. "Maybe they're experiencing a power surge at the plant." He spun on his heels and started to walk toward his car. "I'll call it in. The fire department will be here in less than ten minutes."

"Jake," Devlin called.

"Yeah," he responded over his shoulder.

Devlin frowned then shook his head. "I doona think that's a good idea. No' right now, anyway."

"Doona they close down at night?" Cara asked.

Jake shook his head. "Most factories in this area run twenty-four hours a day. They're not fully staffed, but they do run a skeleton crew in the evening and throughout the night." He frowned and glanced toward the factory. "Are you sure I shouldn't call for back-up? There are people in there, and they could be in trouble."

White streaks merged with the pink and purple flashes and created a pale lavender sky along the skyline.

Devlin shook his head. "Something tells me it isna the factory that's giving us the show."

"Do ye think its Deidra performing one of her funky rituals," Fallon remarked.

Devlin nodded. "I'm getting a strange feeling about all this, and I doona like it. Whether it's a meltdown or

Deidra, I suggest we go in quietly. With the Vampryss running around lose, there's no telling what we could be walking into. Cara, ye and Jake go in from the East. Cameron and Fallon from the West, and I'll take the North."

"Who's coming in from the south?" Fallon asked then chuckled at the confusion his question created.

Devlin grimaced. "Doona be a smartass, Fallon. Unless someone has suddenly learned to fly over tall buildings, that angle is covered by the factory itself."

Cameron grinned, his chest bunched out in pride. "My Anya can fly."

Fallon scowled and slapped him on the shoulder. "Well, Irish. Anya isna here, now is she?"

"Now, that's too bad for me, isna it?" Cameron's eyebrows rose up and down in comical insinuation.

"Oh, shut up," Cara growled, drawing another chuckle from Cameron.

"Once we've surrounded the area, I'll go in first. If there's trouble, wait for my signal," Devlin said.

"What signal would that be?" Cara asked.

Devlin grinned. "Ye'll know when ye see it. Regardless of what happens, ye all are to wait. Got it?"

Cara glanced at Jake. Confusion radiated from his eyes, and he glanced from one guardian to the other.

His eyes narrowed and his back stiffened. After a moment, he shook his head and drew his gun. "I'm not sure what you guys are talking about, and I really don't care. If Aimee is in there, can we go get her now? Or do I have to go myself?"

"Brother," Cara muttered and rolled her eyes at his macho man attitude.

"Okay, guys, knock off the bullshit, and let's go."

Devlin said before he spun away and disappeared into the shadows.

As planned, Cara and Jake traveled around the East boundary of the grounds, before they moved in. When they rounded the corner of the factory, she caught sight of a furry beast. She stuck out a hand, placed it on Jake's chest and brought him to a standstill.

"Get down!" she whispered.

They dropped behind a large pile of wooden crates that lined the alleyway between the factory and the warehouse.

Thank the gods! The werewolf hadn't even looked their way.

Cara peeked over the top of the crates to look at the congregation of vampires and werewolves.

On the outskirts of the circle, Aimee stood beside an older woman she recognized as the woman from her vision, Madame Elena. Her nerves tensed and a cold knot filled her stomach at the tears glistening on Aimee's cheeks.

"Oh, shit!" she muttered, seething with mounting rage.

A large bonfire raged in the center of the circle. Bright flames of reds and oranges billowed into the night sky. Above the circle, the multicolored currents of electricity continued to gyrate and merge to create lavender bolts.

At the head of the group, Deidra towered three feet above the heads of her followers. Upon closer inspection, Cara spied a small wooden box beneath the woman's feet like a pulpit beneath the preacher.

Deidra's gaze shot to the ashen skinned, blue-veined vampire at her side. She inclined her head toward Aimee and Elena. "Bring me the medium," she commanded.

The man hobbled to Elena and grabbed the older woman's arm. With a swift tug, he yanked her away from the circle.

Aimee grabbed the hem of Elena's skirt and started to follow. A large blue-skinned, two hundred pound bully of a man with dark hair and red eyes stepped from the crowd, placed his hand on her shoulder, and stopped her. He yanked her back in the loop. Aimee's eyes widened in fear and her lips trembled.

Elena jerked her arm from his grasp. "Leave me be. I'll go on my own without your filthy hand on my person." She glanced at Aimee, gave her a slight smile and a wink. "It's okay, child. You stay there. I won't be long."

Aimee bit her bottom lip and nodded.

Behind her, Jake fidgeted. He nudged her shoulder. "What's going on out there?" he asked, in an anxious yet irate voice.

"Sh!" Cara muttered and knelt beside him. "Do ye want the whole shit and caboodle lot of them over here?"

"What?" he asked, his forehead creased with confusion. Without waiting for a response, he scooted around her on the pavement and glanced around the crates. "What the—?" he started. Cara slapped her hand across his mouth and muffled his words.

She raised her eyebrows at the angry look in his eyes. "Do ye want Deidra to kill Aimee?" she murmured. "Because she will if ye doona get yer arse back behind these crates and out of sight."

He did as she ordered and moved around her where

he dropped to the pavement. "I don't understand what everyone is waiting for," he grumbled. After a moment, he shook his head and stood. "This is bullshit."

Cara grabbed his arm and yanked him down. "Get down! Stop acting like the spoiled brat who dinna get ice cream after dinner! Ye canna go barreling in there with that chauvinistic male attitude of yers. Wait until the others are in range, then we'll go in and surround them. Besides, Devlin said to wait for a sign."

Jake's brows furrowed. He raised his gun, clicked the metal chamber once then looked at Cara again. Unspoken pain was alive and glowing in his eyes and she ached to smooth the tense lines from his face.

Instead, she ignored him. She had to. Turning around, she glanced over the top of the crate at the congregation. The vampire who had led Elena to Deidra had rejoined the sidelines.

"Now, medium, connect me to my Ághmach. We have plans to make," Deidra said, her eyes alight with excitement.

Suddenly, Deidra froze. Her eyes widened. Cara followed the direction of her stare. Shock flew through her, and she was barely able to control her gasp of surprise.

"What the hell is he doing?" Cara whispered.

Jake stood up beside her and peered over the crates. "He's going to get himself killed," he commented.

Cara chuckled beneath her breath and shook her head. "Nay, he's playing with her, trying to get her to lose her focus." She inclined her head. "Look at her. She's been thrown off balance by his appearance."

"Is that our sign?" Jake whispered.

"No' yet, but keep watching." She glanced across the lot. Movement drew her attention to where Cameron and Fallon advanced closer to the circle to watch the activities.

"Be ready," she muttered, her eyes fixed on Devlin.

Devlin strolled across the lot toward the gathering. Just outside the circle he stopped and inclined his head.

"Now, Dee, ye know I canna let that happen," he said, in a low, composed voice. One corner of his mouth was pulled into a slight smile, but his eyes gleamed like glassy volcanic rock.

A momentary look of discomfort crossed Deidra's face at his words.

And then, a satanic smile spread across Devlin's lips. "Did ye really think I would stand by and let ye destroy the lives of innocent people?"

Deidra shot him a withering look. In the next instant, her gaze shot around the group before returning to him.

Her lips curved and she waved a hand at her followers. "And what do you think you can do against so many? You are only one."

A sudden icy contempt flashed in his eyes. "Do I look concerned?" His eyes bore into her. "Why doona ye return from where ye came and leave this world alone?" His gaze impaled her with the challenge.

Deidra giggled. "I don't want to."

His eyes narrowed. "And there's that spoiled brat I've always known existed." He frowned. "I wilna let ye defile this world as ye did the one ye left behind."

She held up her index finger. "There's one slight misconception in your statement. I dinna leave it. Ye and yer precious gods destroyed it, and then, ye sent me away," Deidra snarled.

"Ye and yer *kind* are a disease. Ye and Ághmach destroyed that world, no' the gods. Ye infected it with yer filth, destroying everything that ye touched," he said in a harsh, raw voice.

Deidra's eyes flash vibrant red. Her lips thinned with anger and her nostril flared.

Cara held her breath when Deidra's spine tensed and hands clenched at her side. She bit back a smile.

Oh, Dev, I hope ye know what ye're doing.

Chapter Thirty-Three

Devlin's nod was barely perceptible, but it was there. Across the lot, Cameron and Fallon stepped onto the paved lot.

Cara glanced over her shoulder at Jake.

"Come on, but doona get close to any of them." She nodded to the weapon in his hand. "Make sure yer aim is true. If it isna and they get their hooks into ye..." She hesitated to allow time for the meaning of her words sink in.

"Don't worry about me, Cara. Just get my daughter." It was a harsh demand, but beneath its exterior, she heard his plea. He was more concerned for his daughter than for himself.

There was no way she'd choose one over the other and vowed to look out for them both.

Leading the way, Cara stepped from the shadows onto the pavement.

Devlin glanced first at the guys then toward her and Jake. She nodded. He turned back to Deidra and smiled.

"Do ye really think I would come to the party without a date?" he asked. With a quick swipe of his hands, he indicated his companions. "In fact, I brought several."

Deidra's eyes flashed brilliant red.

"Daddy," Aimee cried when she saw her father.

295

She ran toward him, but the circle of vampires and werewolves closed in around her and prevented her from exiting the ring. She tried to shove between two pasty white vamps, only to be grabbed and yanked back.

She screamed out in fear.

"Aimee!" Jake shouted as he rushed forward. "Take your filthy hands off her!"

He stopped two feet behind where Cara stood. His body stilled, his shoulders rigid, and his expression angry. His eyes shimmered of iridescent cerulean blue sparks. At first, the flames sizzled, spit then hissed in his irises as if gaining strength. And then, an ember emerged from the depths of his eyes to form a lightning bolt that exploded into the center of the lot. The twisted flame stopped then split into ten to twelve blue mini-flashes blasting the vampires surrounding Aimee.

The bloodsuckers disintegrated. A grayish mist sprayed over the lot.

Stunned, Cara's mouth dropped open. No longer were Jake's eyes the color of sapphire blue. They glowed of electric cobalt neon. Large bolts radiated from their center.

"By the gods," she muttered under her breath. Taking slow steps, she backed toward him, but kept her eyes fixed on the happenings in the lot.

Across the lot, Fallon shifted. His image jiggled then faded. A moment later, he reappeared in front of Aimee. He raised his fists, connecting to the chins of the two vampires who took up guard position over Aimee. They wobbled from the force of the blows.

Fallon spun around, grabbed the child up in his arms, and shifted again.

Cara gasped when he reappeared beside her, the crying child in his arms.

Cara glanced at Jake.

The magical color faded. Jake's eyes returned to their natural blue. She placed her hand on his arm.

"Jake?"

No response.

"Jake, are ye okay?"

He shook his head and glanced at her. His brows were drawn with confusion. "Cara, what happened?"

She smiled. "Ye just took out part of Deidra's entire army with yer baby blues."

"What are you talking about?" he asked, and then he glanced at Fallon and Aimee who's arms stretched for him. His mouth dropped open in surprise. "What'd I miss?"

She laughed, stretched a hand over and, with a brush of her two fingers, snapped it closed. "We'll talk about it later."

After all, they still had Deidra to take care of.

Fallon grinned and walked over to Jake where he dropped the girl into Jake's waiting arms. Aimee sobbed out her relief and hid her face against Jake's chest. He stroked the girl's hair, and pressed a kiss to her forehead.

"Are you okay, munchkin?"

Aimee nodded and sniffed. "I am now."

"Jake, 'tis a good idea to take the girl and leave now," Fallon said.

Cara agreed and rushed to his side. "Jake, get her out of here!" She pressed a soft kiss to Aimee's cheek.

"What about you?" Jake asked.

"Doona worry about us." Cara muttered. "Just get

yer daughter to safety." She swiveled and turned her back on him.

"We can take it from here. Canna we, Cookie?"

Cara nodded, her focus trained on Deidra. They were up against an enemy who could be cunning and quick, and, at the moment, extremely pissed off.

Deidra, stunned by Aimee's sudden disappearance, released a loud bellow of rage that echoed across the lot. Chills spiraled up Cara's backbone, but she held herself stiff, prepared.

Deidra's eyes fixed on Devlin. "Give her back. Now! She's mine."

The eldest guardian laughed aloud. "It'll be a cold day in hell afore that'll happen. Give it up, Dee! Admit it. We've foiled yer plans..." He touched his forehead slightly in a mock salute. "...*once again.*"

Her growl began low, deep in her chest, until it had no choice but to explode as a bellow.

"Shall we go and join the fun, Cookie?" Fallon asked.

"Hell yeah," she replied. A rush of adrenalin surged through her veins. Now that Aimee was safe, Cara could focus all her attention on the upcoming fight.

With unhurried steps, Fallon and Cara walked up to stand beside Devlin.

"Kill them. Kill all of them," Deidra shouted.

Cara pulled the blade from her pocket, spun around, and sliced a charging vampire across the neck. In comical reaction, its head rolled backward, but stayed connected by a few tendons. The head bobbed on top of a body that stumbled with confusion. Cara kicked up her foot, slapped her toes across the hanging appendage, tearing the threads that held it intact. The head rolled to the pavement.

Without waiting for the explosion of ash, she spun around, ready to battle the next.

The snarling face of a long-snouted werewolf pushed through the crowd toward her. Dark, almost black, fur with a sea of silver streaks covered its body. Intelligence burned in his yellowish-brown gaze. The wolf's ears lay flat on its head as it stalked toward her, its gaze fixed on her face.

Every muscle of her body coiled in tight preparation. Inch by inch, the creature crept forward. Cara kept her gaze focused on the werewolf and scrutinized each freeze-frame step that brought it closer to her.

She waited until its muscles bunched beneath the thick fur and prepared to attack.

Cara lunged forward and swung up both of her feet. The bottom of her feet connected with the wolf's chest. The beast flew off it feet and skidded across the pavement in a tangle of teeth, claws and fur. The werewolf growled its hatred and rose up on its hind feet, digging its hind nails into the hard pavement for leverage, then charged again.

Their eyes locked. Cara arched into a half-circle. Her blade ripped deep into the monster's belly. The werewolf fell over. Its sides heaved and blood painted the ground.

Without hesitation, she stabbed the blade into its heart. A howl of agony ripped through the air before it fell silent. The creature stilled.

Out of the corner of her eye, the movement of another seven-foot werewolf drew her attention. She twirled around, blade raised. As it grew near, she raised her arms, and with a quick swipe of her wrist, decapitated the creatures.

An awful stench filled her nose, and a slight scuffle sounded behind her. Without hesitation, she dropped to the ground and with a powerful thrust of her legs flipped over backward.

Unprepared for Cara's acrobatics, the werewolf swiped a paw out. The dagger nails connected to Cara's hip.

She groaned at the fire that shot down her leg.

"Bastard," she muttered.

She leapt to her feet and jumped away as those same claws raked toward her belly. They missed, but the werewolf's breath, hot in her face, made her gag, the stench foul. Malevolent eyes glared into hers.

The creature tried to sink his teeth into her throat, but she slammed her legs into his belly. It growled in pain and bowed over in pain. She brought her hand up. The edge of her blade ripped through the animal's fur.

With another sharp jab, she twisted the knife into the animal. It howled, and then dropped to the ground, dead. Blood smeared across its muzzle.

Cara circled around and snarled. Her lips curled and exposed her incisors. Her hip nearly crumpled under her weight, but she ground her teeth in determination.

She would not falter.

Another werewolf appeared and charged. Sharp claws raked against her ribcage.

She imposed an iron control on her emotions, rolled over and regained her feet, shaking herself from her stupor. The creature rose, whirled back and growled. Cara limped toward the creature. Her sides heaved. Blood coated her hip, her leg and now her side.

Cara groaned and shifted her position, blocking out the pain. She would heal.

Bloody fucking werewolves!

A shot rang out. The werewolf stumbled then fell face first on the pavement. It raised its head, locked eyes with her, and warped its lips in a grimace of hatred. Claws scraped the pavement as it pulled itself toward her.

Cara retrieved her knife where it landed on the pavement after the attack. She roared with rage, twisted around, and stabbed the werewolf through the top of his head. The pointed tip of the blade exited through the animal's chin.

She drew a deep breath and stood upright. Somehow she'd been pushed against the side alley of the lot. On the other side of the parking lot, the other guardians fought Deidra's army of vampires.

Why the fuck did she get all the dogs? And where was Deidra?

Her gaze scanned the lot. Deidra, her lips twisted in anger, stood near the warehouse. She watched the destruction of her faction without even lifting a finger.

"What the hell were those things?"

Cara jumped, startled by Jake's voice. She spun around. "Where's Aimee?"

Jake inclined his head toward the shadows. "She's safe."

Cara's heart skipped. "Go to her, Jake. Stay with her," she demanded in a soft voice. "Doona leave her alone."

When he didn't move, she drew a deep breath to

calm her rising panic before she spoke again.

"Jake, ye need to go look after yer daughter."

In the next moment, Jake's eyes widened, and he raised his gun.

"Look out!" he shouted.

Chapter Thirty-Four

His warning came too late. Excruciating agony ripped through her left shoulder and ran down her arm. Two long, deep slashes in her skin spewed fountains of precious blood to the pavement.

She spun around and faced the werewolf who'd sunk its long canines into her. She slammed her fisted hand in its stomach. It groaned and stumbled to the pavement. It twisted and snarled, throwing its weight sideways in an attempt to roll and regain its footing.

Another shot sounded. Cara jumped. Chills crept up her spine. The werewolf dropped, motionless.

Cara glanced over her shoulder at Jake who held the smoking gun. "Must ye do that?" she asked as she stuck a finger in her ear to ease the sting of the blast.

Jake grinned and shrugged. "What? Saved your life, didn't it?"

Cara shook her head. "Thank ye, but please appease me and go to yer daughter. Keep her safe."

Jake's eyes traveled over her. Concern lit up his expression.

"Are you going to be okay?"

Cara grimaced. Pain racked her body, but she nodded. "Aye, I'll be fine. Remember, I'm a quick healer." She saw the concern in his eyes. "Really, Jake, go to Aimee."

He hesitated. His gaze shot across the lot where the

other guardians still battled. He glanced at her.

"What about them?" he asked with a sharp incline of his head.

She spun around; glanced to the area he indicated and chuckled. "To hell with them. They left me to the bloody dogs."

Two vampires left the battle and headed in their direction, followed by three more.

"Och, bloody hell," Cara grumbled. She stiffened, taking battle stance. Over her shoulder, she glanced at Jake, whose gaze remained fixed on the oncoming trouble.

His eyes sparkled as if stimulated by the advancing vampires. A mixture of blue and white created an azure flame in his irises.

Cara rolled her eyes and crossed her arms over her breast.

"Here we go again," she murmured. A soft smile curved her lips.

As the bloodsuckers drew closer, uncertainty flared through her. Her smile faded. She dropped her arms and stood upright.

What the hell was the matter with him?

Expressionless, Jake stood immobile as the parasites marched toward him.

"Jake!" she screamed.

As if he took her cue, brilliant flashes of lightning flared from Jake's eyes. Splitting mid-air, the wide bolt divided and tore into the bloodthirsty creatures one-by-one, including the ones on the other side of the lot. It was as if they were the magnet that drew the force of Jake's power.

The lot filled with a shower of grayish ash. Within

five minutes, vampires and werewolves vanished, except Deidra. Her eyes widened in shock. She glanced toward him, shook her head in disgust, and disintegrated into a reddish mist that floated toward the sky.

Devlin, Cameron, and Fallon, their eyes wide with surprise, sauntered across the lot.

"Hey, that was neat," Cameron said. "Where did he learn to do that?

"I'm no' even sure he's aware of what he's done," she said as she stared at Jake's vacant expression. He stood on the outskirts of the group, motionless as if paralyzed by some invisible force.

"How is that possible?" Cameron asked.

"I doona know," she replied as she shrugged and walked over to Jake. She waved a hand in front of his face.

Jake shook his head, free of his trance, and glanced around the area. "What happened? Where did they all go?"

She patted his arm. "We'll talk about it later. Why doona ye go get Aimee?"

For a brief second, he stared at her with confusion in his eyes. He shrugged, spun on his heels and headed into the darkness.

They watched him saunter away.

"There's that magic ye were talking about, Cookie," Cameron said. A smile lit up his face. "And, damn, that's a hell of a lot of power to be flashing around without knowing."

Cara's brows creased. Her gaze followed Jake into the shadow. When he disappeared, she turned to Devlin.

"Do ye suppose the gods know anything about this?" she asked.

Devlin shot her a twisted smile and released a heavy sigh. "I'm no' privy to all of their knowledge, Cara. If they do, I'm sure there is a reason why they havena told us."

A pulsing knot within her demanded to know more, but knew she wouldn't get her answers tonight.

Fallon leaned over her and examined her face. His gaze traveled the length of her. "Wow, Cookie, it looks like the wolves took quite a bite out of ye. Mayhap ye should sit down afore ye fall down."

"Fuck ye, Fallon," Cara cursed, a silken thread of warning in her voice. She gazed at the three guardians. "Do ye think any of ye could have left the vamps and given me a hand with the mangy animals?" Without waiting for an answer she knew wouldn't come, she glanced toward the warehouse where she'd seen Deidra standing moments before. "So, where do ye suppose Deidra went this time?"

"Oh, please, look no further. I'm right here."

The four guardians spun around at the sharp female voice. Cara's stomach churned at the sight of Deidra standing behind Jake and Aimee. Her long fingernails jabbed into the artery of Jake's neck. One small movement and she could easily pierce the vein that held his life force.

Cara glanced at Jake's face. For a moment, he studied her with an intent stare, his eyes humorous and tender. And then they changed and turned the vibrant electric blue.

As if sensing the strength of Jake's growing power, Deidra's grip tightened around his throat. "Oh no, no, we can't have that," Deidra said before she tightened her hand and deprived him of oxygen. His face turned blue then gray and he collapsed. Deidra caught him in one arm. She grabbed Aimee with the other hand before the child landed on the pavement.

"Let them go, Dee. It's over," Devlin barked in a tone rich with frustration.

Deidra frowned. "It's over when I say it is. Not before."

And then, she disappeared into the sky as a red mist, taking Aimee and Jake with her.

"No!" Cara screamed.

A moment later a loud whistle drew their attention to the front of the warehouse where Deidra, Jake and Aimee reappeared.

Cara's eyes fixed on Jake and Aimee. He was so pale. His body lay limp in Deidra's grip.

The Vampryss opened her fist and Jake fell to the concrete in a heap. Beside him, Deidra released Aimee and she dropped beside her father. The child's body shook with violent sobs as she leaned over his still body. She gripped the front of his shirt and tugged, trying to get him to wake up.

Deidra smiled at the guardians, winked, and stepped away from the door. A moment later, the heavy metal door slammed shut with a resounding echo.

"Jake! Aimee!" Cara shouted and rushed toward the building.

The other guardians followed close on her heels. Their footsteps slapped the pavement. Devlin grabbed a hold of her arm and yanked her to a stop.

"Cara! Wait!" Devlin shouted. "It could be a trap."

"Let me go," she gritted between her teeth and

yanked her arm from his grip. She spun around to face him. "What do ye want to do, Devlin? Wait? Like before? We could have avoided all this by going to the cemetery when Fallon and Cameron—" Her voice faded.

"Cookie," Cameron stepped forward. "Doona blame Devlin for this." He caressed her arm. "We'll get them back."

Angry tears spilled down Cara's cheeks.

"Aye, I will!" she glanced at Devlin's downturned face. "And if I have to, I'll do it without help from any of ye."

Chapter Thirty-Five

"Daddy, wake up," Aimee cried. She grabbed the front collar of his shirt and shook. "Please wake up."

His daughter's voice echoed as if coming through a long tunnel. Jake struggled to open his eyes.

"It's okay, honey," he whispered in a hoarse, choked tone.

"Where are we, daddy?" she asked.

Jake squinted. He glanced around the room. "I'm not sure, but we'll get out of here."

Through a three-by-two grime covered window, the parking lot came into view. Fallon and Cameron stood off to one side. Cara stood in front of Devlin. Her hands waved in front of his face in a frantic gesture. Even though he couldn't hear them, he knew they exchanged angry words.

"The gods will learn that I am not to be taken lightly."

Jake turned toward the sharp female voice. Deidra appeared from the shadows and blocked the doorway. She gazed out the window. Her lips curved into a twisted smile.

"It would appear there is dissection amongst the ranks, eh?"

Jake almost laughed at the Vampryss' misuse of the clique, but deemed it pointless. Besides, he really didn't care.

Aimee's arms tightened around his neck, and she began to sob. Her small body shook, and he caressed her back with long, gentle swipes of his palm.

"Let my daughter go," he demanded. "She is of no use to you now."

Deidra's eyes glowed vibrant red. "Neither of you is any use to me, but you will grant me one thing."

"What?"

She smiled. Her forked tongue caressed her pointed, sharp fangs.

"Satisfaction," she remarked. "It would appear that the two of you have special meaning to the female guardian."

Jake snorted, hoping his actions proved believable. "We mean nothing to her."

She took an abrupt step toward him. "Do you think I'm stupid?"

Jake held up a hand. "I didn't say that."

She studied his face with her enigmatic gaze for an extra beat before her mouth spread into a thin-lipped smile.

"You really do not understand who I am. Do you?" she asked with a significant lifting of her brows. "I saw what you did out there. The way you took out my army with that blue lightning of yours." She shook her head. "That was amazing, but you must know I cannot allow you to live with that power. And your daughter is just as strong."

He swallowed hard and squared his shoulders. "I don't know what you're talking about," he replied with deceptive calm, although inside, his guts twisted.

Was it possible? Were the powers he possessed as a child coming back to him?

Deidra laughed. "Of course, you don't." Her expression hardened. "You would say anything to save yourself."

"Look, I understand your anger, but I don't give a rat's ass what you think. My main concern here is my little girl. I hope you can appreciate that. Your issues with the gods and with them..." he hesitated, waved his hand toward the guardians outside. "...is not my concern." He lowered his voice. "Let her go," he begged.

"It is a shame you have been drawn into this war," she said, her eyes hard. She raised a long fingernail toward a stack of dry wood in the corner. A moment later, sparks shot from inside the pile, smoldered a moment before they ignited into large flames that raced up the walls and spread across the ceiling.

Oranges. Reds. Yellows. The colors were alive and sucked the oxygen from the room. They rose, hissed, and spit. Smoke swirled through the room in less than a minute.

The fire blocked the only exit from the room. There was no way out. The smoke burned his lungs.

Deidra remained motionless; her gaze fixed on him. She watched him with a look of regret on her face. And then, she evaporated into a reddish mist that floated toward a vent and disappeared out of the room.

"Daddy," Aimee coughed.

"Sh, baby, don't try to talk," he murmured against her hair. He ripped off his T-shirt, and held it out for her. "Put this over your face. Breath slow and easy."

Jake kept low, making sure Aimee stayed below the smoke, but the heat reached out to them with a ravenous hunger. She coughed and choked. Jake shielded her body beneath him as the fire scorched his skin, singing the hair on his arms.

The smell of the fire, the acrid odor overwhelmed him, and he gagged. The oxygen left his lungs, replaced by carbon monoxide. He pulled Aimee against him.

Where were his powers now? When he needed them the most?

Chunks of burning rubble fell as a portion of the ceiling collapsed and crashed to the floor. Glass shattered as the window exploded outward from the heat.

His ears picked up another sound, besides the cracking fire. A loud hissing hum radiated across the air and sent chills up his spine. He glanced around the room. A mist of steam separated the smoke and revealed a fifty-gallon propane tank in the corner.

Oh shit!

"Aimee," he choked.

No response.

"Aimee," he shouted, but the only sound that emerged was a choking cough.

She was already unconscious.

The hiss from the corner intensified. He closed his eyes.

It wouldn't be much longer now.

The shriek of sirens grew in the distance.

And then, he remembered no more.

****

The pavement buckled in front of Cara and a blast of hot air struck her in the face. The force picked her feet off the pavement and shot her through the air in a spiral backward somersault.

Her stomach swirled with nausea. She slammed

into a pile of wooden crates. She groaned when pain speared between her shoulder blades and down her back. The boxes shattered. Slivers of wood exploded around her, and she covered her head when they plunged back to earth like rocks in a landslide.

After a moment, the noise subsided.

She groaned, pushed the splintered wood off her, and struggled to sit up. Her eyes widened and she glanced around the parking lot for the other guardians. Like her, they picked themselves off the ground, their faces masks of stunned surprise.

She stumbled to her feet and stared at the warehouse. Only a pile of smoking debris of the demolished building remained. Red and orange flames shot from the center of the rubble.

Jake! Aimee!

"By the gods! No!" Cara gasped.

She swallowed hard and stumbled forward.

And then, she screamed, but covered her mouth with her hand to silence her agony. She swallowed and tried to process what happened.

This wasn't real. It couldn't be.

A vise clamp squeezed around her chest. The pressure tightened as if someone cranked the lever inch by inch. The piercing pain dropped her to her knees and she covered her chest with both hands.

Bile churned in her stomach like an eddy, burned up her throat, and threatened to explode in a projectile bout of vomit. Her throat raw and her eyes burned from the acrid smell of burning wood.

By the gods, help her. What could she do?

She wanted to scream in denial and race into the flames, certain what happened could only be a nightmare.

Devlin, Fallon and Cameron rushed to her side.

"We've go' to get out of here, lass," Devlin said, his tone anxious.

She shook her head, her eyes fixed on the blood red glow of the fire. From the corner of her eye, movement drew her attention, and she glanced in that direction.

Evacuated factory workers lined the sidewalk. Sirens echoed in the distance.

Ashes scattered and wafted across the breeze. Smoke settled in the air like a nauseating cover.

She refused to leave.

Chapter Thirty-Six

Jake pushed himself into a sitting position. Every bone in his body hurt, and his joints and muscles ached. He groaned in misery and swiped a hand over his sweat-drenched face and drew a deep, oxygenated breath.

Even though his body exuded excruciating agony, a deep, inner peace enveloped him.

Aimee stirred in his arms.

"Thank God," he murmured and glanced into her face. He caressed her cheek with his hand. "Aimee?"

Her eyelids fluttered and she opened her eyes. A smile trembled over her lips, and her cheeks turned a rosy shade of pink as the oxygen rejuvenated her damaged lungs.

"Hi daddy," she said.

Flickers of brilliant lights glittered in the corner of his eye. His stomach lurched, and he squinted and looked around.

A fluffy white mist swirled around him...much different than the bitter, grayish smoke of the warehouse.

Where were they?

Less than ten feet away, glimmering stars twirled in a beautiful rainbow-colored swirl. From the center of the vortex, an iridescent sphere emerged and glowed larger and brighter as it grew nearer.

And then another appeared…and another…

What was going on? Was this heaven?

The orbs floated and spun above their heads for a moment before they whirled ten feet away. The brilliance nearly blinded Jake, and he shielded his eyes from the radiance.

And then, the light faded, replaced by the figures of two men and a woman. All three wore silken robes tied at their waists by braided golden cords.

The woman stepped forward, gorgeous too trivial a word to describe her beauty. Long, midnight-colored hair hung to her waist. A pinkish-rose flush coated her cheekbones and accentuated emerald eyes.

The man on her left stood almost six foot. Curly black hair brushed his shoulder. The other man with light brown hair towered above both, and stood to the right of the woman.

They smiled. The glow in their faces warmed him, and the kindness he read in their eyes humbled him.

Was it a trap?

His arms tightened around Aimee, and she moaned.

"Daddy!" she squealed.

"Sorry," he murmured and eased up.

Aimee pushed herself out of Jake's arms. She rubbed her eyes, lifted her head and glanced around.

"Daddy, where are we?" she asked, in her Aimee-innocent voice. She tucked herself in against his side.

Jake pressed a kiss to her cheek. "It's okay, honey. We're going to be fine." And in that instant, Jake accepted the truth of his own words. They would be all right.

The woman held out a hand to him. He lifted Aimee and set her on her feet.

Without hesitation, he stood and placed his hand in hers. The warmth of her hand closed around his.

She smiled and gave him a firm shake.

"I am Danu," she said then released his hand. With a dainty finger, she pointed to the men at her side. "And this is Dagda and Lugh."

"Where are we?" he asked as he glanced around at the clouds. "Are we dead? Is this heaven?"

"You are in our heaven. We are the gods of the Tuatha Dé Danann, and this place is known as the Otherworld."

Anger rushed through Jake. The blood raged through is veins. "We died in that warehouse fire, didn't we?"

Danu nodded. Her eyes filled with sympathy. "Your physical bodies did, but it is not the end of your life."

"How can you say that?"

The man called Lugh stepped forward. "You are dead only in the human sense of the word."

Jake's brows furrowed. "What are you saying? Are we or aren't we dead, for crying out loud?"

"Your place is to stand beside your mate."

A muscle quivered in his jaw. "My mate?"

Danu tilted her head to one side. Her eyes studied Jake with curiosity. "Aye, your mate. Cahira is your soul mate, your life mate, and you are her life."

"Cara?" His eyes widened in surprise.

All three gods nodded.

Jake shook his head. "I still don't understand any of this. Why me? Why Aimee?"

Aimee had remained silent throughout the interchange, but now, she slipped her hand into Jake's.

He glanced down into her smiling face.

"What, honey?" he asked, surprised at the twinkle in her eyes.

"It is destined, daddy."

"And what do you know of destiny, Aimee. You are only a child."

"Mommy taught me," she said.

Jake's stomach knotted, and he knelt down on one knees. "That's not possible. You were only two when mommy died."

"But she did, daddy. She really did," Aimee insisted.

Awkwardly, he cleared his throat, straightened and faced the gods again. "Did you have something to do with this?"

Danu smiled at Aimee then looked back at Jake. "Your daughter is the descendant of a very powerful witch, and, as such, she possesses strength and wisdom passed from her mother to her while still in her womb. It is a connection that will forever remain with Aimee."

Jake ran an agitated hand through his hair.

Danu continued. "Deidra chose Aimee for the power that runs through her. We chose you for the fire in your blood. Together, you and Cara shall make a powerful match. The Prince of Power, mated to a Síoraí."

"Prince?" Jake stammered. He swallowed hard. "I believe you have chosen the wrong man for that title. I have no powers."

Dagda stepped forward. "But you do, my son. You have been blessed with the power of the blue flame."

He hesitated and blinked with confusion. "Blue flame?" He hurtled back to earth as reality struck.

Hadn't Cara said he'd destroyed Deidra's army with his eyes?

"As in baby blues?" he asked in a choked voice.

Danu nodded.

"But I don't remember any of that."

Lugh smiled and waved a hand in front of Jake's face.

Jake shivered with vivid recollection. The anger that soared through him fueled the flame and made his gifts more powerful.

His eyes widened.

Lugh nodded. "The blue fire is linked to your emotions. Just as our guardians learned to use their powers, you must learn to use yours."

Jake glanced at Aimee. "Why us? And why Cara?"

"You were chosen for this important feat before your birth, just as the Síoraí were chosen centuries ago. That you met and married a Druid to produce a magical child, an extra bonus to our cause." He shrugged. "As for Cara, we had intended all of our guardians to be male, but Cahira's spirit was strong. She called to us."

"What if I don't choose this life for me or my daughter?"

"You have already chosen it, Jake Bradshaw, by letting Cara into your heart. It is a binding that you will not be able to deny."

Jake understood it all now. "So this was all a process. We were pawns...herded like animals to do your bidding."

Danu shook her head. "It is a process to give you everlasting life and love with your one true mate." She held up a hand to halt his bitter response. "When Cara lost her family, she lost a part of herself. You and

Aimee have given her back the reason to keep fighting. There is a battle on the horizon that we cannot deny. We must all be ready."

"Tell me about Cara's husband. Why did he have to die?"

Danu's eyes darkened with sadness. "An unavoidable prerequisite, I'm afraid." Her brows drew together in an agonized expression. "He needed to die for Cara to accept who she is."

This was all too much for Jake to comprehend. He wasn't sure if he should be happy or pissed that his daughter and he had been drawn into this paranormal world of danger.

"Why are we here? Aimee and I?"

"This is the place of your final transformation."

"Transformation?"

"You and your daughter will attain immortality on this day. You will live forever." She smiled and glanced at Aimee. Her eyes twinkled. "However, your little girl there will continue to grow until adulthood. Once she has reached twenty-one, the aging process will stop."

"Does Cara know about this?" he asked.

Lugh shook his head and spun around.

In the process, he raised his hand. Cara's image appeared in the clouds. She sat on the pavement in the parking lot outside the warehouse. Her hand clasped across her stomach. Tears fell down her cheeks and she wept aloud.

Jake's heart hammered in his chest.

Did she cry for him?

"As you are here, she must be there," Lugh answered.

"Is that real?" he asked. His eyes remained fixed

on the picture.

Danu nodded. "It is. There is so much that our guardians must undergo in their journey. This is part of it. They must experience loss to accept their future."

"But isn't that what happened when they received their immortality? You took away everything that made them human? They suffered immeasurable pain at the loss of their loved ones? Why must they endure it again?"

"The first time, they received their immortality and their desires to fight. This is to give them back everything they lost...a new life and a love to cherish. They'll never be alone again." She glanced at him. "Do you deny her? Her love?"

Once again, his eyes landed on Cara surrounded by the white mist. A warm glow flowed through him. He loved her, and no matter what the future brought, he could never deny her any more than he could deny himself.

She made him whole again after Lisa's death.

He turned back to the goddess and gods. As if they heard his thoughts, smiles graced their celestial faces.

Danu nodded. "It is time for you and Aimee to return to your life. Remember, there is a battle on the horizon. Cara will need you when that time comes."

"I'll be there," Jake vowed.

Chapter Thirty-Seven

Cara dropped to the pavement and floundered in an agonizing maelstrom of anguish. Her misery so acute it became a physical pain that exploded throughout her entire body. Her breath shallow, her senses drugged.

This couldn't be happening. Not again.

She wrapped her arms around her knees and dropped her forehead into the valley between them. Deep sobs racked her insides. Her body rocked back and forth.

Grief and despair tore at her heart.

Just like Braedan, her son and her parents. For the second time in her life, everything that made her world real had been ripped away.

By the gods, she couldn't bare it again. Her teeth chattered, her hands trembled, and her throat grew raw with denial.

She gulped hard, tried to swallow past the lump in her throat. Her mouth felt like old paper, dry and dusty.

How had it come to this?

****

"Isna there anything we can do?" Cameron asked.

"Nay," Devlin replied. "'Tis the process she must experience alone. Ye know that, or have ye forgotten?"

Cameron groaned. "I remember all too well, and, if ye remember, I almost killed ye for it."

"But ye dinna," Devlin said and slapped Cameron

on the shoulder.

"Wow, that dinna take long."

Both men glanced up at Fallon's comment.

Devlin smiled and released a deep sigh of relief. At least, her torment wouldn't last long. "Thank the gods," he muttered.

From the midst of the flame engorged building, Jake materialized. He carried his daughter in his arms. Both appeared alive and well.

Devlin strolled over to Cara. Head bowed, her forehead rested on her knees. Her shoulders shook from violent sobs that ravaged her body.

He set his hand on her shoulder and gave her a little shake. "Cara," he said, in a low voice.

She shuddered, and then looked up. Her tear-streaked cheeks pierced his heart. He nodded his head toward the building. "Look."

Her eyes widened in confusion, and she glanced in the direction he indicated. She gasped and jumped to her feet.

"How is this possible?" she asked, her voice shaky.

Without waiting for an answer, Cara ran across the parking lot. She came to an abrupt stop in front of Jake.

****

Cara touched his face with trembling fingertips, tracing every beloved line, the curve of his mouth, his dark eyebrows, and his strong jaw. And then she gazed at Aimee, asleep in her father's arms.

She smiled through her tears, and caressed Aimee's angel soft cheek. The child whispered an endearing sigh against her touch.

"By the gods, I thought ye both were dead," she whispered, her voice choked.

Jake chuckled. "It is by the gods' will that we are here, standing before you."

She tilted her head. Her brows creased in confusion. "I doona understand."

"I'll explain it all to you later," he said, lowering his lips to cover hers in a kiss meant to reassure her.

When he pulled away, she looked into his eyes. "Are ye okay?"

"Never better." He glanced down at Aimee. "We should get her home and in bed. It's been a rough ordeal for her."

****

Devlin, Fallon and Cameron stood up from the couch as he entered the room.

Jake smiled. "She's all tucked in." He walked across the room and held out his hand to Devlin. "I don't know how to thank you," he said. His gaze moved over the three men. "All of you for everything you've done for Aimee and me, and you have my most heartfelt gratitude."

Devlin smiled, shaking his hand. "'Tis our pleasure, Jake." He glanced at Cara. Jake followed his gaze. Cara sat on the end of the couch, her head bowed, hands clenched into fists in her lap. "'Tis time for us to be on our way. I'm sure Fallon and Cameron are anxious to get home."

Fallon stepped forward and offered his hand. "But if ye need us, Cara has the number. Pick up the phone and we'll be here."

Jake clasped his hand. "Thank you."

Cameron knelt in front of Cara. "Hey, Cookie," he said. She glanced up and smiled. "If ye need us, call. Okay?" At her nod, he smiled and drew her into his arms for a quick hug.

After a few more good-byes, the three guardians left Cara alone with Jake.

She refused to look at him. "I'm sorry about all that's happened. I'll leave first thing in the morning, but I've go' to say goodbye to Aimee first." She tilted her face to glance at him. Tears filled her eyes. "I hope that'll be okay?"

Jake's heart skipped a beat, and he swallowed, sitting on the couch beside her. "Why are you leaving?"

She jerked, spun around to look at him, and stared into his eyes for a long moment. "I told ye that once Aimee was home safe, I would leave—" Her voice trailed off and she swallowed hard. "I canna stay. My presence here is a beacon for demons." Tears seeped over her lower lids of her eyes. She brushed them away.

Jake got up from the couch and strolled across the room where he stopped in front of the wall of pictures. His shoulders hunched. "Please don't leave," he pleaded, in a soft, difficult to hear, voice.

Confused, Cara leaned forward. "Are ye saying ye would risk Aimee's life...yer life, just to have me stick around?" He turned to look at her. She shook her head. "I'm sorry, Jake, I canna."

"I'm sorry, Cara. So sorry for everything." He cursed beneath his breath and slammed a solid fist into the palm of his other hand.

She flinched at the sound, but didn't say a word.

"When I think of the things I've said to you. The scornful way I judged everything about you. I accused you of—" He broke off, raised his eyes to the ceiling, as if trying to get himself under control. With slow, careful steps, he crossed the room and knelt in front of her. He gripped her hands in his. "Cara, we need you. Aimee and I *both* need you."

A lump formed in her throat. "Jake, I need ye. Both of ye, but—"

"No buts, Cara. You don't need to worry about us. We'll be fine, as long as you're with us." He must have recognized the disbelief in her expression, and he smiled. "Aimee and I had the pleasure of meeting your gods."

Her eyes widened. "What?"

"Come to find out, Aimee and I are going to be around for the rest of our lives…and yours." He chuckled. "Aimee will continue to grow until she becomes an adult, but then the process will stop."

"Immortal?" she choked out the question on a gasp. "Are ye telling me that ye're both immortal?"

Jake sat beside her, wrapped his arms around her and pulled her into his arms. "Yep. I've been told that we're bound by an immortal bond." His expression turned serious. "I don't want to break the bond, Cara. I only want to make it stronger. Can you accept me for the bastard that I've been?"

He leaned forward. His lips hovered over hers. She laid her hands flat on his chest, halting his descent, and gazed at him. "Are ye sure this is what ye want?"

His answer was a kiss filled with tender passion. The misery that shackled her for weeks fell away like old skin. Under the mastery of his kiss, she was reborn.

He pulled away and glanced into her eyes. "I love you, Cara." He cleared his throat. "I never thought I'd love another woman as much as I loved Lisa, but I was wrong."

"I love you, too." She smiled. "I swore I wouldna

ever fall in love and bind myself to a man. When I lost Braedan, I vowed I'd never let myself hurt like that again. I convinced myself that I was okay on my own, but then I met ye. I canna imagine my life without ye or Aimee in it."

Jake leaned back again the couch and drew her against him. He pressed a kiss to the top of her head. "Well, then, I guess we both have a second chance."

She snuggled against him.

For a moment, they sat in silence enjoying each other's company.

Suddenly, a loud squeal interrupted their moment of quiet comfort.

"Cara!" Aimee squealed and rushed across the room, jumping onto the couch beside Cara.

Cara hugged the child close.

"Hey, Aimee." She looked into Aimee's cheerful face, and her heart burst with love for the cherub-cheeked wee lass.

"Are you going to stay with daddy and me?" she asked. "They said you would."

Over the top of Aimee's head, her questioning eyes met Jake's. He smiled and nodded.

Cara didn't respond to Aimee's question with Jake's answer. Instead, she pulled away. "Will that be okay with ye, Aimee?"

A childish smile lit up her face. "Sure, it is."

Cara laughed and wrapped her arms around her again. "Then I'll stick around awhile."

"Are you going to be my mom?" she asked, in a tiny voice.

A lump formed in Cara's throat. "If ye want me to, I'd be proud to be yer mom."

Aimee looked up at Jake. "Do you think my real mom will mind?"

Jakes smiled. "I don't think she'll mind. Some children only have one woman to call mom. I think she'll be happy that you've got two."

Aimee pulled away from Jake, giggling, and jumped to her feet. "I'm hungry. I'm going to find Mrs. Denton."

Jake laughed as the girl ran across the living room into the kitchen. He pulled Cara back into his arms.

"So, do you think you can put up with me for an eternity?" he asked.

She smiled. "Aye, I surely can."

His face grew serious. "Cara, I know I haven't been—"

She placed a finger over his lips to shush his words. "I love ye, Jake."

"I love ye, too, Cahira O'Leary. Forever." He grinned. "Now let's go feed the munchkin and get her back in bed, so I can take you to bed and show you how much."

****

Mrs. Denton waited for them in the kitchen. Tears filled her eyes when she saw Aimee, and she rushed forward to grab the child in a bear hug. "I heard the commotion, and prayed it was you, child."

Over the top of Aimee's head, she caught Cara's eyes. "Thank you," she mouthed. Cara smiled, nodding in acknowledgement, knowing that inside the aged body resided the mind and spirit of Aimee's young mother, Lisa.

Mrs. Denton stood, walked across the room and wrapped her arms around Cara. "Take care of them,

Cara," she whispered in her ear, and then pulled away, a broad smile on her face.

Mrs. Denton nodded. Her eyes pleaded for understanding. Cara did. It was time.

Cara spun around and glanced at Jake. "I'm going to go take a shower."

He nodded. A twinkle lit up his eyes when he gave her a kiss on the cheek.

Cara leaned down to Aimee who sat at the table, and pressed a kiss to her cheek. "Good-night, lass."

"Night, Cara," Aimee chirped.

****

"But Mrs. Denton, I don't understand," Jake asked. His pulse hammered a path through his veins. Confused, his eyes widened and he stared at the elder, waiting for an explanation.

After pouring Aimee a bowl of cereal, Mrs. Denton pulled him back into the living room, away from Aimee's line of sight.

"Cara is all that you need, Mr. Bradshaw. It is time for me to move on. She will take care of you better than I ever could."

Jake shook his head. "How can you say that? You've been with us for years. We all need you, even Cara, and I'm sure she'll tell you that yourself."

Mrs. Denton's figure wavered. Dizzy, his vision blurred. He clenched his eyes shut then reopened them. Unsteady on his feet, he dropped into the chair and lifted his chin.

The blood drained from his face, and he rubbed a hand over his eyes, afraid to believe what he saw. But the vision remained. It was no longer Mrs. Denton who stood before him, but Lisa, as beautiful as ever, and very much alive.

"L…i…s…a?" His words came out as a strangled gasp. He swallowed hard, blinking again. "But how?"

She smiled and walked toward him. "I've never left you, Jake. I've been nearby to watch out for you and Aimee, but now, I am no longer needed. Cara is the one you need, and she needs you. She's a good woman, and I couldn't be more proud to have her raise Aimee."

"You've been here? This whole time?" he asked in disbelief.

Lisa nodded. "As Mrs. Denton, yes." Her lips curved. "I couldn't tell you or they'd make me leave."

"Who?"

She shook her head. "It doesn't matter. When we started dating, I knew you would only be mine for a short time. It was fated, Jake. I love you, will always love you, but now, you belong to Cara."

"I'm sorry," he murmured.

Lisa's brow rose. "For what?"

Tears filled his eyes. "Your death was my fault. If I hadn't of wanted to nail that bastard—" he stopped when she shook her head.

"If I hadn't died that day, it would have been another day. You need to understand, this was destined." She glanced toward the kitchen, a soft smile on her face. "Our daughter understands this."

"Does she know about you?"

Lisa shook her head. "No, I couldn't tell you, or her, a condition of my becoming Mrs. Denton."

"Did Cara know?" His blood boiled at the thought that Cara might have known and not told him.

Lisa walked over to the pictures on the wall. Her fingertip traced Aimee's infant face in the photo. She smiled and turned to face him. "Our daughter has grown into a beautiful child. Cara will take her into adulthood, and train her to use the powers she has buried inside her." Her eyebrows rose and a smile curved her lips.

"Did she know?" he asked again, needing to know.

"Cara's connection to our daughter is more powerful than you can imagine. She needed to know about me, understand the source of my power. Bless her soul; she understood the need for silence. Do not blame Cara for that. She loves you, Jake, and our daughter, and she understood the importance of my presence…for both of you, as well as for me." She stood in front of him, raised her hand and caressed his cheek. "I can find my peace now, knowing that you found happiness."

"But—"

Lisa placed a finger over his lips. "Love her, Jake, and let her love you in return. Be a family for all time. Let Cara help you to accept your past and the powers you carry inside." At his raised eyebrows, she giggled. "And yes, I have always known about you. Aimee not only carries my heritage, but yours, as well. Protect each other, Jake, for the battle is close on the horizon." She removed her finger and pressed her lips to his cheek in a soft kiss. "Good-bye, Jake," she whispered.

And then she was gone.

"Daddy," Aimee called from the kitchen.

Jake cleared his throat.

"Coming, honey," he called. With one last look around, he went to take care of his daughter.

Chapter Thirty-Eight

Jake hesitated outside the bedroom door, his hand on the knob. A wave of apprehension swept over him, and he drew a deep breath.

He twisted the brass handle and pushed the door open.

When he stepped across the threshold into the room, Cara jumped up from her seated position on the edge of the bed. Her hands twisted in front of her, her faces clouded with uneasiness.

His heart raced a gallop across his breastbone. Wearing one of his white cotton button-up shirts, she was the most beautiful woman he had ever seen. The material stretched mid-thigh, held together over her breasts by a single opaque button.

Her fiery red curls hung loose around her shoulders, slinking down the length of her back.

He never took his gaze from her as he closed the door behind him with a soft *click*.

He hesitated and measured her for a moment. A pensive shimmer shadowed her eyes, and he realized her emotions matched his own…nervous.

Thinking quickly, he grinned. "It took a while, but the munchkin has finally gone back to sleep."

"Is she okay?" she asked then bit her lip.

He nodded. "She'll be fine. That's the thing about children. They're resilient and bounce back." He snapped his fingers. "Just like that."

"And Mrs. Denton?" Cara asked in a hesitant voice.

Jake's expression stilled and grew serious. "Mrs. Denton, aka Lisa, is gone."

"I'm sorry. I couldna tell you," she said in a suffocated whisper.

He cringed, realizing that she feared his reaction. Lisa was right. He loved Cara, and she loved him. Nothing else mattered.

He crossed his arms over his chest and grinned. "Lisa told me that too. Believe me when I tell you, I haven't forgotten how stubborn that woman can be."

Uncertainty lit up her eyes, but when he chuckled aloud, she smiled. "You were lucky to have her."

He nodded and strolled forward where he stopped in front of her. "I know, and now I'm even luckier to have you. That is, if you'll have me?"

A small smile of enchantment touched her lips. "Jake?"

"Cara, look, I know I've been an ass, but with you at my side, we, the three of us, you, me and Aimee can survive anything Deidra throws at us. Will you have us?"

Tears filled her eyes and trembled on her eyelids. "Aye, Jake, I'll have ye and Aimee. I canna imagine my life without either of ye in it."

With his thumbs, he brushed away the tears that found their way down her cheeks. He wrapped his arms around her and held her.

"Thank god," he whispered against her hair.

Suddenly, Cara stiffened and pulled away. Her eyes widened as if she'd just remembered something. "I forgot to ask about Madame Elena. I lost sight of her during the fight. Was she all right?"

Jake grinned and nodded. "She was fine. When all hell broke out, she went into hiding behind a pile of stacked lumber. The guys found her and took her to a friend's house. She'll be safe there."

Cara's shoulders drooped in relief. "Thank the gods."

His brows furrowed. "She was a little shook up, but she's a survivor. In her line of work, I'm sure she's seen stranger things. I'm going to drop by and see her tomorrow."

Cara nodded, stared at him, her heart in her eyes. "Ye're a good man, Jake Bradshaw."

Her soft voice washed over him like a tidal wave. His pulse pounding and his senses reeled.

Jake held out his hand to her, needing to touch her. "And how are you, Cara? When I saw all that blood—" he shuddered.

Her hands dropped to the solitary button and with a quick flick of her wrists, she unbuttoned the closure, and spread the material apart. She smiled. "No more blood, no more wounds. As ye can see, I'm perfectly fine."

He swallowed hard. His breath caught in his throat as his gaze traveled over her nakedness. "I see perfection."

His hands cupped her cheeks, and he tilted her face up to him. He smoothed his thumbs over her lower lip.

Her arms crept around his neck. She leaned her body against his. Her breasts pushed against his chest while her curved molded to his body. His world was filled with her. Passion pounded the blood through his heart, chest, and head.

She spread tiny kisses across his face until she reached his mouth. Her teeth nibbled at his lower lip, and she teased him with lips full of fire, filled with promises.

"You are so beautiful, Cara," he said, scarcely aware of his own voice. And then, uncertainty ripped through him followed by a warning voice in his head. *He loved her more than life itself, but what if he failed her? Would she love him still?*

She drew away. Her emerald eyes locked with his. His stomach clenched. He reached for her, but she backed away and avoided his grasp.

"What's the matter?" he asked, in a hoarse tone.

"I love ye with all of my heart, Jake. Unless ye tell me to leave, I'll stay with ye forever."

His eyes widened. Confusion raced through his veins. Her lips didn't move, but he heard her voice.

How was that possible?

"Our bond has brought our souls together. Our hearts are one. 'Tis a benefit of our connection."

"Bene—?" She stepped forward, covered his lips with the tip of one finger, and shook her head.

"Think the words." She smiled. *"I will hear them."*

"I love you, Cara."

She returned to stand in front of him and wrapped her arms around his shoulders.

"As I love ye," she whispered. Her breath brushed his ear. Tingles shot up and down his spine. With one hand, she unbuttoned his shirt. Leaning forward, she pressed a row of kisses along his muscles. He groaned at the heat of her mouth.

Her heartbeat echoed in his ears. He heard it.

He gripped her under the arms and drew her up the length of his body, covering her lips with his. His tongue explored the soft recesses of her mouth.

After a moment, she drew away, struggling to regain her breath. She looked into his eyes, and he saw her love for him shining in their depths.

"Do ye know what Síoraí means?" she asked. Her voice, deep and sensual, sent a ripple of awareness through him.

He shook his head.

"In ancient Celtic, Síoraí means eternally. My love for ye is powerful and everlasting. Nothing will ever change that. *A chuisle, a chro go Síoraí...my pulse, my heart forever.*"

He caressed her cheek. "I love you Cara, my warrior woman." His lips lowered to hers, but before they covered hers, he whispered, "Forever."